T5-CSA-783

Criminal Intentions

BY THE SAME AUTHOR

The Mark Treasure mysteries:

UNHOLY WRIT
TREASURE BY DEGREES
TREASURE UP IN SMOKE
MURDER FOR TREASURE
COPPER, GOLD & TREASURE
TREASURE PRESERVED
ADVERTISE FOR TREASURE
WEDDING TREASURE
MURDER IN ADVENT
TREASURE IN ROUBLES
DIVIDED TREASURE
TREASURE IN OXFORD
HOLY TREASURE!
PRESCRIPTION FOR MURDER
TREASURE BY POST
PLANNING ON MURDER
BANKING ON MURDER

The Merlin Parry mysteries:

LAST SEEN BREATHING
DEATH OF A PRODIGAL
DEAD IN THE MARKET
A TERMINAL CASE
SUICIDE INTENDED

Criminal Intentions

David Williams

ROBERT HALE · LONDON

© David Williams 2001
First published in Great Britain 2001

ISBN 0 7090 6945 6

Robert Hale Limited
Clerkenwell House
Clerkenwell Green
London EC1R 0HT

The right of David Williams to be identified as
author of this work has been asserted by him
in accordance with the Copyright, Designs and
Patents Act 1988.

2 4 6 8 10 9 7 5 3 1

Typeset by
Derek Doyle & Associates, Liverpool.
Printed in Great Britain by
St Edmundsbury Press, Bury St Edmunds, Suffolk.
Bound by Woolnough Bookbinding Ltd.

This one for
Camilla Hornby

ACKNOWLEDGEMENTS

Acknowledgements are due to *Ellery Queen's Prime Crimes 4* edited by Eleanor Sullivan for MR OLIVER (copyright David Williams 1985), to *Ellery Queen's Mystery Magazine* edited by Eleanor Sullivan for SOMETHING TO DECLARE (copyright David Williams 1988), to *Ellery Queen's Mystery Magazine* edited by Janet Hutchings for SECOND BEST MAN (copyright David Williams 1994), TRICKS OF THE TRADE (David Williams copyright 1997), THE FINAL CHANCE (copyright David Williams 1999), IN CHARITY WITH HER NEIGHBOUR (copyright David Williams 1999), THE EXTORTIONATELY DEAR DEPARTED (copyright David Williams 2000), THE GIFT OF THE GAB (copyright David Williams 2000), THE RUDE AWAKENING OF SYBIL FLITCH (copyright David Williams 2000), to Macmillan *Winter's Crimes 15* edited by George Hardinge for UNCLE'S GIRL (copyright David Williams 1983), to Macmillan *Winter's Crimes 20* edited by Hilary Hale for THE OTHER WOMAN (copyright David Williams, 1988), to Macmillan *Winter's Crimes 21*, edited by Hilary Hale for FREEZE EVERYBODY (copyright David Williams 1989), to Macmillan *Winter's Crimes 24* for TAKE TWO HUSBANDS (copyright David Williams 1992), to Little Brown *Midwinter's Mysteries 5* edited by Hilary Hale for A PUBLIC SERVICE (copyright David Williams, 1995), to Pocket Books *Malice Domestic 6* edited by Anne Perry for SWEET FRUITION (copyright David Williams 1997).

Criminal Intentions

CONTENTS

FREEZE EVERYBODY

The little doctor dismounted at the end of the long gravelled driveway and wiped his forehead. It had been a hot ride from the village. He leaned his bicycle against the outside wall of the substantial, covered porch, and carefully removed his jacket from the wicker basket attached to the handlebars. When he had just as carefully unfolded and donned the jacket, he removed the oblong medical case from the same receptacle. Instinctively he glanced up at the main bedroom window in the east wing of the big Victorian house. This was to the right of the front door, under a heavy pointed gable. Then he ascended the two wide marble steps and rang the bell. It was a rather timid ring, but then he was a rather timid man.

He was glad that it was the maid, Bridget O'Mara, who opened the door.

'Would you be caring to bring your bike inside the porch, Doctor Slansky?' she asked, stuffing a bunched handkerchief into the pocket of her plain black dress.

She was a sturdy, full bodied woman, with dark eyes, a possibly sensuous mouth, and good legs, but she was still no beauty. Her skin was rough, the features coarse, and the short wiry hair unkempt and already flecked with grey. Bridget had been in service in this Norfolk house for twenty-two of her thirty-eight years, and though she had never lost the brogue, it was more than a decade since ever she had thought of Limerick as home, or spinsterhood as anything other than a permanent status.

'The bike should be all right there. Yes. Thank you. Thank

you,' Rudolf Slansky repeated, bobbing his close-cropped head, over grateful as always and now with an added nervous concern. He could tell Bridget had been crying and he was unsure whether it was proper for him to enquire why.

'Shall I go straight up?' he asked, after deciding that the tears were none of his business – regretfully so, because he was naturally compassionate and because he was drawn to rough country women.

'If you please, Madam wants to see you in the drawing-room, doctor.' There, was a little, choking noise at the end of the words which suggested the tears were still, as it were, available on tap.

Bridget closed the door, and without further comment or attempt at pleasantry, led the way through the stone vaulted hall to the drawing-room.

The doctor's worn, leather soled shoes tapped out his progress on the shining, coloured tiles in a way that reduced him to tiptoeing out of inane but acute embarrassment. It was a house that filled him with insensible awe every time he entered it – and this was the fourth visit in the ten days he had been in temporary charge of the medical practice in the village. In the diminished number of practices where he usually got locum work there were few Gothic mansions and none with living-in maids.

'No car today, Doctor Slansky?' Mrs Chalfont questioned when he entered the room, establishing that she had watched part of his slow and demeaning approach to the house from where she was sitting near the open French windows. She regularly pronounced his name as Shlansky, which was wrong, but he would not have dared tell her so. It didn't matter, except her invention seemed to be in some way a product of disdain, like the no more than patronizing smile that regularly passed as her initial greeting.

Maud Chalfont was a widow of nearly sixty, which made her several years older than the doctor, though indubitably better preserved than he. She was slim and erect, with a striking countenance, and a presence and voice that spelt breeding and authority. Her tinted hair seemed always recently arranged. Her clothes were good, though styled to suit the owner, not the current fashion. Today she was wearing a pale blue silk dress, the half sleeves and three quarter length skirt advantaging both her firm forearms, and the well turned ankles gracefully crossed above high heeled, court shoes. A double row of pearls at her neck matched the bracelet on her right wrist.

For Slansky to come before Mrs Chalfont was like having an audience with the Queen, not that he had ever had an audience with the Queen. He imagined the drawing-room at Buckingham Palace would be very similar to this one though – elegant, tidy, crammed with antique furniture, priceless pictures, and with carpet so thick that it put extra effort into walking.

'The car I was to use has broken down again. I'm thinking it's not a very good car,' he said in a strained voice, unable either to prevent both cheeks twitching nervously, nor a reversion to the halting constructions of his refugee days fifteen years before this. 'It's a not very new car, of course,' he added apologetically, eyes blinking too often in the moon shaped face.

'Foreign,' Mrs Chalfont snapped back imperiously.

Slansky felt that the deprecating of the vehicle's origins might easily have been intended to cover his as well. 'It's a Ford. I think it was made—'

No matter,' the other interrupted. 'Doctor Riggle should have left you better provided. Since you don't have a car of your own.' But the last words implied that the lack of a powered conveyance was still due to Slansky's wilful carelessness. 'Sit down, please.' She indicated an armchair somewhat smaller and definitely lower than the one she was occupying.

'Thank you. Thank you.' He nodded his way to the chair, then sat on the edge of the seat cushion, very gently, hoping not to squash it too much, and with his elbows tight to his sides. He kept the bag upright on his lap, as if it were there for use as a means of defence. His sweating hands clasped the handle.

'How much longer will Doctor Riggle be away?' asked Mrs Chalfont.

'Two weeks yet. Two weeks and three days.'

'Good.'

Out of natural humility, the doctor couldn't imagine why she should think it was that. 'I hope Mr Gripp is making progress,' he offered.

'We'll talk of my brother later. Where do you go after this?'

'After this? Back to the village. I have the surgery to take at—'

'I don't mean this afternoon,' she broke in impatiently. 'I mean when Doctor Riggle gets back. Have you another temporary position to go to?'

He swallowed awkwardly. 'Perhaps I will have. Nothing is yet arranged. Then it will be the middle of September. You understand there is not so much need for locums then. Not after the school holidays. But the medical agency—'

'How many weeks have you worked this year, Doctor Slansky?' came as a demand not as a polite enquiry.

He hesitated. 'Quite a lot, I think,' Nervously his left hand moved to cover the frayed, right cuff of his shirt now revealed as buttonless, and as conspicuous as a flag of surrender – a soiled one at that.

'I wonder if you're being quite accurate? You were engaged at very short notice by Doctor Riggle. When the doctor who usually stands in for him had to cancel. So you were available at no notice in the middle of the school holidays, when there is very great demand for locums. Good ones, that is. But evidently no one had demanded you, Doctor Slansky? You are Czech?'

'Yes . . . That is . . . No . . . I'm naturalized British now. Since fourteen years.' The change of subject had thrown him. He leaned forward earnestly over the case. 'Also I re-qualified. Since I am coming here from Prague. After the Russian invasion, you understand?'

'And your family?'

'Family? My mother and father are dead now. A long time ago. I have a brother. In Czechoslovakia still.' He loosened his collar. The button on that came off too as he touched it.

'You're not married?'

He shook his head, wondering if a nearly total lack of buttons had suggested the question. 'It was never possible.'

'And do you have a home anywhere?'

His cheeks twitched again. 'Not at the moment.'

'Why did you leave the permanent practice you were in? In the Midlands, wasn't it?'

He could feel the cold sweat running down his reddening face and neck. The eyes first registered denial, then dulled with resignation before he spoke. 'That was five years ago. I was assistant doctor only in the practice.' He fumbled for his handkerchief 'I wasn't needed any more.'

'After eight years?' She fixed him with a merciless gaze. 'Surely it was because you were struck off the medical register? I have made enquiries.'

He looked down, wiping his face. 'Not struck off, only suspended. I was reinstated after two years.' His head came up again slowly. 'It was not for something immoral. Nothing like that. A wrong diagnosis only.'

'But a fatal one? A patient died, I believe.'

'A very old patient, yes. It was better I took the blame. The other doctor, the senior partner . . .' But he left the sentence unfinished. There was no point in trying to explain to people. It was too complicated. Too undignified.

'And you haven't had a permanent post since that time?'

'No.' He straightened, then gave a little sigh. 'Mrs Chalfont, why are you asking me all this? If you think I'm not a good enough doctor for your brother, I won't come again.'

'On the contrary, Doctor Slansky, I think you're an excellent doctor. So much so, I have an important proposition to put to you.'

'To me?' He looked about as if there might be someone else she was addressing.

'I hope you will agree to become my brother's personal physician, giving your attention entirely to him.'

'Entirely? Just to him?' His mouth dropped. 'But I don't think such an arrangement would be possible. I am staying at Doctor Riggle's house only until—' He was stopped by the dismissive wave of an elegant hand.

'Of course, you'll need to live here. Rent free. There's an unoccupied flat above the garage. It's furnished, and very comfortable. A main meal will be provided.'

'I see. His face was still showing perplexity, but the glimmerings too of something like hope. 'You're very kind, but since I have no money . . .' He shook his head, confused and embarrassed. 'What I mean is—'

'Your salary will be twenty-five thousand pounds a year, paid monthly in advance. But I shall require you to sign a contract letter stipulating you will stay for seven years. At the end of that time there will be a hundred thousand pound bonus in addition to your salary. You will be sixty-five then. An appropriate time to retire, perhaps? You would be wise to make pension arrangements out of your income meantime, but that, of course, is up to you.'

'Yes,' said the doctor making a breathy noise in his throat that was really a strangled shout for joy.

'You will be entitled to four separate weeks' holiday a year. But you must never be absent for more than a week at a time. Never.'

Never,' he repeated with spirit, and as though longer holidays should properly be regarded as sinful.

'You will keep daily written reports on my brother's condition. Noting the times of day you see him, his temperature, his blood pressure at appropriate intervals, the medication you prescribe. So that there's a record.'

'Of course.'

'Good.' Mrs Chalfont gave a gracious nod. 'So do I take it you accept the post, and the conditions?'

'I have to accept so soon?'

'Is there any need for delay on your part?'

He hesitated for a brief moment, then shrugged. 'No, not at all. So, yes, I accept. Thank you.' Then his face clouded. 'Only . . .'

'Only what, doctor?'

'Your brother, Mr Gripp, he's had two strokes. Not so serious as they could have been. Except all strokes are serious. And he's already sixty-six, I think. It's not certain that to have a doctor here all the time will stop him having another stroke. Perhaps one that will be most serious.'

'If you're concerned about keeping my brother alive, you

18

needn't be.' She turned to ring the silver handbell on the table beside her. 'You see, he's dead already. Oh yes, he went very peacefully. Another stroke. When he was asleep. At about this time yesterday. His body is in the deep freeze. I had it put there immediately.'

'More tea, doctor?' Mrs Chalfont asked some minutes later, holding her hand out for his cup. 'So, as I was saying, we have to maintain the pretence that my brother Edwin is alive for the next seven years. If his death were reported now, nearly half the value of his estate would go in taxes. I consider that's nothing less than confiscation, but it's the law.'

Intrigued at Mrs Chalfont's evidently choosey attitude as to what constituted observable law, Doctor Slansky passed over his cup. 'It would be such a lot of money? For the taxes?' he asked, tentatively.

'Several million pounds. Despite the fact that my brother had recently transferred most of his wealth to my two sons and their children. Regrettably, it was necessary for him to live for seven years for his gifts to be free of Inheritance Tax. You'll know enough about Inheritance Tax to understand?' But her expression made it clear she hardly expected him to know more than the minimum – but enough to appreciate the special hardships of the very rich.

'I think so. And it wasn't possible to make the gifts earlier?'

Her mouth tightened. 'It was not until after his wife Rachel died, a year ago, that my brother was free to see reason. I mean in relation to making a just and equitable disposition of his great wealth.'

'That would have been after his first stroke?'

'Yes. It was when I came to live here. To look after him.' She handed him back his cup. 'Rachel always disliked me, and the feeling was mutual. For some reason she resented me my scholarly husband, though she was aware that as a professor at a provincial university his income was quite inadequate. My brother was no intellectual. He made his fortune at a fairly early age. In property development.' She pronounced the last phrase as though the activity rated about level with prostitution and drug trafficking. 'Our father was a general in the army. A fine soldier, but not wealthy, you understand?' It was plain, however, that the general must have had other qualities, no doubt to do with moral not monetary values. 'My sister-in-law was also jealous of our children. She and Edwin were childless. She was a good deal younger than he was, and her death was unexpected. In a car accident. Until then, Edwin had left everything to her. He had naturally expected to die first.'

'She would not have had to pay this Inheritance Tax?' the doctor asked.

'No. It isn't levied on widows. Only on their estates after death. If she had survived, Rachel would have left nothing to me or to my children. It was providential that Edwin survived her. Except he didn't do so for long enough.'

Slansky nodded, but he looked troubled. 'Seven years is a long time to . . . to pretend, Mrs Chalfont.'

'But not if things have been planned properly. I had antici-pated my brother's death might occur too early, though not nearly so early as it has. He seemed to be recovering well enough from the first stroke, but not from the second, as you know. However, I was prepared for the loss. Emotionally and in prac-tical terms.'

'In practical terms,' he echoed involuntarily: it was difficult to picture Mrs Chalfont being emotional.

'I am quite satisfied the body will store satisfactorily where it is.'

'In a deep freezer?'

'A large one. Acquired for the purpose some time ago. It's in the basement. Locked. When the time comes, we shall need to remove the body and allow it to de-frost. I have concluded that no ordinary undertaker is going to suspect what has happened. Provided we are careful. Do you agree?'

The doctor nodded slowly. 'Not an undertaker, no. But if there is an autopsy—'

'There will be no autopsy, doctor. Why should there be? An autopsy is required only if someone dies who hasn't been seen by his doctor for two weeks. Or if the circumstances are unusual or suspicious. Otherwise the attending doctor is perfectly entitled to issue a death certificate. If you were reporting my brother's death today, would you have any doubts about the cause?'

Slansky stared at the little pile of cake crumbs he had made on the plate he was holding. 'No. None. When I saw him two days ago he was not so good. He had made very little recovery since his last cerebro-vascular accident. Another could have happened soon. Or a coronary thrombosis. His death also.'

'Exactly. So you would have issued the certificate. I would have taken it to the Registrar. The funeral would have taken place later this week. Everything would have been normal. What difference is there that we delay the whole matter by seven years?'

The doctor hesitated. 'None really, I suppose.' In truth, the question had made him a good deal more comfortable about the plan. 'Except no one can see him in that time?'

'People will accept that you see him. That I see him. That Bridget will see him. It will appear we shall all be seeing him daily. No one else has been near him since he came back from hospital six weeks ago. No one except Doctor Riggle, before he went on holiday and you took over. It's unlikely anyone else would have seen him. Ever. No matter how long he had survived. He has certainly been in no state to receive visitors, nor shown any signs that he ever would again. Isn't that true?'

'I'm afraid, so. And it's not likely he would have improved much. A little perhaps.'

'Quite. It's why his passing has been a blessing for him. But that's no reason why his heirs should suffer.' Mrs Chalfont nodded decisively. 'You know there are no servants besides Bridget? Not any more. Except for Moffat the gardener, and he doesn't live in. He's in the kitchen from time to time, that's all. Naturally, he's to know nothing about the arrangement.'

'And your sons, Mrs Chalfont? Your two sons?'

'They and their families live far from here. They have never been in the habit of visiting my brother. There's less reason than ever that they should begin now. I shall, of course, visit them from time to time.'

'Will you tell your sons about the . . . the. . . ?'

'The subterfuge? Certainly not. That will be neither appropriate nor necessary.'

'Doctor Riggle—'

'Is no problem,' she interrupted. 'Edwin never really cared for him, and Riggle never relished coming here. It's too out of the way. Too isolated. I shall simply explain that Edwin has taken a great liking to you, so much so that we've decided to retain your services full time.'

'So could I ask, Mrs Chalfont, what would you have done if I hadn't been here?' It had taken some courage for him to put the question.

'I was in the process of finding a doctor similarly placed to yourself. Someone ready to accept the position of personal physician to my brother while he was still alive,' she replied.

'And to carry on, like you've asked me, if he died too soon?'

'Yes. Obviously there would have been a risk. It was imperative I chose the right man. As it happens, I was using the same medical agency as you. I didn't expect Edwin to die so soon, of course, which is why I was overtaken by events. So your presence and your . . . your suitability were both fortuitous.'

Slansky nodded thoughtfully. 'And your maid also knows everything.'

'Bridget was devoted to my brother. It was she who took him to . . . to where he is now. She showed such reverence.' Mrs Chalfont looked out on to the terrace, her eyes indicating stoic forbearance if not actual grief. Naturally, like you, Bridget will benefit immediately and in the long term from the arrangement.

'Naturally,' he repeated, putting his plate on the side table with his cup. 'It is breaking the law, of course.'

'Yes. We shall both be doing that, doctor. If we are discovered, I imagine the consequences for you would be worse than for me. However, I see little possibility of that happening. Even so, it is why I shall need your signed acknowledgement of the terms we have agreed. Just so that we know exactly where we stand.' She paused to be sure that the consequences of her words, like the meaningful look, had registered properly. 'Of course, the rewards for a successful conclusion are ample compensation, don't you agree?'

'Yes, Mrs Chalfont.' He swallowed, steeling himself not to contemplate going back on anything. 'I think I should examine the body now.'

'Quite right. Bridget will show you.' She rang the bell again.

And so began the period of nearly seven years through which three people successfully maintained the apparent survival of Edwin Gripp.

Doctor Slansky gradually settled for a standard of living he had never remotely enjoyed in the whole of his previous and disjointed career. The flat was as comfortable as Mrs Chalfont had claimed. Bridget brought him lunch each day on a tray, and did his laundry, cleaning, and shopping. He indulged his taste for literature and music, building a substantial library of mostly scholarly paperbacks, and tape recordings of classic orchestral works. He had needed to buy a good radio and tape player, but the price had been relatively minor. It was not until the second year that he abandoned bicycling as his normal method of transportation. That was when he acquired a small, reliable second-hand car. Even so, it was some time before he could bring himself easily to accept that he could afford modest luxuries.

The doctor grew not to miss his active professional life. In his way, he had been dedicated to medicine. Yet, since his suspension and reinstatement, the opportunities for work had diminished almost into infinity. If it had not been for Mrs Chalfont's offer he could well have been forced to find another kind of employment, and at his age that would not have been easy. However, he was assiduous in maintaining his fictitious patient's medical records, to the point where they came to be a useful, perhaps even a necessary sublimation. The completeness of the notes was matched by the inventiveness that went into their compiling. In course of time, they built up into a meticulous case study in the care and rehabilitation of a stroke victim. Mrs Chalfont was duly impressed, but in the distant manner to which she had reverted soon after the arrangement had been agreed.

Like a priest repairing to church to say the offices, Slansky twice a day visited Edwin's empty bedroom, each time being sure to appear at the window so that Moffat the gardener, or the postman, the milkman, the garbage collector or those others who regularly came to the house might note his presence in the sickroom.

Bridget regularly took meals up to Edwin's room – trays of genuine food which she stayed there to consume herself, on the pretence that the patient needed help with his eating. In fact this was the way she took most of her own meals, while watching the television set installed at the bedside.

It was this last habit as much as anything else that brought Slansky and Bridget closer together.

The doctor was not gregarious by nature, but after a while the intellectual content of his new life began to pall as his main source of fulfilment. Quite simply, he felt a loneliness, and more, the renewal of a primeval sense of incompleteness that had pervaded his old impecunious existence, but which his present affluence made unnecessary. Naturally, the constrictions of his life were hardly conducive to the making of new friends, and in any case he was basically shy. Mrs Chalfont provided no companionship, indeed she tended to treat him rather as she would an upper servant. After she was satisfied that he was going to further her seven year purpose in a much better than adequate manner, she tended to absent herself from the house more and more, making visits to family and friends. Sometimes she was away for quite long periods.

So there was only Bridget.

At the start, the doctor took to dropping into the kitchen for coffee mid-morning, though that sometimes involved suffering the company of garrulous old Moffat, who did the same, and who was no stimulus to anything. Bridget was usually too busy to linger when she brought the lunch tray, which was why Slansky finally elected to take his lunch with her in Edwin's room. He thus became a fairly frequent viewer of early afternoon television, just as, in course of time, Bridget became an awed listener to taped Mozart and Beethoven: this was after she took to accepting the doctor's regular invitations to wine and light suppers in his flat.

Proximity between sympathetic members of the opposite sex often serves to reveal attractions and to obscure blemishes, the more so with a couple left in isolation. The Irish woman's rough exterior and untutored mind soon ceased to register in the doctor's perception of her. Increasingly he came to see her as someone altogether companionable, and, as time went by, physically desirable as well.

For her part, Bridget came to revere the little refugee doctor, to hang on his every accented word, to marvel at his knowledge, education and culture, and most of all to be overwhelmed at the attention he was paying her.

Even so, the period during which friendship ripened into courtship was a very long one: it was nearly six years before Slansky proposed marriage. But neither party was practised in wooing or being wooed, and both came from backgrounds where protracted courtships had been the rule rather than the exception. Nor was time ever a conscious consideration. What developed into an always chaste romance came to provide the central theme in their lives – something to savour and not to condense, for patience had been a way of life to both since childhood. In truth also, the two had reached ages where the more intimate physical aspects of the affair needed to be approached with some trepidation – on her part out of a modesty born of total innocence, and on his because of an illogical, persistent, and spectral presentiment that when put to the test his sexual capacities might prove less than adequate.

So it was that, even during the year following the formal engagement, Slansky still took no liberties with his future bride.

The wedding finally took place in the middle of the last year of Slansky's contract with Mrs Chalfont. The ceremony was at a registrar's office with only Moffat and his wife present as witnesses.

Mrs Chalfont approved the union, believing that the stronger the dependence between her two conspirators, the more they would be obliged to keep faith with her and each other to the end – the end that was in any case very near.

The honeymoon was spent in Scarborough, and lasted a week. This was the longest time the doctor was permitted to be away, and the only time he and Bridget had ever been absent from the house at the same time. This was a concession on Mrs Chalfont's part since it meant she had to stay at home for the whole week. One of the three had to be there always for fear of fire, or burglary, or some other hazard that could result in outsiders learning that Edwin was no longer alive.

The couple returned with their love strengthened by lusty passion. The doctor's misgivings about his likely performance in bed had been dispelled on the first night, a result more than a little due to an unexpected and enduring influence beyond his own control.

For when it came to the point, Bridget's own demure inhibitions had quite evaporated – dispersed by the triumph of a formidable, natural instinct. Once she had savoured the ecstasy of the sexual act, her appetite for more of the same had become insatiable: despite her inexperience, the woman had proved to be a veritable Aphrodite. It was as though love-making came more easily to this virile Irish housemaid than bed-making ever had – but with many more variations.

The couple had scarcely left their Scarborough hotel room except for meals. In her enthusiasm, Bridget would even have done without the food for most of the time, except that after a little while Slansky clearly needed to increase his calorie intake to maintain his strength.

Nor did Bridget's joy in uninhibited and frequent sexual concourse diminish one bit on their return. There was no more television viewing after lunch in Edwin's room, not when there were livelier things to do in Edwin's empty bed. And the light suppers, in the flat the couple now shared, were consumed in the bedroom not the living-room – still often with wine, and a musical accompaniment, though Bridget had developed a strong preference for the noisier climactic pieces.

It never occurred to this simple woman that so much draining of his manhood might be doing her husband a mischief. Nor

could the now sixty-four-year-old Slansky bring himself to
impugn that very manhood by denying his wife her consuming
pleasure, or even to explain why moderation might be indicated.
In truth, of course, Slansky enjoyed their physical relationship
just as much as his wife did, which is why he took a daringly fatalistic view on what it might be doing to him.

'That pain in your chest is almost certainly mild angina,' said
Doctor Riggle in his surgery, after examining Slansky thoroughly
six months after the marriage. He had agreed to keep the result
of the consultation confidential. Slansky had told Bridget that he
had needed advice about a backache. 'Probably not serious yet,'
Riggle continued, 'but you should see a cardiologist. Meantime,
you ought to take it easier. That new wife of yours is too
demanding perhaps?' he added, but half in jest. No one except
Slansky credited uncomely Bridget with a boundless sexual
appetite.

Slansky promised to do what the other doctor advised, though
he wasn't quite as good as his word. He decided to delay seeing
the heart specialist, and simply to take the pills prescribed, while
conserving his energy as best he could. He determined to eat
carefully, avoiding animal fats, dosing himself with extra vita-
mins, and sneaking as much sleep as possible when Bridget was
busy at her duties in the main house.

Mrs Chalfont had noticed no change in the doctor, but she
never paid much attention to his appearance. And she was
bringing her own grand design to fruition just a few days after he
had been to see Riggle, so there were much more important
considerations than Slansky's health to engage her.

'I telephoned the undertaker, doctor,' she announced on the
day appointed for Edwin's second death: it was a Sunday. 'As I
expected, there was no one there. Only an answering machine.
I'll call again first thing tomorrow. You can date the death certificate for today.'

'Good. And you want the funeral to be on Thursday?'

'Yes. You'd better give me the certificate straight away. And you
can ring Doctor Riggle tonight. About the extra certificate he has
to sign. For the cremation.' She had the order of events set firmly

in her mind – as might have been expected of a general's daughter.

Seven years and six months had passed since Edwin Gripp had formally given away his money to his sister's family. Mrs Chalfont had regarded the extra half year as a nice touch, to allay suspicion at the Inland Revenue.

It was mid-January, and snowing hard – the kind of conditions that prompted people to be concerned more with their own comforts than with the over-zealous execution of official duties. Mrs Chalfont had thought of such things – which included the undertakers being closed on Sundays: that had given her a full day in hand, in case anything had gone wrong.

Slansky and Bridget had removed the body from the deep freezer the night before. It had been left to thaw out slowly in the cellar. Then they had dried it, carried it upstairs and put it to bed.

Everything seemed to be going exactly as planned. That was until a panic-voiced Mrs Chalfont summoned Slansky, over the house telephone in the flat, at three o'clock the next morning.

'I think he's gone too soft. Much too soft,' she clamoured when they were both standing at the bedside. It was quite exceptional for her to show such nervousness. Unable to sleep, she had gone in a few minutes earlier to check on the condition of her brother's corpse. 'I mean he looks as if he might . . . well, flatten out altogether. Like . . . like heated wax. Is it because it's been so long?'

Edwin's face was wan and sunken, but there was every reason for that: he was dead, and Slansky knew the time of his dying had no relevance. 'He's quite normal, Mrs Chalfont. I mean for someone who's . . . He's quite normal.' The doctor had hesitated over stating the obvious, finding words sleepily, and breathing hard. There was a pain in his chest. He had raced to the house half dressed, then hurried up the stairs – and he had been exhausted before Mrs Chalfont had woken him: Bridget was extra demanding at weekends.

'Should we open the windows? To stop him getting too warm?' asked Mrs Chalfont, still on edge.

'If you like. He won't alter now. But it won't do any harm.'

Slansky moved across the room. He had to wrestle with the catch of the heavy casement before he got it to budge. He shivered as the icy wind blew in on him.

'That's all right, then, doctor. I'm sorry I disturbed you. I'll see you in the morning.'

Except it was not all right. Dr Slansky died suddenly a few moments later, on the way back to the flat – in the driveway, in the freezing snow, of a massive heart attack.

It was Bridget who found him, and demented Bridget who then had to be coaxed into saving seven years work from going to waste on the very last day.

'A doubly sad event, Mrs Chalfont,' said the grey haired, venerable Dr Riggle. 'Two deaths in such a short time. Your brother a week ago today. Doctor Slansky this morning. Bridget is bearing up well, as you are.' He shook his head.

It was midday on the following Sunday, a full week since Slansky's true demise. The two were seated in Mrs Chalfont's drawing-room.

'It was good of you to come so promptly, and with the roads still in such terrible condition. Thank you too for attending my brother's funeral on Thursday, doctor.'

'I was glad to pay my respects. There were not many left hereabouts who knew him well.' He paused. 'I understand now why Doctor Slansky wasn't there.'

'He was quite unwell. Throughout the week. He insisted it was only a chill, she put in solemnly. 'Of course, we had no idea he was seriously ill.'

'Hm. When he'd come to consult me I'm afraid he made me swear I'd tell no one what was wrong with him.'

Mrs Chalfont sighed. 'He really shouldn't have ventured out this morning. Neither Bridget nor I knew he was going, of course. We were both here in the house. He should never have gone to the post-box. Not on foot.'

'That's right, I'm afraid. This east wind can play the very devil with angina sufferers.'

'He didn't go out at all in the week. But he wouldn't stay in

29

bed. In case he was needed. In case there were any other formalities to complete over my brother's death. I gather there weren't.' She chilled at the thought of what fresh subterfuges she would have to have invented if any had emerged.

As a last resort she had been going to say that Slansky had been called to Prague urgently. It simply wouldn't have done to have admitted his death so close to that of her brother's. It could so easily have produced enquiries, which, worst of all, could have resulted in someone ordering an autopsy on Edwin. As things now stood, a decent interval had elapsed between the two events.

Altogether though, it had been the worst week of Mrs Chalfont's life. 'Thank you for signing the second certificate approving Edwin's cremation, by the way,' she said.

'Ah, yes, there have to be two doctors for that,' Riggle replied. 'In this case it was only a formality, as Doctor Slansky suggested when he phoned last Sunday. The authorities need to be sure there's nothing fishy, you see? Before a cremation.' He cleared his throat. 'I didn't think it necessary to come out here. Just took a quick glance at the body in the drawer at the undertaker's on Tuesday. I didn't need to . . . to fiddle about with it in any way. I thought you'd like to know that. Relatives usually do.'

'Thank you, doctor.' She had been right in calculating it would have been an insufferably long way for aging Dr Riggle to have come to the house in the snow for a formality. If he had seen the body here instead of in a refrigerated drawer at the undertaker's he might have been prompted to look more closely – even to 'fiddle'. She had taken an extra risk by insisting on a cremation so that there would be nothing to exhume for examination afterwards.

'Indeed, it was a great credit to Doctor Slansky that your brother survived as long as he did,' Riggle observed in a patronizing tone. 'Great credit. Better physician than I took him for, as a matter of fact. Those case notes are almost good enough for publication in a medical journal. I told Bridget as much just now. And I gathered from her—'

'That I am arranging to have them published privately?' the hostess interrupted. 'Yes. The idea seemed to please her.' In fact, it had proved to be Mrs Chalfont's *coup de main*. 'I was deeply grateful to Doctor Slansky. It was a very great comfort to me to have Edwin for all those years more. His mind was quite active you understand? To the end.'

'Yes, the case notes show it.'

Mrs Chalfont rearranged the folds of the black lace dress she had chosen for the occasion of the doctor's visit. 'By the way, will there be an autopsy on Doctor Slansky?'

'Oh no. I examined him only last week.'

'I wondered about that.' It was a gross understatement: she had counted on it – on the rule about two weeks.

'I told him he might have angina. His dying of a heart attack today is no surprise. Classic end from classic symptoms. I've given Bridget the death certificate already.' He sighed. 'Poor simple creature. Heart broken, of course. She'll be all right, I assume? Financially, I mean.'

'Quite all right, yes. I can vouch for that.' Except the simple creature was refusing to accept the money due to her dead husband. It was true she was heart broken, certain that Slansky's death had been divine retribution, because they hadn't been married in a Catholic church. She was sure that meant she had lived in sin like a wanton, wicked woman for all those months, glorying in the weaknesses of the flesh. Mrs Chalfont had at first found this attitude superstitious and difficult to credit, particularly since Bridget had stopped going to mass years before. On the other hand, in a curious way it seemed actually to help with Bridget's stoic acceptance of events. And if she hadn't felt so guilty she would probably not have been ready to accept there was atonement in helping Mrs Chalfont's deserving children and grandchildren. But it had been the offer to publish the case book as a memorial to Doctor Slansky that had finally tipped the balance.

'Well, I must be going.' The doctor rose from the armchair, then gazed for a moment through the window at the snow decked landscape beyond. 'I don't believe Slansky could have suffered at all. But, you know, with his body lying there in these nearly Arctic conditions for anything up to three hours,' he paused and gave a shrug. 'You wouldn't believe, it was as though he'd been in a deep freezer for a week.'

'Oh, I can well believe it,' said Mrs Chalfont earnestly.

SWEET FRUITION

Henry Trublit was a born loser. I should know, I married him. He was Captain Henry Trublit when I first met him, serving in the regular army, in the infantry. He wasn't in one of the grand British regiments, but my parents were impressed all the same when I brought him home to suburban Ealing the first time. He looked like a soldier, an officer, even when he was in civilian clothes. He was tall, dark, and ramrod upright, with a well trimmed, bristly moustache, a plummy accent, and a vacant expression that people mistook for thoughtful.

'You can always tell good breeding,' I remember my mother saying afterwards. Good breeding was one of her things. She kept spaniels, where bad breeding usually meant ear infections. There was nothing wrong with Henry's ears.

'Comes from a long line of army officers, he told me,' my father had put in, narrowing his eyes, and applying the coded inflections they both used to indicate what was socially acceptable and what wasn't.

My father was a clerk in a small, exclusive London bank. Before she married him, my mother had been a hotel receptionist in Park Lane. Both were snobs by inclination, which meant they hadn't been impressed at all by Norman Walsh whom I'd been going out with for the previous two years. Norman was a coach driver – except he owned the coach, or bus as my parents called it, and intended to own more, in fact a whole fleet of luxury coaches. At the time though, it was just the one coach, or bus, and that one only partly paid for. My father was never inspired by Norman or his prospects.

It was shortly after I'd split up with Norman that I met Henry. I suppose you could say I was caught on the rebound, because, to be honest, it was Norman who dropped me, not the other way round.

Henry had come for a meeting at the Chancery Lane legal firm where I worked. It was soon after his father's death, and he was seeing my boss, old Mr Plumley, about the will. He arrived very early, and I'd had the chance to chat him up while he waited for Mr Plumley to come back from an outside appointment. Mr Plumley was the partner who had looked after the Trublit family business for donkey's years. He was impressed with Henry too. 'Fine young man,' he said, when he was giving me dictation, after Henry left. 'Credit to his father, the colonel. Should do better than the old man, too. Yes, definite touch of his grandfather in Henry.' I made a note to look up grandfather straight away. It turned out he'd been Major General Sir Francis Edmund Trublit, MC, DSO.

That started it, especially since, as he was leaving, Henry had plucked up the courage to ask if I'd join him for the evening. He said he was booked to stay the night in a London hotel, didn't know anybody, and would I like to do a theatre and supper.

Not wanting to sound too available, I said it just might be possible, but only if I could arrange to cancel another engagement. I promised to leave a message at his hotel by tea-time, which I did – saying I'd come, of course. Which was probably the biggest mistake of my life.

It was hard to tell from the papers how much family money the Trublits still had. Henry, and his three married sisters, were getting fifteen thousand pounds each from the will. The rest of their father's estate, total value unspecified at the time, but which included the family house in Wiltshire, was to be held in trust for their mother during her lifetime. The house was to go to Henry on her death.

I was twenty-three then, still living at home, and with marriage definitely in mind, though no prospects offering in that direction after the bust up with Norman. If I say so myself, I was quite a looker in those days, and had never lacked for boyfriends. It was just that none of them ever had what my father considered bankable prospects. Henry seemed more than just an eligible bachelor. He was thirty-five, single, good-looking, serious – too serious, but I didn't find that out till later – and a career army officer with good chances of promotion, or so everybody thought, with a house in the country on hold, plus a quarter of whatever else his mother left eventually. There was also the social cachet of the grandfather's knighthood. Even though it was the sort of title that died with the owner, after the engagement my mother bragged to all her friends, and most of her acquaintances, that I was marrying into the aristocracy. After that, everyone seemed to expect I'd end up as Lady Trublit. I didn't do anything to discourage the expectation either, because I knew it would reach Norman Walsh.

Henry had asked me to marry him three months after we met – after a lot of pushing on my part. I can't say that I was ever really in love with him, but he seemed a good catch, and I was getting my own back on Norman, and the slut he took up when he dropped me. There'd been no, what my mother called, hanky panky during the courtship – she had always suspected Norman's intentions in that area, and she'd been right, as well. Henry was too much of a gentleman – she insisted – to impose physically on our relationship before he'd made an honest woman of me. Trouble was, he didn't impose much on the relationship in that way afterwards, either.

Henry's mother never really approved of me. At the time, I'd put that down to his being her only son – that no woman would have been good enough for him in her estimation. One of his sisters told me, years later, that her mother felt he had married me because he was shy of women of his own class, which was hardly a compliment. It was true, though, that he never seemed to have had any girlfriends in the debutante set. Anyway, at the time I figured I wasn't marrying his mother, whose line-up in the snobbery stakes made my parents look like non-starters. For the first twelve years of the marriage Henry was posted abroad most of the time, and I went with him, so we hardly saw his family.

Despite the expectations of Mr Plumley and my father, Henry's promotion prospects seem to wither with time. He did become Major Trublit at thirty nine, but he stayed in that rank until the end of the Cold War, when the British Army started to contract in all directions. You could say Henry became a quite early military economy. He was retired at forty-eight, given a puny pension, and about twenty thousand pounds in redundancy money. But what was an ex-infantry officer of his age supposed to do next? He tried financial services, which was another name for selling insurance, but that fell through because he couldn't sell as much as a funeral expenses policy to even his closest friends, a good many of whom, whether army or civilian, had also been made redundant: there was a world recession beginning at the time.

It was by luck not intention that we'd never had any children, so at least we didn't have extra mouths to think about. Henry had never been what you might call keen in bed, and we kind of drifted past the time when something might have been done to find out why I'd never become pregnant – not counting Henry's simple neglect of the normal method of going about it, of course. I must admit though that kids have never interested me much. If they had done, I suppose the drift wouldn't have been allowed to happen.

Henry's mother died a year after he left the army. She'd made quite a hole in the money her husband had left, so neither he nor his sisters got much out of that. The house turned out to be more of a liability than an asset because of the state it was in. The old lady had avoided spending money on its upkeep for fear of 'running down the family capital', as she put it, something she'd still succeeded in doing pretty effectively in other directions. And the place wasn't an historic country mansion, either, which I'd thought it would be when I first learnt about it. Built of stone, it was early Victorian, all gables and dilapidated outbuildings, with too much land – about fifteen acres all told, most of it let for grazing. We certainly couldn't afford to live in the place. Henry put it up for sale, but nobody even came to see it – not a single person in a whole year.

It was Henry who was sold the idea that we could make our fortune by turning the place into a 'pick-your-own' fruit farm – growing mostly raspberries, with some strawberries, and black-currants thrown in. That kind of thing was all the rage at the time, and I had to admit we owned the basics needed to set up on our own. Tests showed the soil was right, and the property was close enough to several towns to attract customers. There was also a local growers' co-operative that would take any excess fruit and sell it to the London and other big city markets. The experts Henry consulted said that within two years of making the initial investment we ought to clear over five thousand a year – and that was after deducting living and working expenses.

I still wasn't so certain about it all as Henry, but I was more desperate than he was, and five thousand a year clear seemed promising enough. Remember, this was well after the time when I knew he wasn't ever going to be a general, or even a colonel, even if a major war broke out and he was recalled to the colours. I figured that if we could build the business, and spend a bit on the house, we could probably sell it all as a going concern in about four years, with enough out of the proceeds to buy a small place in Spain where property and living were cheap, and the weather fabulous. We were renting a small flat near my parents at this point, and I was making more money as a temporary secretary than Henry was as a clerk with the Ealing Council. But I hated the work. It was all so degrading after those high expectations. The notion of breathing clean country air and being our own masters was appealing too. What tipped the scales for me was seeing adverts for Norman Walsh Coach Tours in the papers – the national papers as well as the local ones. Norman had done well, and, according to my mother's gossip circle, he put it down not just to his own hard work but to the way Fiona, his tarty wife, had dedicated herself to the business. Fiona Slock, as she was before she married, had been in the same year as me at school, and the only thing she'd been dedicated to was chasing boys, otherwise she'd been as bone idle as they come. Well I'd show her what dedication meant.

What Henry's fruit farming advisers hadn't stressed enough –

although he might not have been listening at the time – was the labour that would need to go into the business, and permanently, not just for the first few years. And the only full time labourer we could afford besides Henry was me. Every penny we had was soon tied up in making the house habitable, the outhouses usable, in steel netting our boundaries against rabbits and deer, in paying for chemicals for the ground clearance, and the posts and wiring for the raspberries, and for the fruit stock, and the fertilisers, plus the equipment to handle it all. The list was never ending, and there was certainly nothing left for paid employees.

We cut corners where we could, but there weren't many. Henry bought probably the oldest working tractor in the South of England. Only he and I were allowed to use it, not that there was anyone else available in any case. Our machine had been made before tractors were fitted with roll bars. A new law had stipulated since then that only owners, not employees, could use tractors without roll bars. It was because tractors were supposed to be too easy to turn over: we were lucky if we got this one to start. You had to be an expert to get it to do tricks.

It was five years before we saw any of that promised profit. They'd been five gruelling years too, spent in hard labour out on those fifteen acres during some baking summers and cruel winters, working often from before daybreak and to well after nightfall. Anyone who tells you that soft fruit farming is a three summer months' doddle has never planted ten thousand raspberry canes in mid winter, hammered in posts and wire for them, and pruned, trained, fertilized and mulched them in every subsequent year. And that isn't the half of it, nor even the quarter of it. If raspberries make heavy work, strawberries and blackcurrants are even worse. We ploughed in our half-acre of blackcurrants in the third autumn, wrote off the cost, and replanted with more raspberries.

Work didn't draw Henry and me together either. I was too tired most of the time for anything but sleep, and we never took holidays. Henry put in even more hours on the farming than I did. I compensated for that by keeping the house, and making our meals. Henry compensated by developing a drinking habit.

He insisted rum kept up his strength and his body heat, and helped him to sleep – which was probably all true, but not to the extent he allowed alcohol to take hold of him. Like everything else, I put up with that in the belief that as with the work we did, and the stress we were both under, the end justified the means – even at the times when drinking made him violent, and there were plenty of such times: he always promised next day it wouldn't happen again.

It was at the end of our fifth fruit farming season that I told Henry after supper one night that I seriously thought the time had come for us to sell up.

'Sell up? Just because we're in profit at last?' he answered, apparently dumbfounded.

'In profit for the second year,' I insisted. 'The place is a going concern, now. We always said we'd sell when that happened.'

'Nonsense, we never agreed any such thing,' he said, pouring himself another rum and Coke – his regular tipple since the time he'd been loaned as a training officer to the Trinidad army. 'And anyway, the price of property's still too low for us to think of selling.'

'It's lower still in Spain,' I countered sharply. He was lying, of course, about what we'd agreed, and I was furious with him – the kind of fury that doesn't go away, that turns into fixation. I'd never have stuck it for all those years if the final prospect hadn't been clearly set out from the start. I think that was the first time it went through my mind that a dose of paraquat weed killer in what he was drinking would solve my problems nicely. I suppose it wasn't a very serious thought. It was because I was so angry – and paraquat happens to be the colour of Coke.

We had a big argument that night. It lasted till we went to bed, and we carried it on the next night. Henry insisted he'd never said we'd sell and move to Spain, and he went on insisting we had a thriving business now that would sustain us for years to come, and allow us to save for our old age.

Old age! I was still only forty two – but life seemed to be slipping away from me. I wasn't interested in Spain for my dotage. I wanted us to move there while we could still enjoy sunshine all the year round, and live pretty well on our capital gains and Henry's indexed pension. He was immovable though – or nearly. In the end he agreed at least to consider selling in a year's time, provided the profits kept up. Since two could play at that game, I threatened to leave him then and there unless he took on someone to cope with my part of the strenuous work.

We'd been employing a few casual workers during the height of the previous two summers – to weigh out fruit that customers picked themselves, and also to do the picking of produce we sent to market. These helpers were all women. I said I'd put in more time myself on those jobs if we could employ a man full time. It wasn't a fair swap, and I knew it. One agricultural labourer would cost more than all the seasonal part-timers we'd been using put together, but I still made it an ultimatum and Henry had to agree to it.

The man we hired was Peter Adler whom we already knew by sight. He was thirty four, and had been a farm worker all his life. He wasn't married, and had recently come back to live with his widowed, ailing mother in a rented cottage on the outskirts of the village, on the same side as us. It suited us to have him so close. He leaped at the job because getting to his present work meant cycling eight miles every day. Later the reasons for his staying became centred on me.

Peter was a strapping, blond young man, taller than Henry, strong as an ox, and with arm muscles like steel hawsers. Even so he was a gentle giant. I'll always remember the first time he held me – when he had to lift me down from the tractor. My jeans had got snagged in the seat cover. It had been like floating on air, his grasp around my waist so easy and confident – and so manly. He was quite well educated too, with an immense knowledge and wisdom about country things.

The next winter was heavenly – not as heavenly as winter in Andalusia might have been, but for the first time in five years I was treated like a farmer's wife, not his work horse. Of course, this was mostly because at last there was a real man about the place, not just an introverted, semi-drunkard, given to violent outbursts.

40

Peter and I got on well from the start. He was nearer my age than Henry was. All right, to be exact, he was eight years younger than me, but attitude counts for more than years, I always think, and in those terms he made me feel younger even than he was. He was kind and courteous to me, too, and always around when I really needed his help. They say nearness breeds sexual awareness, and that's what happened in our case. Within six months we were lovers. All of a sudden I was reborn as a woman, and it wasn't too late for this to happen – Peter proved that.

Our sixth year of fruit farming was far and away our most profitable too. At the end of it, I was torn between making Henry honour his promise to sell up and move to Spain, and the certainty that this would mean leaving Peter. That was until Henry remarked one night, without any prompting, what fools we'd have been if we'd done what I wanted the year before, and sold the place. 'It's a little gold mine,' he said. 'Will be for the rest of our days. Taking on Tarzan was a great investment too, not a drain on profit.' Tarzan was his private name for Peter. 'Don't you ever suggest selling again,' he went on in a threatening tone. 'We're here to stay.'

It was his arrogance that upset me most, more even than his ignoring the promise at least to discuss things again. It was only possible to bear because I now had a reason for staying myself, even though Henry didn't know that. Really I wanted the penny and the bun – Peter to love, and a new life in a warm country. My problem, of course, was that Henry owned everything. If I left him, divorced him, all I'd get was half his pension and an even smaller share of the farm income – a very small share if the divorce judge knew I was leaving Henry for another man. I got advice on it all from a lawyer in Salisbury, and that's what he said.

And Peter had nothing but his wages.

'Oh, darling, I do so want to live with you. To marry you. If only Henry wasn't in the way,' I whispered to him impulsively one evening, when we were in bed together. It was in late November, and Henry was at a growers' co-operative dinner twenty miles away. I remember the occasion vividly because of what came next.

Peter didn't answer straight away, but I'll never forget what he said eventually, quite slowly: 'Had an old dog called Henry once. He was in the way as well. Savage sometimes, too. So I put him down. I could do the same with your Henry, that's if you wanted.'

My body went cold all over, then warm, fantastically warm again. 'You do mean . . . do away with him?'

'Sure. Make it look like an accident. Lot of accidents happen on farms. It's expected. Take that old tractor of yours.'

He did away with Henry just after Christmas, when the weather had been wet. Looking back on it now, it was so simple. It was the time of year when some of the raspberry posts and wiring always needed mending or renewing. Henry regularly carried on with this alone after supper when Peter had gone home. We'd had flood lights put in two years before, so there was no problem with it being dark. Usually Henry had drunk too much by that time to get a lot done, but it made him feel indispensable, or self fulfilled, or something.

One Friday, Peter left early in the afternoon to see a dentist in the town. But he came back again, quite late, and joined Henry outside, saying he felt he should make up the time lost. Henry was even more fuddled than usual because, as arranged, I'd laced his drinks at supper. He was rewiring the last line of raspberry canes just below the steep, solid escarpment that ran along our northern boundary, and he had the tractor and trailer with him. After a bit, Peter asked him to move the tractor along to where they needed extra posts from the trailer. Henry, a stickler for observing regulations since army days, never let Peter operate the tractor.

As soon as Henry started the tractor engine, Peter unhitched the trailer behind his back, and leaped up behind him. Before Henry knew what was happening, Peter had put his hand over Henry's on the throttle lever, opened the throttle wide, and swung the steering wheel hard left so that the tractor shot up the steepest part of the escarpment at a crazy angle. Peter leaped off a split second before the huge machine turned itself over, and crashed down the bank with Henry under it, killing him outright.

When he'd made sure Henry was dead, Peter went home across the fields, the way he had come. No one had seen him. His now nearly bedridden mother later swore he'd been home all evening. He'd put a pill in her tea on his return from town, so, in truth, she'd been asleep in front of the television since then.

I didn't see Peter kill Henry, but I didn't regret what he did. I believed Henry deserved what happened to him. It was I who had to 'find' Henry's body much later when, as I told the ambulance crew, he hadn't come in. I didn't mind that either. Of course, I'd pretended to be hysterical when the ambulance arrived. I'd always been good at theatricals.

The coroner's court returned a verdict of accidental death. The coroner himself added a rider about the tractor being out of date, and Henry taking charge of it while under the influence of alcohol. 'A recipe for disaster, I fear,' he said. He was right too.

The police hadn't suspected foul play. Their investigation of the accident scene had been quite thorough, but like the coroner and the pathologist at the hospital, they put what had happened down to Henry being drunk.

Henry's life hadn't been insured, which was a pity, but it had been too late to do anything about that once Peter said he'd kill him – not without risking suspicion later.

Peter and I decided to carry on as usual for the next season, again to avoid suspicion. I played the heartbroken but plucky widow. He was the loyal employee whose devotion to me gradually became more evident as time went on. We married at the end of the following summer. No one in the village was in the least surprised, and that included the vicar who performed the ceremony.

It turned out to be another good year for the farm. Even so, we decided – a bit reluctantly on my part – to give it one more, final year before selling up. This was partly because property prices had dipped again, but were predicted to rise in the following spring, and partly because Peter's mother wasn't expected to last the winter. Prices did rise too, and Peter's mother, who had been moved to a nursing home, died in the February.

I have to say that the first careless rapture of life with Peter had worn off before this. The breathtaking, real excitement in our relationship seemed to end after Henry's death, and went altogether after the marriage. We seemed to settle into the same routine of living that I'd had with Henry – except I was working harder again. Peter had been against hiring anyone to replace himself. He said he could easily do his old work and Henry's, which would mean a huge saving. It did as well, except he didn't seem to notice how much extra effort I had to put in too. Once again, I told myself it was all in a good cause, so I didn't grumble. It was astonishing really – and disappointing – how like the old life the new one became. Peter even took to drinking rum and Coke – not to excess, like Henry, but he was moving in that direction all right. He'd always taken a litre bottle of Coke with him out to where he was working in the warmer weather: it was the rum he added at night that was new – and, for me, uncomfortably reminiscent. And that wasn't to be the only reminder of times past.

It was mid-June when I said to Peter one evening that it was time we put the farm up for sale. He shook his head slowly. 'That'd be a daft thing to do, love,' he replied. 'We're coining it now. What we should be thinking about is buying that extra land. Make a bigger bundle with that, we could, growing more fruit for the market.'

There was a ten-acre field for sale next to our western boundary. It was true that while the 'pick-your-own' business had more or less levelled out, we could easily have sold double the amount of fruit we were then sending to the local markets. 'But all we want is enough to live on in Spain, after we sell up here. Live simply, I mean,' I insisted.

'Who wants a simple life in Spain, doing nothing all day?' he answered. 'Not me. Not if we can make a more comfortable living right here. And for as long as we live.'

I could hardly believe my ears. He hadn't actually mentioned our old age, but he'd got close. Otherwise he'd used almost the same words as Henry had done – and pouring his third rum of the evening while he did it. What's more, we argued the same point for days, and he remained adamant. And this was the man who now owned half my fruit farm. We'd put everything in our joint names when we married. That had been my idea. It seemed only fair at the time. Of course, whichever of us survived, the other inherited everything anyway. We'd taken out a three year joint life and accident insurance policy at the same time as well. It was our broker who advised that, saying it was prudent in case one of us came to grief while we were still working the farm – that Henry and I should have done the same thing. I'm glad we accepted his advice because it did give me some solid consolation later.

Peter's untimely, tragic death occurred during a short heat wave, late in the following spring. That had seemed to me the best time to arrange it.

When the doctor came, I explained, through my tears, that Peter had always stored a handy amount of concentrated, ready mixed paraquat in an old litre bottle of Coke in the tractor shed, and that he could have picked it up in mistake for a new bottle, early in the morning, when it was still fairly dark, and taken it out with him on the tractor. The police inspector agreed later it would have been an easy thing to do, especially after I told him that Peter had kept fresh bottles of Coke in the same shed, only that they'd all been drunk. Peter had been tired, due to over-work, and probably not too aware of his actions: a quite high alcohol level was found in his blood too, showing he had taken more drink than usual the previous evening. I'd arranged that as well, of course. It had been very hot mid-morning on the day, and, being extra thirsty, Peter had sunk a quarter of what was in the bottle before he realized what it was. All this came out again in the coroner's summing up at the inquest.

At the time of his death, Peter had been in the new ten-acre field on the far side of the property. If he'd tried to cry out, there'd been no one close enough to hear him. It was more prob-able, though, that the poison had instantly paralysed his throat and vocal chords. He died within a minute. The coroner said how dangerous it was to keep poisonous substances in unlabelled containers – although he accepted Peter had put a label on the bottle which had fallen off. The police found the label later on the shed floor. I hadn't made it look too evident, but it wasn't too unobtrusive either.

I hadn't been able to attend the inquest. By then I was in a nursing home, under sedation, and had to stay there for several weeks. They said the shock had been too much for me, and I'd suffered what amounted to a nervous breakdown. Everyone was so sympathetic over my double loss.

I sold the fruit farm for a good price as soon as I recovered, and bought a pretty little Spanish house, not too far from Seville. It was a year after that when Norman Walsh got in touch again, then came out to stay for a few nights. His business collapsed in the recession. Fiona divorced him shortly after. Well, she would have, wouldn't she? He seemed so depressed the day before he left, I said we'd have a whale of a party to cheer him up – just the two of us. We ate and drank till the small hours. Then we made love. I hadn't planned that, but it happened. Afterwards he told me, in detail, about his terrible life with Fiona, really let his hair down. I was just as frank with him about the awful dance Henry and Peter had both led me.

'Till you got rid of them both, my clever puss,' he said knowingly. 'So now tell me how you did it.'

And I told him – the truth, also in detail. Well it was that kind of night. He was my oldest, trusted friend – oldest lover. We were both high as kites, and I was pleased and, in a curious way, deeply relieved at having someone to whom I could unburden. By then, I'd pretty well decided to ask Norman back for a longer stay, possibly even a permanent one.

A week after Norman left, two British policemen arrived on my doorstep. A month later I was extradited back to Britain, charged with conspiracy to murder my first husband, and with the actual murder of the second one. Norman had put a miniature tape recorder under the pillow. He hadn't been drunk at all, and he'd been paid by Henry's three poxy sisters to trap me. I was convicted on both counts. Afterwards, the sisters sued me for every penny I got from the fruit farm – and they won.

When Norman had been broke, he'd gone to the sisters saying he'd never been happy about either of my husbands' deaths, and believed he could make me admit I'd killed them both. If he succeeded, and if I was convicted, he told them they could sue me, and he'd settle for half of whatever they got. It was payment by results, and they had nothing to lose, except his travel expenses.

Would you believe, Norman came to see me after the trial? – to make an apology. I asked him why he'd shopped me when, if he'd played his cards right, he could have married me? Cool as could be, he said even if that had happened, as my husband the most he'd have been entitled to in law would have been half my property, and he was getting that anyway, with no hassle – *or any of the risks my other husbands had run.* What a nerve. *And* he went back to Fiona.

My parents were dead right to say Norman shouldn't be trusted.

TRICKS OF THE TRADE

By and large, Mr Arnold Fiskin was an honest, hard working man, who followed the normal practices of his calling. Small, bald, roundish and nearly sixty, appearing always a touch nervous, with an honest gaze and impeccable manners, Mr Fiskin was a dealer in antiques, an activity, it must readily be admitted, in which a degree of artfulness is expected and accepted.

It was a Sunday in mid February when Mr Fiskin made a second visit to a property on the outskirts of Lower Hartley. In his view – partly tutored, partly instinctive – Mucklebury Lodge was the only habitation in the Devonshire village that showed promise of yielding reward for valuable time expended. A solid, dignified stone built house of only modest proportions, it dated probably from around the middle of the eighteenth century, and was showing recent signs of deterioration that had to mean its present occupiers were hard up – a lot more so than their predecessors, otherwise the place would have fallen down long since.

The tall, double iron gates were rusted, crooked on their hinges, and permanently open before a pitted driveway that wound through a substantial, unkempt garden. The porticoed front door, from which the off-white paint was peeling, was flanked by windows on whose frames, unhappily, there was no paint left to peel. A piece of roof ridge was missing, and several tiles looked to be dangerously askew.

Probably a case of genteel poverty, Mr Fiskin had diagnosed on his brief visit the day before, with the rider that if the occupants of the house were feeling the pinch, they were making some effort to maintain their dignity. The net curtains, closed at every downstairs window, were clean, the front steps were swept, and the brasswork on the door had been recently polished.

When, on his first visit, Mr Fiskin's knock had produced no response, he had attempted a cursory examination of the ground floor interior of the house. It had been an unsatisfactory attempt because of the net curtains, but he thought he had discerned enough to support his initial confidence. Today, when Mr Fiskin drove his suitably aged Volvo estate car up to the door, he had observed with satisfaction that smoke was rising from one of the chimneys. It was still some time before his knock was answered, by a woman of formidable size and girth, her grey hair swept back to a bun, though a good deal of it had eluded capture, giving her a windswept look. She was wearing steel framed spectacles with heavy lenses, and she was dressed in layers of unmatched woollens over a long, thick grey skirt. It was difficult to estimate her age – her skin texture, especially that of the cheeks, neck and mittened fingers, seeming not quite to accord with the hair colour.

'My name is Mr Arnold Fiskin,' the caller announced, removing his tweed hat with a flourish, and placing it over his heart as though he was pledging allegiance to something. The hat was a prop he regularly used as an earnest that he subscribed to old fashioned values. 'I called yesterday, but there was no-one in. I left my card in the letterbox . . . with a note saying I'd return today? On the off chance?' he ended questioningly, raising his voice a touch, for fear that the woman might be hard of hearing since her features had not registered any reaction to his opening words.

'Left a card, you say?' she uttered at last, in a broad Devonian accent. 'Ah, yes, to be sure. The General did mention someone might be making a call. Better come in then, hadn't you, m'dear.' The voice, though uncultured, was melodious, and again seemed somehow younger than the slow moving body from which it emanated.

Mr Fiskin wished he could see the woman's eyes properly, but they were shrouded by the spectacles, and then by the dark interior of the house. He assumed she must be some kind of servant. 'Thank you,' he replied, promptly stepping inside. 'Yes, since I was in the area, it seemed a pity not to make myself known to the er . . . to General er . . . ?' he offered tentatively, in the hope of eliciting a name, and with the air more of a visiting clergyman than an avaricious door-step buyer. He wiped his clean shoes, with prolonged and unnecessary zeal, on the worn, coil mat, while making a swift inventory of the hall furniture.

'The general was just going to have his coffee in the drawing-room,' the woman continued affably. 'Expect you'd like some too, wouldn't you?'

'I would indeed. How kind.' He was seldom made so welcome. 'And what a nice house this is. When I first saw it, I felt instinc-tively—'

'Mornin' to you. Arthur . . . er Wiskit, is it?' interrupted the tall stooping figure now framed in an open doorway on the far side of the hall. 'Been expectin' you.' The clipped moustache, and the mannered, nasally diction – not to mention the only near rendering of the caller's name – would have spelled army officer to Mr Fiskin without prompting. He had begun his adult career as a regular soldier in the infantry – and hated the expe-rience.

'Arnold Fiskin, actually, sir,' he now corrected pointedly, 'of Arnold Fiskin Limited, fine antiques and pictures, London.' He held out his hand. London was as much of an address as he ever supplied at the start on these occasions. The card he had left offered no more – not even a telephone number.

'How d'you do. General Sir Percival Amhurst-Cole. Retired now, of course,' the other man provided, examining the prof-fered hand before taking it, as though checking it for contaminates. Afterwards he pushed both his own hands back into the pockets of the long fawn cardigan, making it a good deal longer in the process. He turned about and limped slowly back into the room, worn slippers flapping across bare floorboards. 'Come inside,' he called over his shoulder. 'And take a pew. Mrs Trevenion bringing us coffee, is she?'

'Thank you, Sir Percival, yes,' Mr Fiskin replied deferentially, bringing up the rear, and unsure whether he should address his host as that or as General.

The drawing-room was, if anything, darker than the hall had been. It was a dull day outside, and the still closed net curtains deepened the funereal atmosphere. Mr Fiskin was just able to make out that under a shock of snow white hair the general's tanned face was quite unusually leathered, to a degree that even suggested intervention by some pockmarking type of disease. Not that the dealer was hugely interested in the physical characteristics of either the general or his housekeeper, if that's what she was. He was already too concerned – and dispirited – over the house contents.

Mr Fiskin had rarely entered a home of apparent substance that was so wholly lacking in any vestige of tasteful furnishings. This room, like the hall, looked as though it had been fitted out with rejects from a junk shop. Even what might once have been half good was severely damaged, like the large, Victorian, glass-fronted bookcase on one wall, bereft of books, and with one of its lower doors entirely missing – or the sofa on which the general had motioned the visitor to sit, and whose loose cover proved to be hiding a collection of springs that were looser still.

That there had once been pictures in the room was clear from the oblong, light patches on the wallpaper where they had once hung. But the promising impression that the dealer had gleaned through the windows the day before was to this point proving to be the product of his own wishful thinking. He had seldom been in such a cold house either. Wherever the smoke producing fire was burning, it wasn't in the drawing-room. The only evidence of heating arrangements here was a single element, old-fashioned electric fire set close to the armchair the general was making for, but it wasn't switched on.

'Have you lived here long, sir?' Fiskin had decided to compromise on the form of address for the time being.

The General lifted his eyebrows as though the question surprised him. 'Yes. Since around doomsday. Place is denuded now, as you can see. Most of the old furniture's been sold. Upstairs is worse than down here. Everything had to go for death duties.' He lowered himself into the sagging chair while his visitor wondered how anything upstairs could be worse than the sofa.

'You're looking to buy antiques, of course,' the general went on. 'Won't get any here, I'm afraid. More's the pity. I could use some extra loot.' He sighed heavily. 'Yes, all the good stuff went years ago. Before my dear wife passed on, God rest her.' He blew his nose with a piercing high, trumpeting noise into a large, red silk handkerchief, and then took several seconds to recover from the effort. 'Still, glad to see you,' he added, breathless still, but with a careful smile – as though a less careful one might split the parched, grooved skin of his cheeks, 'I don't entertain any more. Don't know a soul in the village nowadays either, not that I'd want to. They all probably think I died years ago. Or moved.' The second possibility seemed in some way to console him.

'Indeed,' Fiskin responded with a nod. 'The character of the English rural village has changed beyond belief, and not for the better, I'm afraid,' he continued – loftily for someone who lived in a high rise London flat near Vauxhall Bridge. At least, he thought, the old boy would be a willing seller of anything he owned that was worth having, except there was nothing of the kind in sight. 'I buy all kinds of valuables, of course,' he went on, still hopefully. 'Ornaments and jewellery, as well as furniture and pictures. Quite often an owner's got a little gem or two tucked away somewhere. Things that everybody's forgotten about. In the attic or the cellar.' His last words were put more as a question than a comment.

The general lifted himself an inch from the seat, loosened his trousers by tugging at their front, then dropped back on to the creased cushions with a satisfied grunt, his eyes on Fiskin's throughout. 'Can't believe we've got any gems left here,' he said, breathless again from the fresh exercise, but now brushing at the front of his cardigan. 'Still, you're welcome to look for yourself after we've had our coffee. Don't expect me to go round with you, though. And I'd advise you to wear household gloves if you're going in the attic. Damned dirty up there. Least it was the last time anybody looked, and that was probably a decade ago.

Oh, thank you Mrs Trevenion. Mr er . . .' his nose creased. 'Mr Riskit will need a pair of household gloves.'

'Very good, General,' said Mrs Trevenion who had just appeared with a tray of coffee things which she placed carefully on the baize covered bridge table to the general's right.

With an inward sigh, Fiskin admitted to himself that a household unable to produce even two cups, two saucers and a plate for biscuits with no single piece of china matching another had to be truly on its uppers: even the biscuits were broken.

'There's just these few things that took my eye, Sir Percival,' the dealer said when he re-entered the room an hour later, carrying a large open hatbox in his arms. 'I found most of them in the attic, mixed up with the junk there.'

The general took off his glasses, and put down the dog-eared copy of *Country Life* he was reading. 'So it was just as you said, my dear chap. Any good are they?' he completed, with more of diffidence than hope in the tone.

Fiskin placed his burden on the bridge table, and more carefully than Mrs Trevenion had done with the coffee tray earlier. He extracted his small horde of finds from the box, then took off the cotton gloves he had been loaned. Although old, the gloves had been spotlessly clean when given to him, in contrast to the condition they were in now. He placed them beside the two tarnished, silver plated eggcups, the gilt framed miniature water colour of a squinting King Charles spaniel, the cracked Waterford glass decanter, and the translucent bowl. 'I took you at your word, General,' he said. 'Had a pretty thorough rummage around.'

'Absolutely, my dear fellow. So what have you got?' The general leaned forward, his eyebrows moving up and down as he surveyed what was on the table. 'Hm. Can't believe those eggcups are worth anything. I remember the dog picture. Nobody liked it, including the dog.' He looked up and gave a bronchitic chuckle before returning to his examination. 'Thought we'd thrown away that decanter. Still worth a bob or too, is it? What's that dish thing? Don't remember seeing that before.'

'It's a small serving dish, sir, almost certainly jade,' the dealer replied to the general's question. He always kept as near to the truth as he could.

'Valuable, is it?'

Fiskin was doing his best to suppress his excitement. Once in a while, on his provincial tours, he came upon an item that compensated for all the time and money he spent knocking on doors, suffering rebuffs, spending uncomfortable nights in cheap lodgings, battling against wind, rain, and snow, and most of the time to little purpose and less profit. Eleven years ago, for instance, he had paid £50 for what he thought just might have been an oil sketch by John Constable: after experts had proved that it was, he sold it for £20,000. He had taken a risk on that oil sketch which might have proved to have been worthless: he knew too little about pictures to rely solely on his own judgement. But jade was quite a different matter.

After leaving the army, and drifting from job to job, Mr Fiskin had ended up as general dogsbody in the hallowed Bond Street premises of Lichter's, Europe's most respected dealers in fine jade. He had spent ten years at the firm, rising to a position of minor responsibility. It was after this that he had set up on his own as an antique dealer. Rarely since then had he come upon any exceptional item of jade, and hardly ever had he been in a position to buy even averagely good examples. Yet what he had just placed on the general's coffee table was one of the most exquisite, unspoiled nephrite jade serving bowls of immense antiquity that it had ever been his privilege to hold. There was no doubt in his mind, either. Mr Fiskin knew jade better than he knew his own wife.

'It's quite valuable, General, yes.' He responded now. 'Depending on its age and ... er ... You've no idea where it came from? I found it in a wooden box inside one of the cabin trunks. I had a lot of difficulty getting the trunk open.'

'Ah, you would.' The general's eyes lit up. 'Those trunks belonged to my grandfather, the admiral. Haven't been opened for years. Always thought they were full of clothes. Yes, he was Royal Navy. China Station. Jade comes from China does it?'

'Some jade does, yes, General.'

'That's it then, isn't it? It's a piece of jade he picked up on his travels. What's it worth?'

Fiskin was pleased about the convincing, uncomplicated provenance of the piece. 'I'm not an expert, but I'd say several thousand pounds. Maybe as much as . . . five thousand.' He *was* an expert, and he estimated the right buyer could offer seventy thousand for it at least. 'I tell you what, General, you've been so kind and trusting, letting me dig around by myself, I'd like to return the compliment.' He paused for a second. 'I'm prepared to risk it, go on my judgement, and offer you five thousand cash, on the spot. That's including the other items, of course,' he ended earnestly: the other items were worthless.

It was the general's turn to ponder. 'Very decent of you, Fuskit. Very decent indeed,' he responded after some moments, then made movements with his closed lips before he opened them again to say: 'But I don't want you to take a risk like that. And I don't feel I can afford to either. What if the thing is worth even more than you think? I feel we ought to get a . . . a really expert opinion.' The tightened lips wobbled again before he added. 'There's an antique dealer I know in Exeter. Used to handle a lot of ivory, that sort of thing, I remember. Bet he knows about jade. Think I'll ask him over tomorrow and—'

Fiskin's stomach gave an anguished heave. 'I can do better than that, General,' he interrupted. 'Give me a minute, and I'll get on to a friend of mine at his home, on my car phone. He's a world authority on jade. If I describe the dish to him, I'm sure he'll be able to price it. Of course, he may say it's worth less than I've offered, in which case . . .' he gave a theatrically ominous frown, leaving the sentence uncompleted. It was a ploy that sometimes worked – but not on the general.

'Well that'd be my bad luck, wouldn't it, Fostik? And I wouldn't dream of holding you to your offer if your friend says the thing's only worth a few hundred' he replied. 'No, by all means, go and phone him. I'll wait here for the verdict.'

The dealer was not away long. He sat in the car with the doors closed, pretending to use the phone, while he feverishly planned his best policy. It was clear he had to offer the general an enticing price to avoid the Exeter dealer being involved. The question was still, how much.

It was two weeks and a day later that Mr Fiskin again appeared on the doorstep of Mucklebury Lodge. This time he was accompanied by a thickset man of medium height, in his mid-forties. Their knock was answered by a pretty young woman, with tousled blonde hair, and dressed in a roll necked, fisherman's knit sweater with pushed back sleeves, and a pair of tight black slacks. 'Hi,' she said brightly, looking from the men to the Ford parked in the drive.

'Good afternoon, miss. I'm Detective Inspector Merchant, Hampshire CID,' said Mr Fiskin's companion, who had darting eyes, and an understanding smile. He showed the woman his warrant card.

'You're a bit west of your beat,' she observed.

'That's true, miss. Though it didn't take us that long from Winchester using the motorways. This is Mr Arnold Fiskin. He's helping us with our enquiries into the theft of a valuable jade bowl, and its subsequent attempted sale. We're hoping to see General Sir Percival Amhurst-Cole. Is he in?'

'General who?' the woman seemed mystified.

Merchant repeated the name.

'There's no one of that name here,' she answered, shaking her head. 'Our name's Hoplake. That's Peter my husband, and me, I'm Trudy Hoplake. I think you've got the wrong house.'

'No, this is the house all right,' said Mr Fiskin who was studying Mrs Hoplake intently.

'Do you have a housekeeper called Mrs Trevenion, ma'am?' the inspector enquired.

'No. We have no housekeeper. Couldn't afford—'

'Who is it, Trudy?' interrupted a dark haired, gangling young man in check shirt and yellow corduroys. He had appeared from behind her in the hall.

Mrs Hoplake introduced the newcomer as her husband. It was after she had explained their callers' business to him that

Inspector Merchant asked if they might come in. Peter Hoplake shrugged. 'If you think it'll do any good,' he agreed, grudgingly. 'Mr Fiskin says he was admitted to this house mid morning, on Sunday, 19 February. That's two weeks ago yesterday, sir,' said the inspector. 'I'd like him to identify the rooms he was in for me.'

Hoplake frowned. 'Two weeks ago yesterday? But you couldn't have been here that morning, Mr Fiskin. We were out the previous morning, but on the Sunday we were in all day. I was working in the study—'

'And I was busy in the kitchen from eleven onwards, making cakes, and getting the lunch. We had roast beef, and all the trimmings,' put in the ebullient Mrs Hoplake.

'I was first shown into the room over there,' Mr Fiskin insisted. Ignoring what the Hoplakes had said, he had moved past them and made for the drawing-room door.

'Ah, well that proves it's the wrong house,' countered Hoplake. 'That door's kept locked by the landlord, and we don't even have a key to it.'

'Landlord, sir?' questioned the inspector. 'You rent the house, do you?'

'That's right. Took it on a monthly basis last June. It'd been on the market for ages. It's totally unsaleable, or even rentable on a commercial basis. The owners let us have it cheap, basically to keep out the vandals until they can find a buyer. Suits us pretty well. I'm a playwright and TV scriptwriter. Need plenty of hush. This place is glorious in the summer. Freezing in the winter, like now of course, but we only use three rooms, the study, the kitchen, and one bedroom. My wife's usually away in the daytime.'

'I work freelance for cosmetic companies, as an in-store demonstrator. It's not my proper job, but it brings in some lolly,' Mrs Hoplake provided, a touch regretfully.

'But I think I'd be right in saying your proper job is acting, isn't it, ma'am?' said the inspector. 'I've seen you on the stage. Both of you.'

Mrs Hoplake gave a quick glance at her husband, then

answered. 'How clever of you, inspector.' If she had at first seemed fazed by the question, she was obviously flattered at the recognition. 'You probably saw us when we were in the Wessex Players, a touring rep. Great little company – before it folded. We often played Winchester.'

'Shakespeare in the open air, schools, and stately homes. I remember, ma'am. And you were very good, too.' The inspector nodded at her approvingly, before asking her husband. 'So which of these rooms is the study, sir?'

'Through there.' Hoplake pointed to a door on the right. 'Want to see?'

The policeman turned to the deeply silent Fiskin. 'Did you go in there, sir?'

'No, I didn't. The door was locked. The general said it was an empty room. And I didn't go in the kitchen either because he said there'd be nothing of any interest, and Mrs Trevenion objected to outsiders being there.'

'What about our bedroom, Mr Fiskin?' It was Mrs Hoplake who asked the question, in an overly indulgent tone.

'I went in all four of the unoccupied bedrooms. They only had odd bits of worthless furniture in them. All junk.'

'Ours is the one at the top of the stairs on the right,' said Peter Hoplake.

Mr Fiskin was now studying Hoplake's face as searchingly as he had done Mrs Hoplake's earlier. 'The general said that was his room,' he responded. 'And not to go in there because it was too untidy, with nothing for me in it.' He swallowed, and turned to the inspector. 'As a matter fact, I did try to look in, but the door was locked.'

'Incredible. It's never locked. And did our phantom house-keeper have a bedroom?' asked Mrs Hoplake, still humouring Mr Fiskin.

'Mrs Trevenion? No, she didn't,' he answered. 'The general explained she lived in the village.'

'Then shouldn't you try to find her there?' demanded Hoplake, his tone not nearly as understanding as his wife's.

'We did, sir,' replied the inspector, with a glance at Mr Fiskin.

'We asked several people, but no one seems to have heard of her. Or the general, come to that.'

'That doesn't surprise me. The house is owned by a family called Edwards. I believe most of them live in Wales.'

'Mr Fiskin had the same trouble when he asked in the village about who was living in the house. That was on his first visit. On the day before he says he gained admittance to the house.'

'When I expect he found nobody knew our name either. Is that what you discovered today, too, inspector?' Hoplake asked.

'It was, sir, yes.'

'That's because we don't fraternise at all. We don't use the village store even, because it's a rip off.' Hoplake paused briefly before addressing Mr Fiskin directly. 'I don't suppose you went in the attic here, by any chance?' he said.

'Yes. It's where I found the jade bowl we're here about. It was in an old cabin trunk belonging to the general's grandfather. He was an admiral. On the China Station,' he completed, it seemed somewhat lamely, though it could have been because he still seemed preoccupied with something else.

Trudy Hoplake let out a giggle, then quickly covered her mouth with her hands. 'Oh, I'm so sorry, Mr Fiskin,' she cried, 'but it does all sound so unlikely to us.' She was still doing her best to suppress her amusement as she went on. 'You see, the attic is locked as well. The keys are kept by the agents in Exeter. If we absolutely have to go in any of the locked rooms, one of their representatives has to be present. It's a terrible ritual when it does happen. Like when Peter thought there was a wasps' nest up there. The old boy they sent is so meticulous. Except that time he got locked in the attic with the wasps. The draught up the stairs blew the door shut. It was a scream. I mean he wasn't in any danger, because there weren't any wasps after all. But he'd left his bunch of keys in the—'

'Look, why don't you both sit down, and tell us exactly what's supposed to have happened in detail,' Hoplake had cut in sharply on his wife. 'Maybe we can throw some light on the problem after all.'

They were all in the study by this time, a cosy room in its own way, gloriously untidy, with a log fire burning briskly in the grate. There were books and bits of manuscript stacked everywhere, including the floor, with a desk computer and a printer contrasting with the decrepit looking desk – and the even more decrepit armchair behind it which had immediately captured Mr Fiskin's full attention. The two visitors took the upright chairs that Hoplake had just cleared of books and papers, while Trudy Hoplake perched herself on a corner of the desk.

The inspector cleared his throat. 'Ten days ago, Mr Fiskin left a valuable antique jade bowl at Christie's in London. It was to be auctioned by them next month. He instructed that a reserved price should be put on it of sixty thousand pounds. After he left, the alert lady in charge of cataloguing the sale thought she recognized the item. She was right. It happened it had been re-valued by the firm last year, for insurance purposes. Property of Sir Paul Fitzammon, the industrialist, and kept in his country house, Charwood Hall, near Winchester. Sir Paul and his wife have been in America since the middle of February, but a check was made with the gardener and his wife, she's the housekeeper, and then with Sir Paul himself by phone. It seems the bowl had been stolen since he and Lady Fitzammon were last in the house on 17 February.'

'Straight burglary was it?' asked Hoplake.

'Seems so, sir, and we believe we know how and when it was done. Nothing else was missing, which is probably why the absence of the bowl was overlooked by the couple. They live in a cottage in the grounds, not the house itself. Sir Paul has a large collection of jade which he keeps in locked glass display cabinets. It's a well known collection, like other things in Charwood Hall, which is open to the public several times a year, for charity. Oh, and they have theatrical performances in the long gallery. Perhaps you've performed there?'

Hoplake frowned as if searching his memory. 'No I don't believe we have, inspector.' Then, at a glance from his wife, he corrected. 'Oh yes, come to think of it, we did once. But in the Charwood Hall garden, not the house. It was in the summer.' The tone was dismissive.

'Well, I never, sir. Anyway, one of the display cabinets had been neatly forced. The other items in it had simply been moved around slightly to disguise the gap.'

'Doesn't the house have an alarm system?' questioned Mrs Hoplake.

'Yes, ma'am. But it was being updated at the time, along with the electrical wiring of the whole house. It's now pretty certain the thief was a man in overalls, carrying a clip board and a tool case, who walked in early on Saturday the 18th. The people from the electrical contractors assumed he was from the alarm company, except no one from the alarm company was supposed to be there that day. It was all pretty cool, really. And since the loss happened on our patch, it was my job to go to London and find out from Mr Fiskin how he came by the bowl. His story is—'

'The truth of the matter is, Inspector,' Mr Fiskin interrupted in an uncharacteristically insistent voice, 'I bought it in good faith from someone who said he was General Sir Percival Amhurst-Cole in this house two weeks ago.'

'Quite so, sir,' the policeman agreed, 'except the only gentleman of that rank and title died not long ago in retirement, in Florida.'

'But presumably you got a bill of sale, Mr Fiskin?' said Hoplake.

The dealer reddened. 'I paid cash, and . . . and there was no receipt.'

'How much did you pay?'

'Twenty-five thousand pounds,' came the almost whispered reply.

'Wow! D'you always carry that much about you in cash?'

'More, quite often. Cash is . . . is quite common in my trade.'

'But not to get a receipt surely—'

'In this case, I'm afraid, I gave in to the general's plea, his heartfelt plea. He seemed so totally genuine,' replied the hapless Mr Fiskin. 'He er . . . he wanted no record of the sale. He was very anxious to avoid paying capital gains tax on it.'

Hoplake shook his head. 'Could I ask, is Mr Fiskin under arrest, Inspector?'

Merchant looked at Mr Fiskin. 'He's not under arrest, no. As I said before, he's helping us with our inquiries into the matter.' His voice still made it plain that Mr Fiskin could hardly be regarded as some innocent kind of witness.

'Poor Mr Fiskin,' said Mrs Hoplake. 'I wish we could be of help. But really it's a total mystery.'

'If you were here,' said her husband, 'wandering about in rooms that are never used, surely your fingerprints would still be all over the place.'

'No they wouldn't,' Mr Fiskin countered firmly. He had stiffened suddenly, and was wearing a determined expression as though he had just made an important decision. He moved to the edge of his chair, and was staring hard at Hoplake. 'And you know perfectly well why there'll be no fingerprints of mine here. The general gave me gloves to wear. And I was grateful for them. The place was very dusty. And leaving me to go round on my own was masterly, as well. It gave what happened much more believability. It was known I'd be thorough, of course. That I wouldn't miss the jade. Every antique dealer is thorough.' He took a deep breath, then went on. 'Only it wasn't any general who gave me the gloves, was it? It was you, Mr Hoplake. You, made up to look like a ninety year old, and behaving like one, just as your wife turned herself into an outsized housekeeper. No doubt, when I'd left, you both went round wiping everything I touched, before I had the gloves on, and after I'd taken them off. That would have been easy.'

'What nonsense—' Hoplake began.

'It isn't nonsense, Inspector,' Mr Fiskin protested. 'I'd guess he's just an aspiring playwright, living off his wife's meagre earnings. They're obviously both out of work actors. You recognized them. And lucky for me you did, because they might have gone on fooling me. The impersonations, and the make-up, were brilliant, I give them that. But they're professionals, aren't they? It's obvious to me now what happened. Hoplake, acting this time as an electrician, stole the bowl in Winchester, from a house he's just had to admit he knows. Before even he's worked out a way to dispose of it, difficult with stolen goods of this value, he and his wife get home from Winchester to find I'd come along out of the blue, and left my card saying I'd be back. That gave them a day to dress the stage. And I fell for what they did.'

'Oh, pull the other one, Fiskin,' Hoplake interjected dismissively. 'You don't buy any of this do you, Inspector?'

The policeman folded his arms. 'I don't think Mr Fiskin is through yet, sir. I'd like to hear him out, if you don't mind.'

Mrs Hoplake stood up. 'Well I mind a lot,' she put in hotly. 'So how is this man supposed to have bought a jade bowl from us here when he's never been inside the house. He can't even identify any of the rooms he says he was in, because he's never been in them. Neither have we. Not most of them. They're permanently locked.'

'Except you have keys to them all, Mrs Hoplake,' said Mr Fiskin. 'You have to have. The chair your husband is sitting in was in the drawing-room the day I was here.'

'Tosh. It's his favourite chair, and it's always in here. And if it was in the drawing-room, how did we get it out?'

'You needed it as a prop to give credence. There probably wasn't an armchair in the drawing-room. Everything else there was junk,' Mr Fiskin asserted. Then he turned to the inspector. 'I'm positive the Hoplakes have keys to all the rooms.'

'How could we?' demanded Hoplake.

'Well, one way was to take wax impressions of them when you locked the agent's man in the attic that time. Before you interrupted her, your over confident wife was saying he'd left the keys on the outside when the wind conveniently blew the door shut. I think you needed duplicate keys. To see if there was anything worth pinching in any of the rooms. That's why you invented the wasp story.'

'Imaginative, but still nonsense,' Hoplake responded, but his tone was now more blustering than confident. 'I repeat, this man has never been in this house.'

'Do you challenge me to prove the opposite, Mr Hoplake?'

'Certainly, I do.'

'Then can we all go upstairs now?'

Hoplake shrugged, and looked at his wife. 'As you please. But it's not going to prove anything.'

A minute later Mr Fiskin had the group assembled in one of the bedrooms on the next floor. The room was uncarpeted, and what furniture there was in it was arranged haphazardly in the centre.

Mr Fiskin walked over to a large, white painted, bow fronted chest of drawers. 'When I looked in here and saw this piece, I thought it just might be early Georgian, made of mahogany or even rosewood, but painted over by some Victorian half wit. To make sure, I turned it over, got out my penknife, and cut a small piece off the underside where it wouldn't be seen, or do any real damage. It's quite a common practice in the trade. Doesn't affect the value of a piece like this, though I'm afraid the cutting splintered slightly, leaving a jagged edge. Anyway, I pocketed it, meaning to check on it later. Then, in my excitement with the jade, I forgot it. I'm glad I did. The inspector has it now.'

As Mr Fiskin turned the chest of drawers over, Inspector Merchant took a small transparent evidence bag from his pocket. Removing the two inch long sliver of wood from the bag, he knelt down, and first examined the area to which Mr Fiskin was pointing. Then he glanced up at Hoplake. 'I think you'd better come and see this, sir,' he said. And while the others watched, he slipped the small, uneven wood cutting on to the abrasion in the painted surface: the fit was perfect.

The inspector got to his feet again, and faced Hoplake. 'Do you have anything to add to what you've told me already, sir? Or you ma'am?' he asked, and when there was no immediate response, he added. 'Or would either of you like to alter anything you've said?'

'Certainly not,' Hoplake replied in an arrogant tone.

'But you do understand, sir, that Mr Fiskin has just proved he must have been in the house, so that the rest of his story and his conclusions—'

'This is obviously a fit up,' Hoplake shouted, red in the face, and looking from the inspector to Mr Fiskin. 'Neither of us will say anything else at all until we have a solicitor present.'

'As you please, sir. But I'm afraid I'll have to ask both of you to come back to Winchester Police Station with me to answer further questions,' said the inspector. He turned to Mr Fiskin. 'Have you anything you want to add, sir?'

Mr Fiskin grinned, fingering the wood cutting in his hand. 'Only to thank God, Inspector, for the tricks of the trade.'

UNCLE'S GIRL

I went down to see Uncle Ted in November. Christmas was on the way. As his only living relative I thought he should have me in the front of his mind.

Strictly speaking, he wasn't a real uncle: more of a cousin twice removed – a rich, elderly, childless, widower cousin. He'd pay for attention the older he got. If you follow me.

He was going on seventy-nine with failing everything, especially his eyesight. He'd been a fishmonger in South London: made a packet my mother used to say. He and his wife retired to the Sussex coast. When she died he sold up and moved to this residential hotel between Brighton and Worthing: gloomsville and a swine to get to, especially without a car. It had fourteen guest rooms, two with private baths, and uncle didn't have either of those. He wouldn't. Still, the tighter he was with his loot the more there'd be to leave.

The divorce had cost me a packet. That was the year before. I'd had to give my ex-wife Doris half of everything, even though we didn't have kids. Barbara and I took on a flat in Clapham. It didn't work out – with Barbara I mean, not the flat. I still had the flat. She left after six months. I got lumbered with the whole of the mortgage and a load of debts she'd run up when it was all sweetness and light.

My job was in insurance – middle management at head office in London. It was lower middle-management really with no prospects at thirty-nine if they had started passing you over for promotion at thirty-five. I should have taken exams. I accepted that when it was too late – and too early to be thinking about my indexed pension.

What I'd always fancied was a franchise – like a launderette, perhaps – where you're your own boss. But you have to have starting capital. Doris never bought the idea: too risky. National Savings Certificates were too risky for bloody Doris. Barbara was keen enough till she found out she'd be cooking the beef-burgers herself – that was to do with the fast-food franchise I enquired about. Anyway, they wanted married couples and our 'trial marriage' was on the way to failing by then. We should have got properly hooked when the divorce came through. At the time I wasn't keen; later she wasn't.

There were a lot of things I should have done.

Uncle was fairly pleased to see me: less than he should have been with the cost of the train fare from London Bridge plus what they were charging for the 'winter weekend break' at the Westside Hotel. I'd been hoping uncle would pick up the tab for that.

He'd been a big man, but he'd shrunk, the way old people do. His collar was too big. He stooped too. 'They throw in meals, except Sunday lunch,' he said as he went into dinner on Friday, just after I'd arrived. 'They'll charge extra for Sunday lunch if you have it here.'

'I'll probably have to go Sunday morning, uncle.' It wasn't true: just a precaution.

'Well, check the bill when you pay it.' Now it was true. 'See you aren't charged extra for lunch tomorrow. It's all in. Except Sunday lunch.' He kept repeating things. 'I'll speak to Miss Evans if you like.' He was quite eager about the last bit.

Miss Evans was the manageress, and what you might call a bit of all right. Not exactly flashy and no spring chicken – about thirty-five, I'd guessed: ample figure, maturing nicely. I remembered her from the time Doris and I had come down for the day in the Mini eighteen months before. Dark Celtic type, black wavy hair, wet lips and come-on brown eyes that bored into yours daring you to snatch a glance at the bare cleavage lower down.

It was hard to understand what she was doing at the Westside.

Doris had said that. The place was half empty now. It hadn't been much better that summer. The regular inmates were all practically geriatric. People wanting a weekend break with no ulterior motive like me wouldn't pick a dump like this. There were no shops, nothing to do, no proper promenade and the beach across the main road was just a narrow bit of shingle. It was an in-between sort of place, as I said. I was the only non permanent in the dining-room. Of course, all the others got special rates for endurance.

'Marvellous woman,' said uncle. He was straining through the pebble glasses to watch Miss Evans and missing his mouth with the Brown Windsor soup. She seemed to be doing most of the serving and all the drink orders. She'd been behind the little bar in the lounge before dinner. Uncle had bought us a sherry each – no choice offered. Still, I enjoy sherry for a change.

'Short-handed?' I asked.

Uncle nodded. 'They always let half the staff go at the end of the summer. There's only Gwen – that's Miss Evans – and four others full time now. One chamber maid, the waitress in here and two people in the kitchen. The chef's Jamaican.'

So it was Gwen, I thought. He hadn't called her that in the bar. Out loud I said, 'Wonder why she sticks it here?'

'Vocation,' he answered loftily, as though she was a nun and he was stating a grave and fundamental truth.

I watched the ministering angel. Uncle's idea did her credit, but her legs were too good for a nun. She wasn't averting her gaze from me either. Mark you, I was the youngest male around by about four decades – except for the chef. You could see him in his tall white hat through the serving hatch. He was a big, beaming black man, late twenties with a pointed beard. His name was Alec Nelson, uncle told me (twice); brought up in England. He'd got a college diploma in catering. The fish cakes we had weren't bad.

That night we watched TV in the bar till uncle and the other oldies went to bed straight after the ten o'clock news – like there was a curfew. It was too early for me. Anyhow, I had ideas about chatting up Miss Evans.

She'd been doing paperwork at the reception desk in the hall since dinner. When she came in to lock up the bar I bought her a gin, with a whisky for me. Then we got talking. She sat on a stool behind the bar like the one I was using in front. It was cosy – heads together sort of thing from the start.

She was wearing a V-necked, button through, black wool cardigan next to the skin. The top two buttons had been open all evening. As she poured the whisky she'd deliberately undone the next two with a little sigh of relief – as though she was going off duty: relaxing.

We talked for nearly an hour. Uncle had told her a bit about me. She seemed to like me. I'm no Robert Redford. More an Alan Ladd, if you remember him – with glasses, and my hair's gone a bit in the front. I don't bowl every girl over, but I get my share.

The way she told it, Gwen Evans had had a tough life. She came from Cardiff. Her father had died in an accident when she was little. After that her mother had gone back to hotel house-keeping – abroad some of the time. Gwen's schooling had been messed up a lot. Then her mother had snuffed it. It was a compli-cated story and a bit boring so I wasn't listening that carefully; just looking and weighing up the chances.

I remember she said she was insecure. That was why she didn't move on: knew she could cope with the Westside. She enjoyed looking after old people. So uncle was right. I got the idea she wasn't against young ones though – men anyway.

'I'm for bed,' I said around eleven-thirty. We'd both had a few drinks by then. 'How about joining me, baby?' It was more of a joke than a come-on really – but it worked.

'If you like,' she answered, just as if I'd offered her another drink, 'Your room's best.'

And that was it. One night of bliss for the asking. She'd left before I woke in the morning. I saw her at the reception desk when I came down for breakfast. She was advising a couple of old biddies about something. She glanced up and smiled at me, asked if I'd slept well. There were plenty of flip answers to that one, all unusable at the time.

I spent the day dancing attendance on uncle, trying to bring the conversation round to my inheriting his money. He was hedging on that one. I was a disappointment. No children, no prospects, and a broken marriage – that was me. And uncle didn't approve of divorce either.

Except for Gwen it looked like being a wasted journey. I guessed she'd be about after dinner but she wasn't. When the others trooped off to bed it was Nelson, the chef, who came in to lock the bar. I asked where Miss Evans was. 'Out,' he said, and did I want anything. Yes, but nothing he could give me. I hung around for a bit, then I turned in.

She was there when I left in the morning. Gave me my bill but there was no chance to speak privately. I'd given her meaning looks in the dining-room during breakfast, and when I was paying. There was no what you might call keen response, but uncle was with me all the time watching her as usual. He didn't seem to mind that I was going early.

The following week I rang a few times. She seemed glad to hear me but she was always too busy to chat. I asked her to come up to London. She said she'd let me know: she never did.

Two things happened in the February. First, I was made redundant. Ten thousand pounds compensation for being replaced by a silicon chip. There were more than two million unemployed in the country at the time. I was still reeling from that little surprise when uncle's letter arrived on the tenth. He had married Miss Evans the previous day at the Brighton Register Office.

'So it's my baby,' I said to her as we walked along the sea front after lunch two Saturdays later. Uncle was feeling the need to rest every afternoon since the honeymoon. Serve him right, the silly old sod, was my private reaction to that. 'But why didn't you tell me? You had the address.'

'Take advantage, you mean? I couldn't have done that.'

She had a lovely voice: low pitched with that soft Welsh accent. She was right too. I'd told her about my money problems that night in November. Taking on a woman with child was the last thing I'd have wanted – even before I got the sack. Still, I'd have felt an obligation.

It was her fault, of course. I'd asked about precautions at the time. She'd said not to worry, so I hadn't.

What she'd done might be best for her. Mark you, it was me who might be paying in the long run. The chances of coming into any of uncle's money had gone from the remote to the non-existent. And all because he'd been tricked into thinking he was the father of my child.

She'd got worried before Christmas, she explained. It was on Boxing Day she let him have his way with her, as she put it, though God knows what happened. He looked too frail to spit. What I didn't know was he'd been after her for ages, though I might have guessed. There was no encouragement required: he'd just needed the 'off'.

After waiting a month she'd gone to uncle sobbing with a pregnancy note from her doctor. Uncle hadn't checked dates or anything – just got a special marriage licence, and that was it.

'My idea was to keep it in the family, like,' she said.

'You mean you think the boy will look like uncle?' I asked. 'But I don't look like uncle, so why should . . .'

'That's only part of it, silly,' I remember her interrupting. 'When Ted dies there'll be no death duties. His money will stay intact. Pass to me. That's an improvement for both of us – and our little baby.'

The Welsh are good on death. I'd noticed it before. She was right. If uncle had stayed a widower there'd have been big taxes to pay on his estate when he snuffed it. Even if he'd left it all to me, at the time the lion's share would have gone to the Revenue. We sold policies to protect people from that sort of thing – to shield deserving dependants: uncle wouldn't have bought one.

I watched her smiling into the wind. Suddenly the penny dropped. 'You mean . . . you mean you'll marry me when . . .'

'If you like.'

If I'd like! I damned nearly jumped in the bloody ocean: jumped for joy. I threw my arms around her.

'Not where they might see us from the hotel,' she said, pushing me away. 'All that'll have to wait.'

'OK, darling.' What a twist: this woman was a genius. I was

about to marry a genius. 'You know how much he's worth?'

'Something over half a million pounds,' she answered, quick as a flash. That was a lot of money at the time. 'Just be patient, Arthur.'

Of course, that was the problem.

I went to see them again the second weekend in March. She'd arranged it. Uncle looked older; well, you can understand it. Mentally he was all right, and still tickled pink about the baby. His sight seemed to have got worse.

Gwen had insisted she kept her job, that they went on living at the hotel.

'How else can anyone afford servants these days?' uncle asked.

Well, he could for a start, the stupid old miser. But I wasn't one to suggest he went carving into 'our' fortune.

We were having a sherry before lunch on the Saturday. Gwen was busy somewhere. 'She's a wise woman,' uncle went on, as if I didn't know. 'Expect I'll die before her.' He said it as though there was room for doubt. 'If the child isn't grown up' – meaning if uncle failed to reach a hundred – 'Gwen will still have new money coming in. With inflation she may need it. Naturally I'll leave her everything I have.' He leaned over to peer at me. He was making sure I got his meaning. 'All of it.' That was to leave no possible doubt. There was no finesse with uncle.

I didn't let it stick in my throat. 'Quite right,' I said. 'Able woman like that needs to keep busy, even with a child. And if you go first there'll be her job to fall back on, apart from what you leave.'

It was a funny arrangement. He'd moved from the first floor to the third – a room next to Gwen's. It meant he had the use of her bathroom and a cramped sitting-room she had up there. But they weren't sharing a bedroom. He said his snoring kept her awake and it was just as easy for her to pop in when required. He made it sound as if she did all the requiring: that her demand was insatiable.

Really he was still just another hotel guest with a few special privileges – well one anyway. Good thing there was a lift, other-wise the stairs to the top floor might have done for him, I thought. The lift was the Westside's single salute to the advance of technology. It was also the way they kept the worn-out guests; even so, it was always breaking down.

'Arthur, darling, I do need you so much,' she said to me as soon as we were out of the hotel after lunch. The afternoon walks seemed to be routine when I was down. The passionate plea was new, but very acceptable. 'I think of you all the time. The life we'll have together. One day, that is.' Now she was pouting.

'Won't be so long,' I comforted without much conviction. 'I don't know why you don't come up to Clapham, to the flat, for the odd night.' I'd pressed her often enough. She thought it was too risky – that uncle might find out.

I was still working out my six months' redundancy notice. After that I wanted to do a crash course in hotel management. We'd talked about taking on a hotel with uncle's money – even buying the Westside and tarting it up. The owners were a small Lancashire firm. Gwen thought they'd sell us it cheap if she threatened to leave otherwise.

'He'll last for years.' She sighed.

'Doesn't look that spry,' I said.

'You'd be surprised. Saves up his energy.' She looked at me with meaning: almost accusingly. She knew I found that bit of their relationship disgusting. She took my arm for a minute. 'Tonight will be all right though, lover.'

It was too. I don't know what she'd done to uncle but she came to my room at midnight. It was the first time since – well, the first time.

After, when we were lying in bed smoking, she started telling me about the humiliations. Uncle had his kinky side. Funny, you'd never guess. It made me angry, but what could I do?

'He ought to be put down,' I said.

'How?' she asked. She put her cigarette out and drew her nails slowly across my stomach.

What I'd said wasn't meant to be serious. Now she got me thinking. 'Push him over Beachy Head?' It wasn't far along the coast. 'Point him in the right direction he'd walk over by himself.'

'Down the lift shaft'll be easier.' It sounded as though she'd just thought of it.

'But it's got automatic doors. They won't open without the cage being there.' It was a cheap looking lift but still modern.

'You can open them when the power's off. There's a little catch release. They'll be doing repairs tomorrow.'

'But it hasn't broken down.'

'It will tomorrow.' She came closer to me.

'But it's Sunday.'

'They'll come. The emergency service's seven days a week. They're very good.'

Then she told me how we were going to murder uncle.

Next day we all had sherry before lunch in her sitting-room. Uncle had been grousing about climbing the stairs after chapel because the lift was broken again. He was sure it broke down when he needed it.

Even though they'd had a civil marriage (to please Gwen he'd told me), Uncle was a Methodist – a lustful one by all accounts, the old hypocrite. There was a taxi that took him to chapel and back every Sunday. I was glad he'd been this Sunday. Apart from sort of settling his mind for the longer journey it gave me a chance to rehearse.

Gwen was in and out of the room; mostly out. At one-twenty she came back for a minute. 'The lift's working,' she said. 'I'm giving the engineer lunch in the kitchen now. That way if it goes wrong again he'll still be here.'

'Thinks of everything,' said uncle. He was right.

'You two come down sharp at half-past. Sharp now,' she ordered. The other guests would be nearly through with their food by then. The idea was Gwen could eat with us without having to cope with the serving.

At half-past I went on ahead, passed the stairs and along the corridor to the lift. Uncle had gone to the bathroom. The corridor was narrow and quite dark.

There was a sagging chain hung across the lift. It was about knee-high in the middle. There was a metal notice on it saying 'under repair'. I pushed the doors. They rolled open.

I could have called it off right then: nearly did. I looked down the shaft. You couldn't see the bottom, but I knew the cage was four floors down in the basement. 'What if he lived to be ninety-five?' she'd said. 'People do.'

I unhooked the chain on one side.

The waiting was something terrible. What if someone came? There was only one other person on this floor – an old lady. She had flu. Her meals were being sent up. Gwen had already fixed her. Still I sweated.

When uncle came I stood aside for him. 'Thank heaven we don't have to walk down,'he said as he stepped into space. 'The light's out . . .'

He didn't shout or anything; didn't finish what he was saying either. Surprise probably. He just went. I heard the dull crunch as he hit the bottom.

My first thought was to get to the stairs. I was supposed to be walking down. As I turned round there was Alec Nelson standing right behind me. He was holding the old girl's dirty tray, but he hadn't come from her room. He must have been in the empty one opposite the lift.

I tried to speak but there was no voice. I was terrified. He must have seen the whole thing. Then he winked. Winked! 'Get down the stairs, man,' he said quietly. I watched him do up the chain again. I was supposed to have done that.

The verdict of the Coroner's Court was death by misadventure. They blamed uncle's failing sight. It came out he was waiting for new glasses. Gwen had taken him to the oculist's the week before. His old glasses were shown and that clinched it. They looked like those thick leaded light windows you see in places like Stratford-on-Avon.

The coroner didn't blame the lift people or the hotel. They'd taken proper precautions, he said. Uncle knew the lift was broken but must have forgotten. He'd pushed the doors open himself and tripped over the chain put there to warn people. The court's sympathy went out to the deeply distressed widow. Black really suited Gwen.

I was there for the inquest and the funeral a few days earlier. The solicitor from Brighton read the will out loud in Gwen's sitting-room. That was after we came back from the cemetery. Uncle had left me his watch, and his cuff links. I looked grateful. The solicitor looked relieved. I think he was afraid I'd protest.

Uncle carved up to six hundred and twenty thousand pounds. The will was only two months' old. Gwen was a very new wife. Being the only known relative I might have been awkward. But I was all sweetness and light; not too sweet on the widow, of course. We'd agreed on that. I was understanding in a lofty sort of way. I gave out that the last thing I expected was a fat cut of uncle's money.

I'd got the word on Alec Nelson by then – or thought I had, and not before time. Straight after the 'accident' I didn't know if he was going to shop me or not. It was worse than standing at that lift waiting for uncle to come, especially when the police arrived. Then, bold as brass, and as if we'd fixed it between us, he said we were passing on the stairs when we both heard the thud. He was my alibi, but not for nothing.

I had left for London on the evening of uncle's death. That was something we'd arranged in advance. We'd decided to do what we'd have done naturally – if it had been a real accident, I mean. Alec had kept out of my way, but as soon as I told Gwen what had happened she'd said she'd cope with him. She knew him pretty well. Next day she rang me to say he'd settled for five thousand quid to keep his mouth shut. She said I wasn't to worry about him. She trusted him and we could afford his price. He hadn't liked uncle or something. I had to believe she was right.

I made one visit in April and another in May: just for the day each time. I'd bought a little car by then, on hire purchase. There was no need to economize. I had the redundancy money coming but Gwen insisted we shouldn't do anything to make people suspicious. Leave things 'a decent interval' she kept saying – till after the baby was born. There was too much at stake to run risks now. I thought she meant the many happy years ahead together, but after the will was proved it was only me who mentioned them.

The premature birth happened late afternoon on the first

Saturday in June. One of the old biddies in the hotel got my number and rang me. None of her business, she said, but she knew I was uncle's only relative and all that. I drove straight to the hospital.

Gwen was pretty bad. There'd been complications. The Ward Sister was very understanding. She was West Indian. She said I'd just missed Mr Nelson. I remember thinking it was nice of him to have come. Then she told me.

You had to hand it to Gwen, even if you were bitter. She was clever, especially the way she'd thought two jumps ahead all the time. Seducing me, getting pregnant, bedding uncle so he'd marry her: brilliant. I had to OK the marriage since the child was mine. And after she'd promised to marry me when uncle was dead, she'd set me up not to query the will – at least till it was too late.

The only hitch was uncle didn't expire on cue. She had counted on the stairs and the raving sex life wiping him out fast. They hadn't. It was only his sight that weakened. She got impatient after that.

Gwen could have done uncle in without me, but why miss a trick? If I did the murder, with a witness she could handle thrown in, she was laughing. After that she didn't need to speak to me, let alone marry me, to keep me quiet for ever.

She was getting better when they let me see her the next day: well enough to tell me to get lost. There was to be ten thousand pounds for me, enough for the ice-cream franchise. It's what I still do – sell branded ice-cream from a van. That was my payoff. And lucky, Gwen said, since there was no obligation.

I still couldn't believe it. 'What would you have said to me when the baby was born?' I asked. It was a still-birth, by the way: seven months Sister said.

'What would I have said? What I'm saying now, boyo.'

I asked for that one. 'All right. What if uncle had been alive? What if Sister had told him what she told me yesterday?'

'Well, if nothing else had killed him that would've, wouldn't it?'

She was probably right. What Sister had said was, 'Such a

perfect baby too. Pity the father's gone.' She'd paused then, as if in memory. 'She was so keen to have the baby. Came here to pre-natal clinic. Never missed.' She did a bit of tutting. 'Being a close relative you'll know they'd set their hearts on running a hotel in Montego Bay with their little family.'

Uncle had never told me. 'I remember,' I'd said, to keep up appearances.

'So sad.' Sister had shaken her head. 'It was such a lovely baby. Such a lovely little black baby boy.'

A PUBLIC SERVICE

The four men had played bridge on the first Monday of every month for several years. They met in the basement cardroom of the Renaissance Club in London's Pall Mall at six, and played until ten, breaking for drinks and sandwiches at around eight. If one of them was away, a stand-in was sometimes recruited to make a fourth for the game, but more often the meeting would be cancelled. The four were close friends who in truth valued each other's company more than they did the bridge.

All of the four lived in London, and each was distinguished in his own field. Sir Roger Godber was a Crown Court Judge. Felix Rice, recently created Lord Rice, had once been a cabinet minister, but was now chairman of one large public company and a director of several others. Richard Steen was a senior Harley Street cardiologist. Clive Wallace was a prominent architect, and a widower, which made him the only unmarried member of the group.

'But Clive's hypothesis is quite simple. It assumes one of us is told he's going to die in three months. That he can use the chance to rid the world of someone or something vile. In short to perform a . . . a public service. Isn't that right Clive?' questioned Rice, the ex-politician, in his deep, resonant voice. He took a tentative sip of the claret which had just been poured, raised the glass a foot in front of his eyes, twisted the stem, admired the colour of the wine against the light, then treated himself to a more serious draught. Rice was a heavy man, with a well-fed face, prominent ears, domineering eyebrows and an avuncular expression that had mesmerized a majority of the voters in a Surrey constituency over two decades.

'That's more or less the idea, yes,' Clive Wallace answered, but hesitantly. 'Assuming that if the action is illegal, that even if he's found out, it won't matter because there'll be no time for trial and punishment. Naturally, he'd have to leave a confession to be read after his death. To stop anyone else being blamed for what he'd done.'

'Naturally,' Rice echoed vigorously in the practised politician's reflex manner of agreeing to anything virtuous on principle.

It was the first Monday in a freezing February. The friends had played two rubbers and had stopped for refreshments which had appeared on the cleared card table without summons. Perkins, the wiry, attentive cardroom night steward, was normally stationed in the small dispense bar and buttery between the card-room and the library. He had brought the laden silver tray through after checking the progress of the bridge game by partly opening a sliding wooden panel behind the seat in his eerie.

It was common for stimulating discussion to break out between the four friends at this point. If the present topic was on the surface more serious than some had been in the past, it appeared also to be fairly academic – and no less so to His Honour Judge Godber than to the others.

Godber was a small, neat man. His voice was high and pene-trating, and he clipped his consonants. Now he sniffed and made a steeple with sensitive, well manicured fingers. 'But if one of us had really been told he'd contracted some wasting or anyway terminal condition, and that death was so imminent, why should it follow he should contemplate murder?' he demanded. He jerked his head back as if it were controlled by cogs, then his quizzical gaze swept the others as he continued. 'In such circum-stances, for my part, I'd be inclined to divide the time left to me between riotous living and earnest communing with my Maker. Mark you, I'm not sure in what proportion the time would be allocated between the two.' He gave the self indulgent smile of a judge overly amused by his own double drollery, and who expected others to be equally entertained.

'The idea of assassination as a public service followed what Felix was saying earlier about ridding the world of despots,' said Wallace. 'I can think of . . .'

'It would still mean taking the law into one's own hands, of course,' Godber interrupted, leaning forward for his glass, his words more considered than before. 'No one can do that with impunity, particularly if it involves taking another's life. Dangerous thinking altogether.'

'And very likely impossible in a deeply ill man.' This was Steen, the physician, speaking for the first time since he had thus far been too involved in eating and drinking to do anything else. Tall, dark, slim, and polished in appearance as well as manner, he had the urbane, chiselled features of a well preserved, if matured matinée idol. 'Setting off to shoot some dictator in a far off land would hardly be within the scope of a seriously weakened patient.' He wiped his mouth with his napkin. 'These spiced chicken sandwiches are very moorish. I'm going to order an extra round,' he completed, hand moving forward energetically to help himself to the last of the delicacies.

'Don't know how you keep so slim,' grumbled Rice. 'You're right, though, Richard. I couldn't begin to match the energy and fire power of an SAS man, even without being seriously weakened by illness.' He gave a despairing glance at his bulging waistcoat with its gold watchchain and fob adornments.

Clive Wallace shook his head which had a frieze of unruly hair standing up straight above it. This helped make his long thin face with its rough skin and sharply pointed chin vaguely reminiscent of a dried up carrot. He was altogether less well turned out than the others. This was partly because he no longer had a wife to care for him, but more because he was unkempt by nature. 'I didn't suppose assassination would be the only choice. I did say the elimination of someone or *something* vile.'

'Murder of some dictator was the natural first choice though,' said Rice.

'Might be in your case, Felix,' remarked Steen with his mouth full. 'But remember, I've taken the Hippocratic oath.'

'Not to kill people, you mean? Not on purpose anyway,' Rice responded with a chuckle.

'Well, if a dying member of this club couldn't think of a more worthy last act than shooting a political gangster, I wish I'd never joined it. I mean, the Renaissance is supposed to be dedicated to defending aesthetic values,' said Wallace crossly, and reddening alarmingly. It was apparent he had been unusually irritated at the others' levity. 'I mean, a dictator would probably only last another five to ten years anyway,' he went on. 'For God's sake, there are perfectly monstrous buildings all over the place that'll stand for hundreds of years, insulting the aesthetic sensibilities and degrading the tastes of whole generations, unless someone blows them up. Why not make your last act the destruction of one of those? Or even several?' He took a large gulp of wine.

Covert, baffled glances were being exchanged between Godber and Steen as Rice observed soothingly. 'Yes, there's a good deal of sense in that, Clive.'

'I agree,' Godber volunteered, and, like the others, disturbed by the architect's unusual fury. 'The buildings would need to be empty of people, of course.'

'Oh, and of fine works of art,' agreed Wallace, now calmer and lighting a cigarette. 'That still leaves dozens of monstrosities to choose from.'

'The choice would remain a matter of artistic opinion, I suppose?' Rice debated, but choosing his words carefully so as not to upset Wallace again.

'Yes, but of an elementary kind. Would you like my first twenty eyesores to be going along with?' Wallace asked promptly.

'Well, let's say your first four, old chap,' put in Steen. 'I don't think I'd contemplate blowing up more than four buildings. Not if I was seriously under par. And that's apart from not knowing where to get the dynamite, though I suppose you would, Clive, wouldn't you? Oh, well done Perkins.' He nodded warmly at the steward who had brought in his extra chicken sandwich.

'First choice has to be the Council Offices in Broncaster. Completed in 1961. A colossal concrete abortion,' announced

Wallace with decision, puffing out smoke, then self-consciously waving it away from the others.

'Don't know the building. Hardly know Broncaster. Never in the North East,' Godber commented, pouring himself more claret.

'Well I have to be up there every week at the moment,' Wallace countered. 'You can take my word for it, that building takes the biscuit for unredeemed ghastliness.'

'Right, off with it's head,' cried Steen, waving a hand with his sandwich knife in it.

'Late at night, when there's nobody there,' Rice added.

'Of course,' Wallace agreed. 'Then there's St Mary's Church, Seldon. That's in Strathclyde.'

'Oh, steady on. Can't blow up a church,' protested Rice, as always on the side of the angels, publicly at least.

'I could blow up this one,' offered Judge Godber unexpectedly. 'Funny, I was shown pictures of it only the other day, by someone who took the same view of it as Clive. Another sixties blot on the landscape all right. A quite brutal structure that certainly does nothing to glorify God, inside or out. Parishioners hate it apparently, but they can't afford to knock it down and build a new church.'

'It'll be insured though,' said Wallace quietly.

'Hm,' Rice uttered to excuse real commitment.

'Right. Down with St Mary's,' announced Steen, the self appointed arbiter.

'Then there's the Gwent Shipping Insurance Company's headquarters in Cardiff.'

'But that's been there since my grandmother's time,' Rice demurred, adding gratuitously, 'She was Welsh, you know?'

'And it's likely to be there beyond your great grandchildren's time, Felix,' said Wallace. 'They put a preservation order on it last year. Its only alleged virtues are that it's red brick and Victorian.'

'I know the building. It's hideous,' said Godber. 'Even Betjeman thought as much.'

'So that's another one for the chop,' Steen pronounced

promptly. 'And your last candidate, Clive? Remember you've had one in England, one in Scotland, and one in Wales. Will you go for Ireland now?'

Wallace shook his head. 'Not if I'm restricted to four. The last will be a lot nearer home. It's the old Waterwood Tyre factory on the Great West Road. Empty now, but it's a protected building, and the innards are being converted to a different use. We were offered the job, but refused it on principle.'

'I remember reading the Ministry had added it to the protected list,' put in Rice. 'God knows why. All those white tiles, and that gimcrack tower. Looks like a giant public convenience. I agree, thoroughly bad taste. Always was.'

'Good. That's the lot then. Can we get back to the bridge? My deal, I think,' said Steen who'd had his fill of wine and sandwiches – and what he considered to have been a somewhat vacuous discussion.

'Meant to say, extraordinary coincidence that church being blown up yesterday. In Seldon. I mean, only four days after the Broncaster Council Offices were burnt to the ground,' remarked Lord Rice, before returning to his fish soup.

It was two weeks later. Rice and Steen were lunching together at the Renaissance Club.

'Extraordinary, yes. Suggests Clive Wallace was pretty perceptive in his choice of awful buildings.'

Rice looked up, his laden soup spoon poised unsteadily between plate and mouth. 'You don't mean you think there's a gang of sort of . . . aesthetic saboteurs at work?'

The heart specialist grinned. 'No, that'd be too much of a coincidence. Though I think the church may have been destroyed on purpose.'

'So do the police and the insurance company. *The Times* says they're mounting a joint investigation.'

'Hm. More likely it was vandals than parishioners wanting a new church, at no expense to themselves.' Steen whisked up the last small slither of smoked salmon from his plate with a look of regret.

'Probably,' Rice agreed. 'And I expect the Broncaster fire was an accident. Still, two out of four's a pretty good score.' He cleared his throat. 'I er . . . I suppose old Clive's all right, is he?' he added, watching the other man's face.

'Let's hope so,' Steen responded enigmatically, even though he knew better than that.

It had been on the Thursday after the last Monday bridge evening that Clive Wallace had consulted Richard Steen professionally, at the urgent request of Wallace's own general practitioner. What the GP and the specialist had both provisionally diagnosed as angina had proved to be just that following an immediate stress test, and an angiagram the next day.

Steen had advised his sixty-two year old friend and patient that heart by-pass surgery was indicated without delay, followed by three months of recuperation. Wallace had pleaded that he had too many important projects on the go that couldn't be abandoned straight away. The physician, even at his most adamant, had failed to shift the other's obstinate attitude over this, but eventually it had been agreed that Wallace would have the operation in six weeks. Meantime he promised to give up smoking, to take pills as prescribed, to carry an alleviating inhalant against emergencies, and to avoid being provoked. Steen's first inkling of Wallace's likely problem had been the way the architect's face had so suddenly suffused with anger that evening when the others had upset him.

It was ten days after Steen and Rice had lunch together that Wallace's third nominated building was destroyed by fire. The Cardiff offices of Gwent Shipping Insurance had been set alight by four incendiary bombs timed to detonate in the middle of the Friday night. As with the two buildings already demolished, there had been no loss of life, and no damage to other property – nor any likelihood of either hazard. The insurance company's headquarters had been empty – and, again just like the others, it had stood alone on an island site. These assuaging facts were not nearly assuaging enough for the agitated Lord Rice when he telephoned Sir Roger Godber first thing on the Saturday morning.

'You've heard the news of the Cardiff fire, Roger?'

'Yes, Felix, on the wireless when I was shaving.' The judge nearly added that he would have preferred to have finished his breakfast before coming to the phone to discuss the matter, but he didn't.

'You realize this is the third of Clive Wallace's buildings to be burnt down?'

'The church was blown up, wasn't it?' Godber corrected with a lawyer's exactitude. He was speaking into the wall telephone in the kitchen, and making signs to his wife to bring him his coffee cup from the table, except she was too engrossed in the newspaper crossword puzzle to notice.

'Burned or bombed, it's all the same. They've been irresponsibly destroyed, and we know exactly who's done it,' thundered Rice.

'I thought you were quite approving of Clive's list?'

'Nonsense. That was just during a . . . a frivolous discussion. Nobody took it seriously.'

'Except Clive, you think?'

'Well, don't you?'

'What I may think and what I know of the matter are quite separate considerations,' Godber pronounced in a measured way, beaming at his wife who had at last seen his signal.

'Oh, stop being so bloody pedantic, Felix. You're as bad as Richard Steen.'

'Richard's being pedantic about Clive?'

'No, evasive. He's pretending he knows nothing about Clive's state of health, but I found out Clive's been to see him recently.'

'Clive told you that?'

There was a loud clearing of the throat from the other end. 'Not exactly. I er . . . I rang him to make a lunch date shortly after the second fire – I mean the bombing of the Seldon church,' Rice corrected quickly. 'He wasn't in London. His secretary said he was in Glasgow for two days. You realise Seldon's only twelve miles from there? And guess where he'd been the week before?'

'In Broncaster, probably. He told us he went there every week, don't you remember?'

'No.' There was a brief pause. 'Well, perhaps I do. Anyway, he was there the night of the fire. And if he was in Cardiff yesterday, that would clinch it wouldn't it?'

'Was he in Cardiff yesterday?' the judge asked cautiously.

'I don't know,' was the strained reply. 'But I mean to find out.'

'Good. You can ask him on Monday. It's our bridge night.'

'He may not come. Anyway, it may be too late by then. And remember, Clive's seen Richard. That was just after the February bridge night.'

'He saw him professionally, you mean?'

There was some more throat clearing from Rice. 'He saw him, that's all I can say. It came up in my conversation with his secretary.'

'So he could have been seeing him for lunch, or golf?'

'Look Felix, you're a High Court judge and if . . .'

'Crown Court, actually,' Godber corrected automatically and with feeling. He had expected to be promoted to the higher court in June, but had been disappointed.

'Well, you're a judge anyway. It'll be a pretty state of affairs if it comes out you knew Clive's been dynamiting buildings . . .'

'I have no such knowledge, Felix,' Godber retaliated hotly. 'I was merely present when we light-heartedly discussed what one might do in one's last days, if one succumbed to a terminal illness. Clive said that he'd demolish some ugly buildings. I'm not aware that he has since become terminally ill. If he has, I'm deeply sorry, but I very much doubt he'd actually carry through such a frivolous resolve.'

'Well, I'm absolutely certain he would. Don't you remember how serious he sounded? Anyway, it'd look awful in the papers if it came out. You, a judge, tacitly condoning . . .'

'I've condoned nothing, tacitly or otherwise, and in any case you'd be just as culpable as I am.'

'Culpable. That's the word all right. But I'm not a judge.'

'But you're an ex-cabinet minister, and on the boards of I don't know how many companies.'

'That's different. Readers of the gutter press assume all politicians and company directors are liars who withhold the truth for private gain. They expect judges to have higher standards. Altogether, I think you should do something without delay.'

'Like what?' Godber was beginning to admit to himself that there was something in what Rice had been saying, though he was equally certain the man was more concerned for his own reputation than anyone else's.

'You could go and see Clive. He's only round the corner from you.' Godber and Wallace both lived in South Kensington, while Rice's house was in Hampstead. 'You could face him with the evidence.'

'Coincidence isn't evidence.'

'Three buildings destroyed is more than coincidence. Well, if you don't feel like tackling Clive, at least you could call Richard Steen.'

'So could you.'

'He wouldn't tell me if he knew Clive was dying. Doctors treat patient information as if they'd heard it in the confessional.'

'I should hope so too. So why should Richard confide in me?'

'Because judges are bound by the same sort of code, aren't they?'

'First I've heard of it.' Godber paused, frowning into his now empty coffee cup. 'All right, I'll do what I can. No promises.'

'Good man. Let me know . . .'

'I said no promises, Felix. Cheerio, and . . . and love to Madge.'

An hour later, Godber and Steen met by telephoned arrangement in the broad walk in Kensington Gardens. They had come from opposite directions. Steen lived in Bayswater, just north of the park. Although both men were well wrapped up against the east wind – Godber in a British-warm overcoat, Steen in a too pristine, waxed shooting jacket – the sky was clear and blue, the sun shining, and the early morning frost had almost evaporated.

'You haven't spoken to Felix again?' Steen enquired after the two had removed gloves briefly to shake hands, and then turned to stride eastwards toward the Round Pond.

'Certainly not. Not since I called in on Clive at nine. I must say, he looked fitter than I've seen him for some time.'

'Hm, I'm glad to hear it.'

'He's given up smoking as you ordered. Said it was a lot easier than he'd expected.'

'In his case easier than the possible dire consequences of not giving it up. Surprising how the risk of death concentrates the resolve. Anyway, I'm glad he told you about his heart problem, and the operation. You understood, I couldn't have told you myself?'

'Naturally. Is his condition very dangerous?'

Steen sniffed. 'It's not immediately life threatening.'

'But might he think it was?'

'Possibly. I had to put the fear of God into him to get him to agree to the operation. I see what you're getting at. D'you really believe it's he who's destroying these buildings? As he said, a final act in the public service, and all that?'

'He denies it vehemently.'

'I suppose he'd have to. Apart from anything else, to protect the rest of us. Could we in any way be considered er . . . accessories to his crimes?'

'Hardly. Just bloody fools, if it came out. Which, in a way, is worse. That's assuming he's committed any crimes.'

'But with three out of the four buildings on his list gone already. I mean, it does seem rather more than coincidence.'

'That's what Felix said, of course. But you could both be wrong.' The judge rearranged the red muffler he was wearing as he went on. 'If Clive has frequent occasion currently to be visiting Glasgow, Broncaster, and . . . and perhaps Cardiff, it's not surprising his most unfavourite buildings in those places would be the first ones he'd have nominated for destruction in a . . . in a . . .' The speaker hesitated, making an airy circle with one hand. 'In a fanciful kind of way.'

'Because he'd have them in the front of his mind, you mean?'

'Precisely.'

'Is he coming to the club on Monday night?'

'I imagine so.' If one of the group had to miss a bridge

91

evening, it was usual for the individual concerned to phone Godber.

'Well, I'm sure it'll help us all if he tells us he's not responsible for the mayhem.' Steen paused, then added. 'You mentioned Cardiff. He hasn't actually been there too?'

Godber's shoulders moved from side to side uneasily. 'I don't propose we tell Felix Rice,' he said, 'but, yes, I'm afraid Clive was near there yesterday. He drove back late last night. He told me as much, though I confess he did so a touch reluctantly.'

Steen stopped in his tracks, hands thrust deep into the patch pockets of his jacket. 'But was he actually in Cardiff? Where the fire was last night?'

'No, further west, in Swansea. He's supervising some rebuilding there.'

'But he must have driven back through Cardiff?'

'Round it certainly. On the M4 motorway.' They fell into step again, taking a path that leads across to Lancaster Walk as Godber continued. 'Clive swears he had nothing to do with the fire there. But if Felix knew Clive had been anywhere near South Wales, I shudder to think what action he might take. He was threatening this morning to tell the owners of the Waterwood building to have it guarded at night.' The speaker made a face, squeezing his eyes tightly together. 'It's unsettling to accept that it might be the prudent thing to do, of course.'

'On the contrary, it could be disastrous for Clive. If the police had reason to question him. To accuse him of anything,' the cardiologist pronounced with great firmness 'His heart's just not up to that kind of trauma.'

'But there's no reason why he should be questioned. The police don't know anything about our discussion at the club.'

'Not yet they don't.' Steen shook his head. 'Felix is so unpredictable. If he was asked to explain how he knew the Waterwood place was in danger, he could easily give the whole thing away.'

'I see.' The judge straightened his small frame even more as the two turned right on to the main concrete walk. There was calculation in his gaze too, which was fixed on the recently refurbished Albert Memorial lying a few hundred yards in front of them. 'Very well,' he resolved. 'I'll tell Felix that I'll warn the Waterwood people myself about possible danger to the building. That's what he really wants in any case.'

'But how will you explain you know?'

'I shan't.'

'But if the police are told, they'll press you for an explanation, surely?'

Godber's eyebrows moved up and down. 'In that event I shall tell them what policemen have been telling me in my court with impunity for many years past. I'll say an informer told me. A snout.' The judge nodded, looking extremely pleased with himself.

It was late on the evening of the following day, Sunday, that the old Waterwood factory on the Great West Road was burnt to a cinder, and early on the Monday morning that firemen searching through the debris discovered the charred remains of a human body.

'There's still no reply from his flat,' said Felix Rice, rejoining the others in the otherwise empty cardroom of the Renaissance Club. It was just after six thirty on Monday evening. Rice, Steen and Godber had all arrived before the hour. It was unusual for any of the bridge players to be seriously late, and when there had been no sign of Wallace at six twenty-five, it was Rice who had gone to telephone his flat from one of the payphones in the main hall.

'His office . . .' Godber began.

'Have been saying since this morning they didn't expect him in today,' Rice interrupted. 'I rang them three times.'

'And they'd no idea where he could be reached?' enquired Steen.

'I told you, none,' answered Rice, picking up the whisky he had abandoned earlier. 'His secretary's away, but the woman I kept speaking to said there were no appointments in his diary either. Surely even an architect wouldn't go a whole weekday without checking at least once with his office?' continued a man who prided himself on the orderliness of his life. 'Well it's clear to me he's destroyed that building like the others, except this time he's stayed in it on purpose. Didn't want to face the operation, I expect, nor life as some kind of invalid. I'm positive it's his body they've found,' he completed.

'Well, no one else is. The police aren't for a start,' Steen insisted. 'The report on the radio said there was no quick way of identifying the body from what was left.'

'It couldn't have been a caretaker because there wasn't one. They said that too. There was only a mobile security patrol that called by once a night,' said Godber in a morose tone. He had intended to telephone the owners of the building with his warning immediately after the weekend, but immediately after the weekend had proved to be too late.

'Teeth survive fires, don't they?' asked Rice suddenly. 'Did Clive still have his own teeth?'

'Yes, and if the dead body's his, his dental records will no doubt prove it,' Steen answered.

'So we should put the police on to his dentist right away,' said Rice. 'D'you know who that is, Richard?'

'I do, yes. Chap in Upper Wimpole Street. I'd thought of that already, but it's too early. Once we alert the police, if the body isn't Clive's, he's still implicated. Better to wait a day or two, in case the authorities come up with other takers. And if it is Clive's body, there'll be a letter from him to someone, explaining things. One of us possibly. I'm sure of it.'

'I agree,' offered Godber swiftly, temporarily forestalling Rice who, judging from the expression on his face, was strongly against delay.

'Well I see no purpose in prevarication. We should accept our bounden duty in the matter,' Rice insisted, with righteous fervour. 'One of us must inform the authorities now that he's reason to believe it's Clive Wallace's body they've found, and that it was Clive Wallace who set fire to the building. I think it should be you, Roger. No need to tell them how you know, of course.' He cleared his throat, folded his arms across his chest, and glanced around defiantly at the others in the manner of a man who had dutifully passed a heavy responsibility on to someone else.

It was at that moment that Clive Wallace himself appeared in the doorway of the cardroom. He looked more dishevelled than usual, seriously out of breath, but far from dead. 'I'm dreadfully sorry to be so late,' he uttered, closing the door, and slumping into the empty chair at the card table with a deep sigh. 'There's the mother and father of all traffic jams in Holborn. Would you believe, my taxi's taken fifty minutes to get here from Euston station? I'd no chance to ring you, of course.'

It was Godber who broke the following uncomfortable silence. 'Been north, have you Clive?' he enquired, with an earnestness indicating that Wallace's response would be of more than passing interest.

The architect grinned sheepishly. 'Manchester actually. It's where my secretary's parents live. You see, er . . . she and I, er . . . well, we got married this morning.'

There was a further silence, this time more stunned than uncomfortable as each of the other three debated the reasons why a putative arsonist on the brink of death should decide to embark on matrimony.

'Congratulations,' offered Rice eventually, forcing a smile while speculating about which of Manchester's less attractive buildings Wallace might have singled out for firing while he happened to be in the area. The others made supportive noises.

'You're probably wondering what came over me,' said Wallace with searing accuracy. 'Fact is, Eve and I, that's her name, Eve, we've been talking of marriage for some time. She's no bimbo, you understand? In her early fifties, actually. Divorced some years back.' He gave a weak, embarrassed cough. 'Well, when Richard here gave me the bad news you all know about, we decided to speed things up. I mean, if I fall off the perch as a result of this heart thing, or because of the operation, at least Eve will inherit my estate, such as it is. There's no one else, you see? I've no family at all. We made the final decision a fortnight ago. Got a special licence. Today was the earliest time it could be used.' He paused to take a deep breath. 'We did the deed at the Dewsbury Register Office. It was just the two of us, with her parents and her brother and his wife as witnesses. Didn't want any fuss. It's why we didn't tell our friends. Not anyone.' He looked around guiltily at the other three. 'I'm sorry. And for being late tonight.'

'We all understand, of course,' said Godber swallowing awkwardly. 'But er . . . is your wife with you?' He looked about him, as though the lady might have entered the room unobserved, although if she had she would have been trespassing in a members only section of the club.

'No,' Wallace replied. 'Seems daft, I know, but it's only the actual ceremony we covered today. I've got a load of work on for the rest of this week, most of it out of the office. Then there's the operation. We've decided to delay the honeymoon till I'm far enough into recuperation for us to go on a long cruise. Eve's staying on with her parents till midweek.'

'Good. Sound thinking,' said Steen with genuine and professionally underwritten enthusiasm. He got up and pressed the service bell at the side of the fireplace. 'Meantime, a glass of celebratory champagne will do you no harm. We can't holler for things tonight, unfortunately. Perkins isn't here for some reason. We're having to order everything through the main bar.'

'There's just one thing, Clive,' said Rice carefully. 'Er, you must have heard that the Waterwood building was destroyed by fire last night. Since that's another of your . . .'

'Ah, Mr Wallace, got a letter for you, sir. Didn't know you were here,' said Merit, the club's senior night steward who had just entered in response to the bell. Garrulous by nature, he was old, increasingly hard of hearing, and was unaware that he had interrupted anyone. He searched in the side pocket of his white jacket, produced an envelope and handed it to Wallace. 'It's from Ernest Perkins, sir. You know he's retired through ill health? Well perhaps you didn't, not any of you, not if you haven't been in of an evening since this time last month. Very sudden it was, three weeks ago. It's cancer, I'm afraid, with not much time left to him, according to his doctor. Bachelor he is, with no dependants. There was talk of him getting into one of those hospice places, but he isn't keen.' The old man shook his head. 'Been with us twenty years. Nearly as long as me. That's since he left the regular army, of course. Sergeant he was there.

Thinks the world of you four gentlemen he does, especially you, Mr Wallace. Dead keen on fine buildings see? Goes to look at all your buildings, he does, and not just the ones in London either.'

His face drawn, Wallace looked up from reading the letter which he passed to Godber. It was hand written, short, and to the point – a combined confession and suicide note. It left no doubt about who had destroyed the four eyesores and whose body would be found in the Waterwood building.

'I never knew Perkins was an ex-regular soldier,' said Wallace slowly. 'What outfit was he in, do you know?'

'Royal Engineers, sir,' Merit replied. 'Specialist he was. In demolition and bomb disposal. Nothing he doesn't know about that kind of thing.'

'I'm sure there . . . wasn't,' Godber agreed with a sigh, partly in sorrow, but also in some relief.

TAKE TWO HUSBANDS

'This paper's got nothing but sex in it,' plain Maud Guttins protested, noisily turning the pages.

'Court reports, is it, dear?' her husband Lancelot Guttins commented tentatively. He vaguely wished she might be right, but knew she wasn't. He put more marmalade on his breakfast toast. It was too much to hope that the *Tidcombe Times* had gone over entirely to pornography.

'Too many of the court reports simply cater for the prurient,' Maud went on. 'It's not even normal sex either. Not most of it.'

You had to admire the way she could complain, and read, and slurp up Weetabix all more or less at the same time. 'Can I have some more coffee, dear?' he asked, wondering exactly what, in view of her limited experience, Maud would recognize as abnormal sex.

She took his cup, and poured the coffee.

It was at that moment that he saw the kitchen door fly open. Then he watched, powerless, as a group of shouting, leather jacketed junkies burst in, overturned the table, and forced the screaming Maud to the floor, ripping off her clothes, and ravishing her in front of him.

This sequence was Mr Guttins's favourite Maud imagining. The intruders were sometimes American Indians in full war paint, or jackbooted Nazi SS, or fiends from outer space. What followed after their entry was always more or less the same.

'Of course, sex before marriage is the absolute norm these days,' Maud went on, unaware of the awful fate that had just befallen her, and handing back the cup. 'The absolute norm.'

Mr Guttins sighed quietly. It was sex *after* marriage that had been upsetting Maud for the last twenty-five of her forty-eight years. Pretty well since she had given birth to Kevin – after doing her bit, as her mother had put it so cogently at the time. Kevin was married himself now. An engineer, he had emigrated to Australia, which was just as well because his wife hadn't got on with Maud.

'Isn't it time you were going, Lancelot?'

'Yes, dear.'

Dark, with plenty of hair still, a small moustache, and kind eyes, Mr Guttins was a wiry man, and small, a touch smaller even than his wife, but more energetic. There was a spring in his step as he got outside into the June sunshine. He was dressed conservatively in the style he thought befitted a retail pharmacist. He stopped to pluck a yellow rosebud from one of the floribunda bushes along the drive, doing so expertly with the penknife from his pocket. Gardening was his nominal hobby. But for real escape he relied on erotic fantasy.

He looked back at the house as he closed the gate behind him. It was solid, detached, double gabled, and redbrick, standing in its own bit of garden like its identical neighbours in this solid, redbrick seaside town in the South of England. You couldn't see the ocean from here, in inappositely named Nelson Avenue, but you could smell it when the wind was right.

Mr Guttins fixed the rose in the lapel of his clerical grey jacket, adjusted the black banded straw hat on his head, and made off down the Avenue with short, quick steps. It was an eleven and a half minute steady walk to Pembroke's, the chemist shop he managed on the eastern side of the town, near the sea front. He was not obliged to walk. There was a frequent bus service from the corner which he sometimes used in the winter, and very occasionally Maud drove him to work in their year old Rover 200. Mostly though he chose to walk. He said it was healthier. In fact it was because he could thus more easily attend to the needs of the young women along the route who daily begged him to undress them – as well as to do other things to them afterwards.

Of course, the begging was in the same category of imagining

as the leather jacketed junkies. Mr Guttins was a pathetically frus-
trated middle-aged husband with a frigid wife. The exciting sex
life he led was entirely in his mind.

Fourteen minutes after leaving the house he was inserting the
key in the front door of the shop. The walk had taken longer
than need be on account of an extra two minute interlude, nomi-
nally to tighten both his shoelaces alongside the municipal
tennis courts. *Two nubile, and already minimally clothed girls had been
out for an early game at the courts. He had indulged their brazen plead-
ings to strip them both, meeting their entreaties with deft, practised hand
movements. He had enjoyed revealing the stark and lovely flesh, but left
the creatures begging for the more intimate satisfactions which they had
wanted next.*

'Excuse me? Do say you're opening the shop now?'

The stunning young woman who had spoken was struggling to
get out of the low Mercedes Coupé parked at the curb across the
narrow pavement in front of Pembroke's. Mr Guttins turned in
her direction at the very moment when her long legs – clad in
sheer black panty-hose under the shortest of red skirts – had
parted, a trifle indelicately, to ease the movement of the rest of
her remarkable body.

It was a moment before he could utter. His thoughts had still
been savouring his adventure with the abandoned tennis players.
He pointed to the notice on the door and without taking his eyes
off this fresh, real personification of loveliness, not to mention
lust. 'Officially we're not open till nine,' he said at last, already in
his mind wresting the last flimsy garment from her willing body.
Then he smiled nervously and doffed his hat, feeling his cheeks
redden in response to the exciting contraction in his loins as she
stood before him, to his perception, naked and unashamed.

'It's a prescription. For . . .' she paused momentarily, the big
brown eyes considering Mr Guttins more carefully than before,
'for my husband. For his heart. I tried to get it filled last night.
The chemist I went to didn't have it in stock.' Standing beside
him, she shook the mass of bouffant blonde hair before opening
her white leather hand-bag. She pouted a little as she searched
for something in the bag, her tongue running around her lips

and making them shine. 'Here it is,' she said, looking up. Her white, V-necked, collarless blouse was bursting at the front, revealing under the two top, open buttons not only a generous amount of cleavage but also a breathtaking treat of firm, genuinely unencumbered bosom.

Mr Guttins started undressing her all over again.

'Urgent is it?' he asked, swallowing and taking the prescription from the long, tapering fingers that touched his with a quite electric effect. The perfume she was wearing was for him more provocative than any advertisement could have claimed for it, and it smelt more expensive than anything stocked at Pembroke's.

'It's terribly urgent.' She moved even closer to him, as if they were sheltering from a sudden shower under the narrow lintel above the shop door.

'I see it's a repeat private prescription.' He pretended to re-read the words so that his eyes could continue to feast on the genuinely unencumbered bosom.

'From my husband's Harley Street doctor. For quite a small amount of—'

'Digoxin syrup. Yes. It's not a proprietary. I mean I'll have to make it up for you.' He went on seeming to study the writing. 'It's just for a week's supply.'

She nodded. 'That's why I'm always having to get a fresh lot.'

'Well it's quite strong stuff. You don't want too much of it lying about.' He glanced at his watch. It was 8.41. 'Come inside won't you? I think we can manage it all right.'

He ushered her through into the shop ahead of him – *thrusting himself into her in response to her insistent cries for more.*

'I'll have to close the door again, I'm afraid. My assistant doesn't get here till nine. There's a chair if you want. I'll just . . . yes.' He went behind the counter, then unlocked the glass door into the dispensary beyond.

'I'm intruding on your quiet time, I expect?'

'No, no, not at all. That is—' He looked up to find her standing in the dispensary doorway. 'Oh, I'm afraid—'

'I mustn't come any further? Of course not. It's just that I

102

adore the atmosphere of chemist shops. Especially a small one like this. With such a dear little, old-fashioned dispensary.'

'We're old-fashioned all right.' He took off his suit jacket, *then, nonchalantly, everything else he had on.* He hung up the jacket and, turning full frontal to face her, languidly put on his white cotton working jacket – treating it like the sexy silk dressing-gown he imagined it had become. *He heard her catch her breath*: well, that was understandable.

Indeed, Mr Guttins was not in the least surprised at the increasingly approving gaze that in reality the woman was keeping on him: it came so close to the way she looked at him in his fantasy.

'Old Mr Pembroke, the owner, won't change anything if he can help it. Or modernize. He has three shops like this one,' the pharmacist continued, perfectly able to carry on normal conversations and mundane activities while indulging in an imaginary orgy.

'Quite a little chain.'

'Along the coast, yes. This is the only one in Tidcombe.' He did up the lower button of the white jacket while imagining he was loosely knotting the dressing-gown sash.

'A gold mine, is it?'

His hands gave an uncertain gesture as he looked along a line of drawers above the dispensing table. 'That's not my province, I'm afraid. I make this shop pay. I've been here over fifteen years. It suits me,' he ended lamely.

'Good for you. You're married I see.'

He glanced down at the wedding ring she had noticed. 'Yes. For a little longer than fifteen years.' He gave a chuckle, not knowing quite why, then his expression changed. 'Oh, dear, I'm afraid I don't have enough Dixogin to fill the prescription.'

'Oh sh ... too bad,' she responded, the tapered fingers pulling at the long gold chain that was glinting enticingly in her cleavage – unaware that Mr Guttins had whipped her bare buttocks with it while they'd still been out on the pavement.

'Look, why not take what I can make up? That's about a day's dosage. Then come back this afternoon for the rest?' he suggested. 'I can easily get a fresh supply during the day. I mean if that's convenient.'

She frowned. 'It means driving down again from Hightops. And you know what the traffic's like in the afternoon. I think I'd better—'

'Hightops? That's on my route home. Or nearly,' he put in quickly, and inaccurately. Hightops was the exclusive section of town, a good deal out of his way, and a steep climb – except Mr Guttins would have scaled Everest barefoot for the chance of seeing this vision again. 'I could bring the rest of the prescription with me. That's if you wouldn't mind paying for all of it now?' He still remembered to ensure observance of the shop rules.

'Could you? You are sweet. Of course I'll pay now. Tell me how much.' She opened her bag again. 'And I'll give you directions to the house. Our names Hallier, by the way. Well you can see that from the prescription. I'm Kate Hallier.'

It was a little after 5.45 when the sweating Mr Guttins arrived at the house in Hightops. The steep, bending drive was cut deep into the chalk soil – banked, and sheltered by conifers on both sides. The visitor came upon the north, entrance front of the building quite suddenly, and, despite his determination, it must be admitted gratefully, as he emerged beyond the last line of trees. It was a substantial house, too high up to be overlooked – a 1930's flat roofed villa, rendered in white, with a splendid view of the sea to the south.

'You walked? You poor lamb. I thought—'

'I like to walk.' He was carrying his jacket when she opened the door to him. 'I've brought the prescription.'

'Never mind that. Come in for a drink. Unless you have to hurry home. To your wife. I'm sitting by the pool. It's still lovely and hot there.'

Mrs Hallier was wearing a thigh length, diaphanous yellow wrap which she was still tying in a bow at the neck. Underneath Mr Guttins could make out the briefest of matching bikini briefs through the parting in the wrap. It didn't seem that she had the bikini top on, but it was difficult to be sure the way the wrap

104

material was bunched. But because she was so close to being unclothed already, he had no need to make believe he was stripping her.

'Thank you. I'd like that. I'd like that very much. My wife has her bridge always on Tuesdays. And . . . and on Wednesdays,' he added unnecessarily. He had started to sweat again, but now it wasn't from the exertion of the climb.

'And this is Tuesday.' She smiled tolerantly.

'Yes. So there's no hurry. None at all. What a very nice house.'

'We like it. We're renting it this year, with a view to buying. It's *very* private.' She took his arm as she guided him through the square hall, across the drawing-room, and through sliding windows on to a wide paved terrace. A kidney-shaped swimming pool was sheltered and suntrapped below the terrace, down some curved stone steps. 'My husband's supposed to be living in a warm climate. We should have gone to Florida or Italy, but he insists on carrying on with his business. And he doesn't like flying any more. Or being too far from his British doctors. He's older than me. Seventy-six.' Mr Guttins, in thrall to the grip on his arm, calculated this made her husband older by about half a century. 'Tidcombe's the compromise,' she added.

'Could I ask what business your husband's in?'

'Antique furniture. The pricey kind. He has a gallery in Bond Street. He's there now. Seeing an American client.'

'Oh, from what you said this morning, I thought—'

'He left at lunch time. With . . . with the chauffeur. Back Thursday. That's his routine mid-week. We have a flat above the gallery. But I hate London. Especially in summer.'

'He'll need his Digoxin syrup?'

'No, he has enough to last him. With what you gave me this morning,' she said as they went down the steps to the poolside. 'Let me take your jacket. Would you like a swim? The water's heated to a sinful ninety degrees.'

'I . . . I haven't brought a costume.'

She shrugged. 'That really doesn't matter up here. If you want, I expect there's a spare one in the changing-room over there.'

'Next time perhaps.' He was ashamed at his lack of courage.

'If that's a promise. With your physique, I'll bet you're a fabulous swimmer.' She smiled, squeezed his arm muscle, then stood away from him a little to look him up and down, still in her warmly appraising way.

'Hardly that,' he replied with more justification than he intended. 'I used to swim a lot. Tennis was . . . is my sport really.'

'I like tennis too. Pity we don't have a court here. Sit over there then, and I'll get you that drink. Whisky, gin?' She waved her hand at a raffia bound, glass drinks trolley behind them near the steps.

'Gin and tonic. Thank you.' He sat awkwardly and sideways on one of two long white matressed lounger chairs set only inches apart, and half shaded by a huge sun umbrella. He was feeling over dressed and aware he should at least remove his shoes if he was going to sit properly. He had dealt with the shoes but was still trying to settle himself on the chair when she came back with his drink.

'Topless doesn't embarrass you does it? You being a medical man? The English generally are so prudish about that kind of thing.'

'No, no . . . I mean, not at all,' he answered weakly in a strained voice, while trying to cloak both his embarrassment and his excitement.

She had discarded the wrap and was now standing over him quite naked except for the slim bikini briefs. Her breasts were firm and bronzed like the rest of her. He swallowed and took the glass. This was the most erotic experience of his whole life – and it beat the hell out of his fantasies.

On Mr Guttins's second visit, on the following Tuesday at the same time, Mrs Hallier casually led her guest into a mutual exchange of intimate confidences about their lives. This revealed that they were equally disenchanted with their marriages.

It was not until Mr Guttins's third visit, on Wednesday the day after that, and when there could be no pretence that he was bringing a prescription for her husband, that the intimate exchanges took the form of actions, as well as words. This might have happened earlier, but Mrs Hallier had been determined not to rush things unduly. Now the lounger chairs were pushed tightly together like a double bed. Mr Guttins had arrived in time for the light lunch she'd prepared by the pool – smoked salmon, then strawberries, with champagne to drink. It was early closing in Tidcombe on Wednesdays. He had told Maud he wouldn't be home for lunch because he was stock taking: Maud was at her bridge club from four o'clock to seven.

'But I told you, I've always preferred older men,' Kate Hallier protested later as they lay naked, side by side in the sun, still sipping the champagne. Earlier he had been wearing the swimming shorts she had found for him the day before. He assumed they belonged to her husband. They had been a touch too big for him – but easy for her to pull off him, when they had been playing in the pool. 'Well slightly older men,' she enlarged. 'Men your age, for instance. It's just that Cedric's too old for . . . well, you know . . . almost everything really.' She ran a hand down his hairless chest, then on to his thigh.

Mr Guttins gave a contented moan. 'But he's rich,' he said. Cedric Hallier was certainly decrepit looking as well as old. Kate had produced a photograph of herself with the old boy taken at the pool. She had been hugging him like a sugar daddy: Mr Guttins had found the picture obscene.

'Being rich isn't everything,' said Kate. 'You're much better off than he is really. You're the perfect age. You have your health and strength, a good job, nice home, I expect, despite—'

'But I don't have a gorgeous wife like you to have . . . to have sex with.' He still had to force out the franker phrases. He had never before talked to a woman in the way he talked to this one. His fantasies had not involved much conversation. The present experience was as liberating as making love to Kate – or almost.

'That's easily fixed, silly. You could divorce Maud. Marriage doesn't have to be for ever, you know?'

'But I've no one else to go to.'

'Aren't I good enough? I'd marry you. Or live with you.'

'But you hardly know me?'

She put her glass to one side and, leaning over him, kissed him slowly on the lips. 'Except I was crazy about you the moment I

107

saw you. Didn't you notice? I don't go in for casual affairs. Not my style, darling. But you are.' Her finger traced an outline on his forehead, then his cheek. 'This is the first time I've ever been unfaithful to Cedric. I've been tempted, of course. I've told you how awful it's been for me all these years.' There was a catch in her throat so that he thought she might be about to cry, until she went on more firmly. 'I've been waiting for you to come along. For longer than I can tell you. You're perfect, my sweet. We're perfect together.' She kissed him again.

Of course, he wanted to believe her. She had made his imaginings come true: all of them – and better than just true. 'But you wouldn't divorce Cedric for me?' It was less a question than a supplication.

She lay her head back on the cushion. 'You said the Pembroke shops are for sale.' Her tone was thoughtful, and implied that she wasn't changing the subject.

'Mr Pembroke wants to sell, yes. It's common knowledge in the town. But he can't get his price.'

'Wouldn't you like to be the buyer?'

'Yes,' he answered boldly. 'And . . . and I'd know how to run the shops too. I mean much better than they're being run now.' In fact he'd never once thought of himself in the role of proprietor of anything. Simply, she had the effect of spurring him on recklessly to undreamed of goals – to a new kind of fantasy.

Kate sighed. 'What an idyllic life. To own a nice little group of chemist's shops. Traditional ones. And live right here.'

'No chance of that, I'm afraid,' he responded. 'Mr Pembroke wants nearly a million pounds for the three. He won't sell them separately either.'

'Cedric's worth ten times that.'

Mr Guttins gave a despondent murmur. 'But he's not likely to buy them for me is he?' he offered flatly.

'But I will, when Cedric's dead. I promise. I inherit everything.' She rolled her body back toward his. Her hand moved down his chest. 'Pity we can't kind of hurry him along.'

'To his . . . to his death, you mean?' Although he had hesitated over the word death, for some reason such an appalling proposal didn't seem appalling to him at all, not at that moment. It was like one of his imaginings, where there were no consequences.

'Yes. It'd be doing him a favour. He's getting no pleasure out of life, and he's often in great pain. But they won't operate on his heart. He wouldn't survive. Well that says it doesn't it?' She pressed herself even closer to him as her hand moved lower. 'He's just longing for the end, really. The work keeps his mind off things, that's all. Yes, it'd be a kindness. I know just the way to do it too.'

'You mean you'd want me to—'

'No darling, I'd handle it alone. It'd be nothing to do with you. Not the actual ending.'

'But how—?'

She stopped his words by placing her other hand over his mouth. 'Tell you later,' she murmured, kneeling astride him, then bending down to run her tongue slowly down his stomach. 'This is more urgent, isn't it?'

'You'd need to make up two prescriptions that look the same, with the same dates on the labels. But one would be his normal Digoxin, and the other very high strength Digoxin. Lethal strength. It'll need to be that.' She seemed to savour the word lethal.

They were lying side by side again in the sunshine as she went on. 'I'd put the normal strength bottle in his bathroom cabinet on the first night. That'd be a Thursday.'

'You have separate bathrooms? And . . . and bedrooms?'

'Er . . . yes. Because of Cedric's snoring. He'd take the dose as usual, so his fingerprints would be on the bottle. That could be important. He takes just the one dose at night. Well, you know that. On the Friday, I'd switch the bottle for the high strength one. After pouring out enough of what's in it to make the levels the same. So he couldn't notice any difference.' She paused. 'Then when . . . when it's all over, when he's gone, I get rid of the second bottle, and put the first one in its place. That's after I've poured away most of what's in it. It'll just look as if he's taken too much.'

'By mistake or on purpose?' Mr Guttins asked quickly.

'No one could ever know for certain, could they?' She stretched her arms above her head. 'He likes the taste. I always think he's going to take too much anyway.' She turned her head to look at Mr Guttins. 'That'd work wouldn't it?'

He swallowed. He was in awe at the way she had everything so clear in her mind. 'Yes, it should work all right,' he said. 'And it's so simple. Is it too simple, d'you think?'

'Simple schemes are always the best. No complicated trimmings to go wrong.' She had answered with the same authority as before.

'You say he's never been to a doctor in Tidcombe?'

'No. Only in London.'

'In that case, if he died here there'd have to be a post-mortem.'

She pushed herself up on her elbows. 'So they'd find he'd taken too much of his syrup. It's what they'd be expecting. It'd be his fault he'd taken too much.'

'So long as they didn't think you'd given him an overdose.'

'How could I do that? Hold him down and pour it into him? Lace his coffee with it? Nearly a whole bottle? It'd take that much wouldn't it.'

'In the normal strength, yes.'

'So he'd have known straight away. Anyone would with that quantity. And it has a very distinctive taste. And smell.'

'That's true.' It still bothered him that she could be suspect. But he wanted her plan to work more than anything else in the world. He was already imagining life with her in this house. 'People won't think it odd when we get married later?' He asked, but confident that she'd have the answer to that too.

'Only if we did it straight away. Of course, we'd have to wait a while.'

'But how would we sort of . . . come together, even then? I mean, when would I leave Maud?'

'Oh, that's easy. Once Cedric's gone, I'd have my solicitors buy all the shops from Mr Pembroke. As a straightforward investment. I'd appoint you general manager, so we'd have to meet.

Often. At the shops and here. One thing would lead to another. We'd fall in love. You'd leave Maud. She'd divorce you. We'd marry, and live here happily ever after.'

'Yes,'he said eagerly. 'Yes,' willing it all to come true – imagining that it had.

'Yes, of course, Doctor Chalcott, I'll come right away. It's no trouble,' Mr Guttins had said into the telephone ten minutes before this. It had been just after six-thirty on Saturday morning. 'No I understand perfectly, doctor. Better to get it cleared up straight away. Less distressing for the relatives . . . Yes, I agree. See you shortly then.'

The call had woken him. They usually slept in an extra half hour on Saturdays because he opened the shop later that day. Maud, in the other bed, had wanted to know why Dr Chalcott was calling. She knew Dr Chalcott. He wasn't the Guttins's doctor, but he practised in the town, in the Hightops district.

Mr Guttins had explained things briefly to his wife. A Mr Cedric Hallier had died suddenly. He had a prescription for the treatment of a heart condition filled at Pembroke's every week. Dr Chalcott had been called in. He was at the dead man's house now and wanted the prescription identified. That had satisfied Maud who had gone back to sleep.

Mr Guttins had dressed quickly and was now in the Rover driving to the house in Hightops. He hadn't been there for ten days – not since his fourth visit which Kate had made even more memorable than the others. That had been two Wednesdays ago, a week after Kate had proposed the plan to have Cedric kill himself. Mr Guttins had thought then that despite his desire for Kate, that once he was away from her, his resolve to see the thing through might crumble. But on his visit a week later he had been keener than ever.

He had accepted that he hardly ran any risk at all. The only danger was still that Kate might be suspected of giving the overdose. But in a wishful thinking way, Mr Guttins had managed to detach himself from the consequences of that happening.

It was on that final visit that he had delivered the extra strong prescription of Digoxin. He had dated the label for the second Thursday following – and put a smudge of red ink in the label's right hand corner. That had been to make it easy for Kate to identify. It wouldn't do to mix the two bottles.

No one he knew had ever seen Mr Guttins enter or leave the sheltered driveway of the house at Hightops. Kate had questioned him carefully on that, but he'd been quite sure. The road had very few houses in it, and he'd remembered distinctly it having been empty on his first visit. On subsequent visits he had been feeling far too guilty to enter when anyone was looking. And he had never told Heather, his unglamorous assistant in the shop, about the special deliveries either.

Kate had come in to the shop for the normal Digoxin prescription on Thursday, two days ago. It had been mid-morning and she had handed the form to Heather who had passed it to Mr Guttins. He had been in the dispensary at the time and had remarked pointedly to Heather that Mrs Hallier had been in before for the same reason. He had even come out of the dispensary to wish Mrs Hallier the time of day after he had prepared the bottle of syrup.

And now, he assured himself, it was all over bar the shouting. He could hardly believe it.

The Rover took the steep drive in its stride, soaring to the top with the same sort of zest that its driver was experiencing. He parked beside Dr Chalcott's big Volvo. It was Dr Chalcott he had told Kate to call when the time came. He was one of the older practitioners in the town, a bluff individual who could be relied on to draw the obvious inferences from the facts presented. And the doctor had made that plain enough to Mr Guttins on the telephone.

'Come in, old chap. Nice to see you. Sorry to get you out of bed.' It was Chalcott who answered the door. 'A word in your ear.' The benign, heavily built doctor drew the pharmacist aside in the hall before continuing in a lowered voice. 'Probably a simple cardiac arrest, but he just could have swallowed too much of that anti-congestive you've been supplying.'

'Signs of that, you said?' the pharmacist commented, in the

professional tone he used in the shop when old ladies asked for advice on the best choice of cough mixture.

'Hm, some signs.' The doctor sniffed. 'Possibly just my suspicious mind. Chap's heart condition finally did for him, I expect. Knew him did you?'

'No. Mrs Hallier picked up the prescription every week.'

'Did she now? Attractive woman. Very distressed she's been. They must have been close. More so than you'd expect, really.' The doctor's eyebrows rose in a questioning way to punctuate what, to Mr Guttins, had seemed slightly curious observations. 'She showed me the prescription. From some Harley Street quack. Limited to a week's supply, presumably because the old boy wasn't to be trusted with more. In case he did himself a mischief? That's the thing that made me wonder. I see you've dated the prescription on the back each time you've dispensed it. Very proper.'

'The last time was on Thursday. So you think he might have taken an overdose?'

The doctor made a noise with his tongue like water dripping on to stone. 'Post-mortem will show it if he did. There'll have to be one, of course. I gather he was wealthy.' He made the dripping noise again. 'Another reason to be sure everything's er . . . on the up and up. So if you could just have a look at that Digoxin, then the body can go straight to the hospital morgue. We're in the kitchen. There's coffee going.' He led the way along the hall.

'It's Mr Guttins, isn't it?' said Kate as they entered the kitchen. She was seated at the table. A dark, handsome man of about her own age was standing behind her. Mr Guttins assumed that this was the chauffeur who, of course, he hadn't met, although there was something vaguely familiar about the face. There was a coffee pot and several cups on the table. Kate and the man were both in dressing gowns – Kate's being a frilly, glamorous affair in white nylon. She looked as if she had been crying.

To Mr Guttins Kate looked like the most desirable woman on earth – and she was all his, no kidding, no fantasies. 'Good morning, Mrs Hallier,' he responded. 'I'm sorry to hear the sad news.'

'You're very kind.' She touched her eyes with the tissue in her hand. 'He seemed so well last night. Then Jack took him a cup of tea early, as usual, and found him dead.' She looked up at the man behind her. 'It was a terrible shock for us both.'

'We won't keep you much longer, Mrs Hallier,' said the doctor. 'I just want Mr Guttins to have a look at the bottle of Digoxin over here.' He moved across to the working top under the window and picked up the brown glass container. 'Dated the fifteenth,' he said. 'That's two days ago.' He held the bottle up to the light. 'And a quarter of the contents consumed. Or a bit less than that. Which is as it should be.' He handed the bottle to the pharmacist. 'Shows the patient hadn't taken too much by mistake. Certainly not from this bottle. That about right, Mr Guttins?'

Mr Guttins stared at the bottle, opened his mouth, but no words came out. He had been disturbed at how full the bottle was. Now his gaze was riveted on the red ink smudge on the label. It was the bottle with the high strength mixture.

'So it was a heart attack, doctor?' asked the man behind Kate. It dimly registered with the preoccupied Mr Guttins that the accent was more cultured than you would normally expect in a chauffeur. 'Perhaps my father should have been taking more of the medicine, after all. My wife was always impressing on him not to over-do that stuff, weren't you, darling?' He put both his hands on Kate's shoulders.

'Patients like the taste of Digoxin syrup, Mr Hallier,' the doctor replied with a half smile. 'If he did take . . . a touch too much, the post mortem would show it.'

'Oh, father wouldn't have risked a serious overdose. Much too fond of life for that. And fit for his age.' The man who so resembled the old man in the picture with Kate, and who had so clearly identified himself as that man's son, as well as Kate's husband, now shook his head. 'Funny, Kate's been complaining for years because he wouldn't hand over the business to me. Now it'll all be mine, and we can sell it, and live abroad as Kate wants, but I'm going to miss him like anything. I loved my father very much.'

This patently genuine statement impressed Dr Chalcott, but not nearly so much as it did Mr Guttins.

'The business was run as a partnership between you and your father, Mr Hallier?' the doctor asked, conversationally.

'No. I've just been a salaried dogsbody, secretary, chauffeur, you name it. Should have made me resentful, I suppose, but it didn't. Kate found it harder to take. Especially as it seemed father intended living for ever. And now this has happened, I can't help feeling guilty, as if—'

'He was so lively yesterday,' Kate interrupted loudly. She had moved one hand up to her shoulder to squeeze her husband's fingers, 'we wondered if the Digoxin could have been stronger than usual, didn't we Jack?'

Dr Chalcott looked across at Mr Guttins who still hadn't uttered a word. 'Mr Guttins here is much too careful a pharmacist to make a mistake with a prescription,' said the doctor.

'Oh, I didn't mean to suggest that,' said Kate carefully, her eyes quite dry now. 'Not precisely. But, as you said, from what's left in the bottle, my father-in-law couldn't have taken too much. All I meant was, pharmacists are such busy, overworked people. They must make occasional mistakes, like everybody else.'

'We're all human, of course,' the doctor agreed blandly, sipping his coffee.

Kate smiled. 'And if anything goes wrong,' she went on, 'I suppose a pharmacist just gets a ticking off, doesn't he? That's only fair because of the enormous responsibility he carries every day. I mean there wouldn't be a criminal charge? Not over one professional error?'

'What are you getting at, Kate?' her husband asked, frowning.

'Nothing. Really, I just got carried away. Sorry.' She had been looking at Mr Guttins' trembling hands as he held the bottle. 'I'm sure Mr Guttins doesn't make mistakes, it was just that . . . Are you all right, Mr Guttins?' she added next, in a concerned voice, and getting up. 'You look terribly hot. Why don't you sit down? Here, let me help you off with your jacket.'

IN CHARITY WITH HER NEIGHBOUR

'Choosing neighbours isn't normally a proposition, Mrs Rigby. In your situation, it's pretty well impossible, you being the existing resident,' the dapper, middle aged Terence Snell explained with too much finality. Realizing this, he compensated by adopting a look of profound concern – though frustration was what he was really feeling. Naturally I'll do everything I can to help you. But, really, my hands are tied,' he completed in the well bred accent that was a little less contrived than the facial expression. Leaning forward over his desk in the manner of a benign clergyman, he brought his hands together in a prayerful kind of way.

As senior partner of Upshot and Snell, the larger of the two real estate agencies in the thriving commuter village of Comer, Snell was always at pains to accommodate even the most eccentric wishes of the locals. He tried even harder with older locals whose properties, in the natural order of things, were likely to come on the market sooner rather than later – whether at their owners' instigation or that of their executors. And not to put a finer point on it, Phyllis Rigby was well over ninety.

'My late husband used to say that nothing is impossible until someone else has done it, Mr Snell, by which time it's too late,' the lady responded in a high, even voice, each consonant emerging with exquisite clarity.

The patrician Edith Rigby was a tall, slight but prepossessing figure, still unbending, with a parched, weather-beaten face, alert, pale blue eyes, and steel grey hair pulled back tightly into

117

a bun that was presently sheltering under a narrow-brimmed, tip-tilted straw hat. The plucked eyebrows had been replaced with perfectly arched, auburn pencilling, and the thin mouth was just as clearly defined with bold red lipstick. She was wearing a calf-length, short-sleeved lilac silk dress with a pleated skirt, white cotton gloves and court shoes to match. The dress was now hardly the height of fashion, but it had been three decades earlier when Mrs Rigby had bought it – at Harrods.

'And your husband was right, Mrs Rigby, as he so often was. What a brilliant man. And still sorely missed in the community.' Snell paused to allow the compliment to be savoured. 'The success of this business confirms the very comment you've quoted,' he continued confidently, gazing with pride around his private office, and absently smoothing a finger across his mous-tache, while still making up his mind how to cope with a delicate and, if he wasn't careful, promisingly loss-making situation. 'I've stopped counting the times we've been told by clients that we've achieved the impossible. But that's why they retain us. To do what others can't. Not surprisingly, we do twice the business of our competitors.'

'Indeed, Mr Snell. Then I still fail to see why you can't make sure that Richmount isn't sold to a Japanese buyer. As I've said, if the opposite should happen, I'd never again be able to sleep in my bed at Foresters.'

In which case, dear lady, Snell mused silently, the best course would be for me to sell up for you, while you move to an expen-sive retirement home. His more realistic second thought was that if Mrs Rigby was impelled to move, she'd hardly be likely to have him act for her if he'd been involved in the impelling. That was where the potential loss making came in.

Richmount was the only property that shared a boundary with Foresters, Mrs Rigby's own house which occupied a corner site on the internationally renowned Comer Golf Course Estate – one of the most exclusive residential areas in the English Home Counties. Set high in its own sloping five acres, Richmount had just been expensively refurbished and enlarged, prior to its being offered for sale with vacant possession.

Mrs Rigby's Foresters was bounded by roads to the north and west, and by a woodland belt to the south. A smaller building than the neighbouring one, it occupied more land, but, in greater contrast, had been slowly decaying for the quarter of a century since the death of Mrs Rigby's spouse. When the place eventually changed hands, it would almost certainly be knocked down and rebuilt – but would fetch a handsome price all the same. The estate agent gave a sickly smile intended to imply the reassurance he couldn't offer in words. 'As I said, we've had more than a dozen prospective buyers looking at Richmount, Mrs Rigby. Naturally a number have been well-to-do people from abroad. Directors of foreign companies working in this country. Comer deservedly gets the pick of such people, of course, being so close to London . . .' He had intended adding more from his standard sales patter about the attractions of the golf, the frequent train service to London, the relative closeness of the M40 Motorway, Heathrow Airport, Windsor, Ascot and even Oxford, all of them attractive features to a foreign buyer – information Mrs Rigby knew as well as he did, which was one of the reasons she interrupted him.

'I am not troubled with the numbers of possible buyers, Mr Rigby. I am deeply concerned that Godlock my gardener saw a . . .' she took a long breath . . . 'a Japanese couple going over the house yesterday.' Mrs Rigby clutched harder at her white leather handbag, as though there was a sudden and immediate danger of its being snatched from her.

Snell moved uncomfortably in his chair. He knew Godlock, a lazy, gossipy fellow, who was long past retirement age and who spent more time leaning on garden implements than using them, a shortcoming evidenced by the state of the Foresters garden, or what could be seen of it down the overgrown, crumbling driveway. 'I believe there was a Japanese couple there yesterday,' he offered with calculated vagueness. 'Also some Russians, and, the day before, an American, as well as two lots of prospective buyers from Hong Kong . . .'

'Only the Japanese concern me, Mr Snell,' the lady broke in again impatiently. 'As neighbours of that . . . of that specific nationality would certainly concern you, if you and your wife had spent three and a half years in Malayan prison camps from 1942 to 1945, as my husband and I did.'

'Of course, that must have been a . . . a harrowing experience for you both,' the estate agent offered solemnly.

'Harrowing, Mr Snell? Harrowing?' Mrs Rigby repeated in a rising, scandalized voice. 'It was hell on earth. An experience you can't begin to understand if you didn't go through it. An experience I relive vividly every time I set eyes on . . . on one of those people.'

'But nowadays, surely there are any number of Japanese members of the golf club, Mrs Rigby?'

'Whom I never see because my trees shield the house and grounds from a view of the course. I presently go about very little, and I've long since given up my club membership,' the lady explained shortly, then continued: 'It's the prospect of having a Japanese family living next door that fills me with horror. Yes, horror, Mr Snell. Understand that and you will understand why I am here.' A slight tremble went through her body before she added, in a more rational voice: 'I am willing to pay you.'

There was a moment's silence while Snell dismally reflected on a further disappointment. 'You mean if I arrange for the house not to be sold to a Japanese?'

'Certainly. We can call it a consultant's fee. In cash, if you wish. A private arrangement between us.' Mrs Rigby had outlined the somewhat discreditable terms of her offer with an indifference implying that while they were alien to her own standards they probably met Snell's well enough – assuming he possessed standards.

All of which might have constituted a licence for her listener to print money for himself. In fairness, he'd have had scruples about meeting Mrs Rigby's request, at least in quite the blatant form in which she had put it. But there might have been a creative way around that – if only she had come to him sooner.

He shook his head. 'But what you suggest wouldn't be ethical. I'd never do such a thing.' Making virtue out of necessity was also part of Snell's stock in trade. But there was no joy in his mouthing what amounted to cant on this occasion.

If only he hadn't promised the property developers who had entrusted him with the sale of Richmount that he could get such a high price for the house. It had been so outrageously high that, despite his bragging, countless viewers had either been frightened off by it or had made offers well below it. The only potential buyer the asking price hadn't fazed was the one who had agreed to accept it the day before, and who had already had his deposit notarised, which legally secured him the property.

The buyer's name was Isamu Nakashima.

'I am quite sure, sergeant, that the robbery was carried out by the person who moved into Richmount three months ago. Just like the other robbery here last month.'

'But Mrs Rigby, because of your suspicions, we've interviewed Mr Nakashima twice. Yesterday, and soon after the first robbery,' Detective Sergeant Holladay of the Thames Valley CID responded quietly. 'It's quite clear he had nothing to do with either burglary.'

'He has a wife and three children.'

'But they weren't involved either, ma'am. I give you my word on that.'

The clean-cut, sports jacketed, thirty-two-year-old policeman shifted on the cushion under him in a vain attempt to flatten the lump pressing into his upper leg. He stole a further glance around the oak panelled drawing-room, which, like the rest of the house, he found eerie, stifling, and deeply oppressive. The two were sitting in semi-darkness although it was broad daylight outside. This was because the threadbare brocade curtains at the three pairs of leaded windows were more than half closed. Holladay calculated that moving them might have risked their collapsing on to the furniture below, which included a delicate, inlaid escritoire horribly bleached after exposure there for too many summers. Everywhere there was blemish and decay. An antique chaisse longue, under the window closest to him, and covered in what had once been a pink fabric, had the stuffing spewing from its innards in several places. Not that the couch had offered a place to sit since it was in use as a depository for mounds of yellowing correspondence.

A sizeable, semi-circular inlaid side table on Holladay's right was crammed with precious ornaments, including a tall white porcelain bird on a branch which the policeman was in dread of knocking over. There had been no room there to set anything down, nor was there any on the long low table in front of him which was stacked haphazardly with more aging documents, books, and magazines with curled up covers. This was why he was still holding the china cup and saucer he'd been handed. They were doubtless part of a once important set, but with the cup now so stained and cracked he had so far hesitated to put his lips to its contents. Thankfully, Mrs Rigby had seemed not to notice his abstinence. She was sitting very straight in a parched leather winged chair that nearly matched the slightly less worn one he was occupying. He balanced the tea in one hand, with his note-book on his knee, and held both his elbows tightly against his sides.

'Mr Nakashima is European Chief Executive of the Minato Corporation, Mrs Rigby,' the sergeant continued. 'It's a huge outfit. His salary probably runs into . . . into half a million at least. I know your garden statues and your Georgian silver were extremely valuable, but really he doesn't need to steal things.'

Mrs Rigby gave a bitter smile. 'Of course he doesn't. That's not the purpose of the robberies. Any fool can see that. Don't you realize, he's persecuting me? He wants me out of this house. He'll never forgive me for trying to stop him owning Richmount. In the end, you know, I offered to buy it myself, but he wouldn't give up his claim.'

Holladay frowned. He'd had it on good authority that the price had been too rich for the lady. 'You know, I'm sure you're wrong about Mr Nakashima, ma'am,' he offered. 'Incidentally, he told me he came here to see you. That was after the final row you had with him and his lawyer, at the estate agents.'

'He told you of that did he? Hmph.'

'Yes. You know, he very much wanted to make things up after-wards.'

122

'Which he could have done by not buying the house.'

'Except he'd bought it already by then, ma'am.'

'So he and that fool Snell insist.'

'We gather that was true, Mrs Rigby. Anyway, he wanted to be a good neighbour and all that, but . . .'

'But I refused to talk to him. I turned him away at the door. His wife too. She came later.' Recalling the episodes seemed to provide the speaker with a good deal of satisfaction.

'They have tried, ma'am.' He wondered why he was doing community liaison work when he was paid to investigate crime.

'Correction, Sergeant. They give the appearance of trying. You don't understand the oriental mind. He lost face when I told him he'd committed an unforgivable error in etiquette by challenging the intention and the veracity of an English widowed lady. Since I wouldn't accept his apology, he has no alternative but to oust me from my home. He wants me out because the sight of me perpetuates his shame.'

'From what he and his wife have told me, I can't believe . . .'

'What they've told you is balderdash, Sergeant,' Mrs Rigby broke in. 'You realize too that they simply constitute a . . . a vanguard. The Japanese abroad live in tightly knit groups. The Nakashima's are only the first to buy property on the Comer estate. Others will follow. And the next house they plan to acquire is this one. But over my dead body.'

'With respect, ma'am, I'm sure that's wrong. About their trying to get you out, I mean. Mr Nakashima and his wife impressed on me how keen they are to meld into the community here. They're already active members of the golf club, and the children will be going to local schools in September, after the holidays.'

'All a lot of humbug, sergeant,' came the disdainful response. 'And do you have any better theory than mine about who's been burgling my house?'

'As a matter of fact we do, ma'am, and that's really why I'm here. You see this property is so unprotected by present day standards.'

'I have a burglar alarm,' she retorted with spirit.

'But you've told us you never switch it on, ma'am.'

The lady lifted her chin. 'That's because the wretched thing keeps going wrong. The bell sets itself off for no reason.' This time her words sounded more defensive than convincing.

'That's possibly because it's old and er . . . cumbersome to operate, ma'am. They're much more' – he stopped himself from saying fool-proof – 'much more reliable these days.'

'So they should be. I'm charged a fortune by the alarm company when they come to reset the thing. That's after it's gone off of its own accord.'

The sergeant tutted in apparent sympathy before continuing. 'I notice a lot of your boundary road fencing is broken down, ma'am, and you don't have a gate to the main drive any more.'

'That collapsed with age. In any case, at my time of life, it's far too much bother to open a heavy gate every time I take the car out.'

'You could have an electric gate fitted, ma'am. It would stop any vehicle getting on to the property. That puts off a lot of intruders, not having the means of a quick get away handy, and having to carry the loot any distance.'

'An electric gate would be far too expensive.'

'The fact remains ma'am, and without wanting to alarm you in any way, we believe this property may now be well known to a specialist bunch of thieves. The first haul was valuable garden sculpture . . .'

'On which my husband was an expert as well as a collector.'

'Indeed, ma'am? Pretty valuable stuff these days, I expect. The second burglary was antique silver.'

'Yes. And they only took the best. Like my Georgian tea service. Which is why I'm sorry we're taking tea from an aluminium pot.' She nodded at the object which was placed at a drunken angle on a long foot stool in front of her. Beside the teapot, and poised quite as unevenly, was a sugar bowl, a slop basin, and a saucer of sliced lemon sections, mostly in unmatching china. The thieves had relieved her of her silver tray as well, and she had baulked at using a plastic one from the kitchen for formal entertaining, even for formally entertaining a policeman. In truth, it was a long time since she had offered hospitality to anyone else.

'Excellent tea all the same, ma'am,' he said after closing his eyes and risking a gulp of it. 'And I gather you have a fine collection of pictures. Well, I can see that from here. Plus a collection of carved ivories.'

'They were others of my husband's interests.'

'Is that right?'

'And all impossible to insure these days, sergeant, except at ridiculous premiums. So far, I've been offered derisory sums from the insurance company for my losses. I'm challenging, of course.'

'My point, ma'am, is that there may well be more burglary attempts. A lot of professional thieves these days are experts. They take just the things they know have a high value, which they can dispose of quickly through crooked dealers. And they sell information to each other as well. The thieves who took the silver will have noted the other good stuff you have. They may even have taken photos of it, to pass on to mates or dealers who specialise in pictures, ivories . . .'

'So Mr Nakashima is able to organize an orchestrated stripping of my possessions,' she broke in. 'Which will probably end up in their attempting to murder me in my bed. I was asleep during the first two raids. Well, let them try me again, and see what they get.' The sentence was punctuated by a stiffening of the finely boned jaw.

'It's very unlikely you'll be assaulted by the sort of thieves I'm describing, ma'am. And, I repeat, I'm sure Mr Nakashima isn't involved.'

'I was never burgled before he and his family moved in.'

Holladay accepted that the last remark was as lacking in logic as it was impossible to refute. 'I gather you don't have anyone living in, ma'am?' he said slowly, trying a new tack. 'A housekeeper or a companion?'

'Certainly not. The inconvenience would be unbearable, and the cost prohibitive. As it is, I have a daily woman who breaks practically everything she touches. To have someone like her living in the house would ruin me, and cause me great anguish into the bargain.' She drank from her cup. 'Godlock, my gardener, is here three days every week. The break-ins don't occur in the day time, no doubt for that reason. But at night, thieves naturally assume everyone in the house would be asleep, and they'd be right. So what would be the point of filling the place with costly staff? And all because of a vendetta against me.'

'But you can still do a lot about improving security here, ma'am,' the sergeant insisted, purposely not rising to the bait of her last comment.

There was silence for a moment until Mrs Rigby offered: 'I understand, Sergeant. And I promise I'll look into it.' Her tone had become both peremptory and dismissive. She also seemed very tired.

The sergeant left a few minutes later fairly certain he'd achieved nothing by the visit, just as he was too objective a policeman entirely to place all the onus for that on the old lady. Of course she was being stubborn. He understood her ingrained prejudice against her new neighbours without at all condoning it, and he blamed himself for not being able to persuade her that at her age, and with her relative affluence, the mere cost of home protection should not be the prime consideration. The fact remained, she was a relic of a golden age when gates were ornamental, when front doors, like garages, could be left unlocked, and when a burglar alarm was so unnecessary as to be considered a social climbing affectation. He had a grandmother nearly as old as Mrs Rigby who was quite as obstinate, and even more careful with her money – though she had a good deal less of it than the owner of Foresters. The principle was the same though. They'd both survived the rigours of life in general and of wars in particular with their own ideals intact, and were resentful of the current calamitous drop in moral attitudes.

Nor did Holladay really believe what he had told her about burglars being non-violent, because some were, and some weren't. If she chose to confront one, or more likely two, it was a toss up how she'd be treated. That was what bothered him most.

*

It was midnight on Friday, over a week later. Isamu Nakashima was leaning on the balustrade of the balcony to his upper floor, west-facing study at Richmount. He was wearing an evening dress shirt and trousers, the shirt open at the neck. He had come outside, before turning in, to savour the stillness of the moonlit night and the tranquillity of the country. His wife Michiko had gone straight to bed with a headache on their return from a formal dinner in London an hour before. There had been some paper work waiting which he'd needed to look over before sending a brief fax to Tokyo. To avoid disturbing Michiko, he was going to sleep in his dressing-room.

Everything was as good as it could be for the forty-eight-year-old Mr Nakashima. The Minato Corporation in Europe was doing well under his management. Michiko and the children, already attuned to life in the UK before they had moved to Comer from the London apartment, were settling down well in the new environment. He was sure rural life was better for the whole family than living in town. As for himself, his golf handicap had come down, he had taken up tennis again, and he swam regularly in the Richmount pool. Nor did he resent the extra weekday travelling. The company headquarters were in north west London, and to avoid the worst traffic, he needed to leave the house at six, getting back usually around eight at the earliest. But he had a company driver, and now did the bulk of his reading in the car. It was all worth it to have the weekends here.

The single local problem, well, the single permanent vexation in Mr Nakashima's life was Mrs Rigby, and it irritated him that he still hadn't been able to dismiss it from his consciousness. He actually worried about Mrs Rigby as much as if she had been his own mother who had died three years before.

Mr Nakashima looked across Richmount's manicured lawns and borders toward the tree lined boundary with Foresters, the moon making shadows on the scene like the sun in daytime. He gave an impatient sigh. If only that cantankerous, magnificent, stubborn, splendid old British Empire survivor would see sense. Apart from anything else, at her age, and living alone, she badly needed caring neighbours. And the Nakashimas were ready to be just that. He well understood the root of her problem, but the past was past, and she was denying herself a better present. It wasn't good for her to be alone. He'd gathered from the police sergeant and from older golf club members that she had no children or other family, and it didn't seem that she had many friends left alive either. In all the weeks they had been neighbours, no member of the family had ever noticed anyone visit the house except tradesmen – never once seen a private car turn into the drive.

But it was while the last thought was still in Mr Nakashima's mind that a private car did turn into the unobstructed gateway of Foresters. The fleeting look he got of it suggested it might be a four wheel drive vehicle: the reflection from side windows meant it couldn't be a van, but it was too high to be a salon car. Curiously, he hadn't heard it approach along the road. Apart from the trees and vegetation that broke up the view, the vehicle was travelling without lights and creeping forward slowly with no sound of the engine revving. But Mr Nakashima had sharp eyesight, and he followed the progress between the trees, until the moving object disappeared where the drive swung toward the house front.

Two minutes later the strongly built Japanese was himself moving fast on foot up the Foresters drive, a heavy duty, rubberised flashlight in one hand and a metal golf club in the other. He had delayed only to pull on trainers and to instruct his bleary eyed wife to call the police.

A Range Rover was parked outside the house facing down the driveway. Its tail gate was open and Mr Nakashima could see one large and one small framed oil painting lying on some sheeting inside. As he expected, the front door to the house opened to his touch. Stepping inside he stood still for a moment, eyes closed, acclimatising to the nearly pitch darkness. Soon he could make out a hall with a broad staircase at the rear that seemed to descend directly into a large drawing-room, with only an open archway between the two. Then, better able to distinguish obstacles in his path, he moved silently under the arch and into the room that was only a fraction better lit than the hallway.

Two figures with their backs to him, one standing on a chair, were lifting another picture from the wall. As they both turned about, with the heavy frame held between them, Mr Nakashima switched on his torch, quickly shining the powerful, piercing beam in the eyes of both men in turn. They reacted like dazzled hares.

'Armed police. Freeze,' thundered the Japanese in an accent and tone indistinguishable from native English delivered with convincing inbred authority. 'Put the picture against the wall. Now, both of you, on the floor, face down, arms and legs spread. Do it!'

To his relief his orders were obeyed to the letter – for the few seconds that elapsed before the scene changed dramatically.

'He's not police. He's by himself. We can take him.' The voice had emanated from the middle of the staircase.

Mr Nakashima swung the torch beam in the direction of the new threat, as, with a deep throated roar, he launched himself up the steps, golf club poised. But when he and his quarry were two treads apart, the whole area was suddenly flooded with light, and Mrs Rigby was revealed standing stalwart and imperious above the top step. She was in an ankle-length house coat, her arms outstretched, with both hands determinedly clasping a service revolver.

Taken off guard by the lights, Mr Nakashima mistimed the flailing with his makeshift weapon, allowing the third burglar – now solely concerned with escape – to duck and attempt to plunge past him. Except the man tripped over his would-be assailant's foot and grabbed at his shirt to prevent his own fall. The increased momentum carried both figures down the stairs together. To a fresh observer, it just could have seemed that the two were allies who had become accidentally entangled during a hasty flight.

Mrs Rigby was not only a fresh observer, but also a prejudiced one. 'Rob a defenceless woman, would you! Well take what you deserve. Japanese scum,' she cried shrilly, and started shooting. The first two bullets, both aimed at Mr Nakashima, missed him, the second lodging in his assailant's left buttock as he attempted to rise from the foot of the stairs. But the plucky lady's targeting – or luck – improved with practice, despite the way the gun bucked in her hand with every shot. The third bullet hit her friendly neighbour in the right shoulder as he too was scrambling to his feet.

'Mrs Rigby, it's me, Nakashima. Stop shooting,' he cried as she aimed at him again.

'I know who it is, you swine. You and your hired underlings,' she cried with maniacal intensity, before the gun exploded again. Mrs Rigby was on a high. This time the bullet narrowly missed Mr Nakashima's head, ricocheted off a now reverberating copper gong, suspended below the stair-well, before it homed in the right calf of one of the other two burglars who were now racing for the door. All four of Mrs Rigby's unwelcome callers were now trying to quit the premises – Mr Nakashima, mentally as well as physically wounded by her actions, with as much alacrity as the criminals.

It was the leading and so far unscathed burglar who threw open the front door – and promptly hurled himself into the arms of a burly uniformed policeman.

It was nine o'clock in the morning when Mr Nakashima, patched up and discharged from hospital, had presented himself on the doorstep of Foresters, alongside Sergeant Holladay. Mrs Rigby had already been interviewed – and rehearsed – by the sergeant, before he had gone to fetch her neighbour.

The drawing-room, in which they were now seated, had been very little changed by the night's drama. If anything, its appearance was neater following the attentions of the policemen and women who had descended on the place to collect evidence, and who, before their departure, had tidied up some of the owner's private chaos, believing it might have been made by themselves – or the intruders. Certainly there was more daylight flooding into the room than there had been on the sergeant's previous visit, though the now wide open window drapes looked even more perilously poised.

'Sergeant Holladay has explained all the circumstances to me,

Mr Nakashima. I'm . . . I'm much obliged to you. Intervening in the way you did was very brave,' Mrs Rigby uttered slowly and precisely, as if each word was being reluctantly squeezed from her body like the last slivers of tooth paste from an as good as spent tube.

'Anyone else would have done the same, Mrs Rigby,' the recipient of this tribute replied politely, twice bowing his head energetically as he spoke. The lady's gratitude was being accepted with more grace than had been entirely discernible in its offering.

Holladay cleared his throat loudly, at the same time fixing Mrs Rigby with an expectant lift of one eyebrow. This was a reminder that her planned performance was not yet completed.

She met the sergeant's gaze stolidly, and smoothed her skirt across her legs with both hands. 'I am also very sorry indeed for . . . for shooting you, Mr Nakashima. Shooting you in error. It was unforgivable on my part,' she added, her voice even more strained than before.

'Think nothing of it, Mrs Rigby. In the circumstances, it was a natural mistake. It's only a flesh wound.' The speaker had again punctuated his responses with courteous inflections of his head.

'And Mr Nakashima and his lawyer have told us they won't be bringing charges against you, ma'am, for assault with a deadly weapon,' the policeman interposed, with heavy emphasis on his last words. For the old lady's benefit, he had been anxious to have the reprieve on record, and unchallenged. As for the two wounded criminals, they were slightly more incapacitated than Mr Nakashima, but unlikely to test any judge's sense of common justice by attempting to sue their nonagenarian burgled victim. They had also been made aware that their abjurance in this might earn some mitigation in the matter of their own defenceless wrong doing.

There remained the fact that the gun had been unregistered as well as unregisterable: private possession of such firearms was no longer permitted under British law. Even so, the sergeant believed that, in the circumstances, Mrs Rigby would be let off with a fine and a warning, not the customary jail sentence.

Mrs Rigby did not verbally acknowledge the news of her alleged good fortune which, in any case, she regarded merely as her just desert. Any words of gratitude in this context would accordingly have stuck in her throat. Instead, she emulated her neighbour's bowing, but, in her case, with a not very low bow, performed only the once – and stiffly.

'My wife, Michiko, hopes you're recovered from the ordeal, Mrs Rigby. If there's anything we can do—'

'Please thank your wife for her enquiry. There's nothing . . .' she'd interrupted too soon, and had hesitated because the sergeant had pointedly cleared his throat again. 'But if there is anything, I'll let you know,' she completed.

There was a moment's uncomfortable silence before Mrs Rigby, brought up to know it was a hostess's duty to bridge such awkward impasses, enquired. 'I understand your home is in Kyoto, Mr Nakashima? I'm told that's a very historic, sacred city. Is your wife from there too?'

The businessman smiled. 'Not from Kyoto, no. Michiko's parents both came from two hundred miles west of Kyoto. From . . . from Hiroshima,' he completed quietly.

'Indeed.' There was a briefer but decidedly more pregnant silence before Mrs Rigby asked, this time as if the answer concerned her a little more. 'They were not in Hiroshima at . . . at the end of the war?'

'They lived there, yes, but it happened they were away when the bomb was dropped. They were on their honeymoon.' He gave a wan smile. 'Their own parents were not so lucky. They all died.'

Mrs Rigby blinked several times. 'That was devastating for your wife's parents.' This was delivered as a statement not as a question.

'I gather it was. Heartbreaking.' Mr Nakashima looked steadily into the lady's eyes. 'But that's a long time ago. Before Michiko and I were born. All is now . . .'

Before he could use the word on his lips, Mrs Rigby provided it, and again with great certainty: 'Forgiven,' she said.

'Exactly, Mrs Rigby.' His face and voice livened as he added. 'Today we are all good neighbours with our old adversaries, of course.'

'Of course.' If either of her hearers was expecting an utter-
ance more handsome he was disappointed. At this point, actions
were more expressive than words for Mrs Rigby who now looked
about in her most majesterial manner. It was as though she
intended ordering a servant to do something, then, since there
wasn't a servant, she enquired. 'Would either of you care for
coffee? It would be no trouble.'

Both men refused politely, and got up to leave. As she offered
her hand to her neighbour with no evident hesitation, Mrs Rigby
said: 'I shall write to your wife directly, Mr Nakashima, and invite
her to come here with the children for tea on Tuesday. My
garden is wilder than yours, but children enjoy that don't they?'

'Thank you, Mrs Rigby, I'm sure they'll all be delighted.'

The sergeant smiled to himself. He hoped there was an
uncracked tea set for treaty signing occasions.

SOMETHING TO DECLARE

Percy Crickle had been married to Sybil for seventeen years before he determined to do away with her. The decision was triggered by her attitude over the winnings. It was the sheer ingratitude that stung Percy, coming on top of the massive disappointment she had caused him.

From the very beginning, Percy's mother had insisted he was marrying beneath him. His late father had been an underpaid schoolmaster. Sybil's father was a retail grocer whom Mrs Crickle (Senior) invariably and pointedly referred to as a tradesman. She described over-weight Sybil as a pudding, also as graceless and untutored. She had never understood what a good-looking boy like Percy saw in the girl – or woman rather, since Sybil was already pushing thirty-four at the time of the wedding.

But Percy had been taking the long view. He was then nearly thirty himself, and still living at home. Nor had he quite settled on a career – discounting several false starts as a professional trainee. His mother had put those down to experience, which was inaccurate or, at best, paradoxical. Meaningful work experience was to elude Percy throughout his adult life: he partially made up for the lack with a just sustaining sort of cunning. He figured that marriage to Sybil would be bearable, and better than that when she came into her inheritance.

For her part, God-fearing and trusting Sybil was genuinely in love with Percy. This was a sentiment quite separate from the incautious and transitory pleasure she felt about getting a husband well after the point where she considered marriage a serious prospect.

As for the inheritance, Sybil was a late and only child, with parents who were hard-working, appearing prosperous – and quite old. It had seemed to Percy to be only a matter of time before the fruits of their labours fell to their offspring. When that day arrived he dreamed he would retire from his work – type unspecified – to devote himself to personal improvement of a vaguely academic nature.

In the years following the marriage, it was Sybil who brought in the larger part of their income. She had gone on working in her father's shop which was in a once very affluent part of Liverpool. Percy meantime elected to become a salesman, though with small success. But career set-backs never seriously perturbed him: after all he was only marking time. There were no children of the marriage.

After sixteen years, Sybil's father died suddenly. Then it was revealed that the grocery business had been on the brink of bankruptcy for some time. Sybil's mother sold the shop, exchanging the modest sum it fetched for a life annuity. So it was doubly unfortunate that she also died soon after: the annuity died with her. That was the end of Sybil's expectancy.

Since it was the prospect of the retail fortune that had kept Percy going, its failure to materialise upset him severely: the year that followed was the most depressing in his life. It burned in him too that Sybil continued to earn considerably more than he did. She had become chief check-out assistant in a supermarket.

But it was the sense of injustice that hurt Percy most – and he made no bones about that. He no longer bothered to conceal from Sybil that he had married her for her father's money, now that it was clear her father had had no money. It was no good Sybil reminding Percy that her father's engagement present to her had been the house they still lived in. Percy had now taken to denouncing that very act of benevolence as a mere stratagem, alleging bizarrely that if her scheming father had not provided a roof for her, Sybil would probably by now have been living in a hostel for indigent spinsters.

There had really been no end to Percy's calculated unkind-nesses. They made Sybil very sad and dejected, and this prompted her to eat more, so that she became even fatter than before. But if she had been disillusioned about the reason for her marriage, and left in no doubt about why it survived at all (the house being in her name, Percy had nowhere else to live), Sybil's love for her husband still miraculously endured. If she was miserable in herself, in charity she was also deeply sorry for Percy whose values she now realized had always been horribly distorted. She prayed over that.

Sybil had never let on that she risked a modest stake on the National Lottery each week. So it came as nothing less than a miracle to Percy when she quietly announced one day that she had won a shared first prize – just under a million pounds The sum far exceeded what Percy had expected Sybil might have inherited from her father. He was overjoyed, magnanimously allowing that her past failure to meet his financial goals could now be overlooked. He also made arrangements to quit his latest job as a local government clerk – too early, as it proved.

If Percy's attitude to Sybil had altered, so had hers toward him. Now she was in the ascendant position she determined to stay there, while striving to put some goodness, unselfishness and a right balance into his nature. To begin with, instead of depositing her winnings in their joint bank account, she opened a new account with it in her sole name at a quite different bank. She refused also to consider moving to a larger house, to relin-quish her job, or to fund any drastic change in their style of living. She did give Percy a small weekly allowance – but only so long as he stayed in work. The regular donations she started making to deserving charities she explained were uplifting thank offerings on behalf of both of them.

Far from being uplifted, Percy came to feel even more cheated than before, though this time he hesitated to say as much. And no amount of gentle persuasion on his part would alter Sybil's attitudes. He even started to accompany her to church, something he had never done before and which he did now only to show how his values had changed. Certainly this did impress his wife, and increased her trust in him.

But Sybil continued to insist that the new money would be needed to protect them in their old age: she remained oblivious to Percy's plea that there was quite enough to cover middle-age as well, starting immediately. Sybil had her own reasons for cautioning him that some day one of them would be left to survive alone – possibly to a great age. There she had made a mistake, for it was thinking about that very thing that put homicide into Percy's mind.

Sybil's other mistake was her one significant concession. She determined to indulge a lifelong aspiration by taking a cruise. After a great deal of searching through brochures she settled on a two-week, late spring voyage in the Bay of Bengal, because it was cheaper than most others, and because she had always wanted to see India and Burma. Percy was welcome to go with her if he wished, although since he distrusted foreigners and loathed foreign countries, as an alternative she offered to pay for him to spend the same period at a three-star hotel in Torquay, a resort he had always favoured.

Percy chose the cruise with an avidity he had difficulty in disguising, but disguise it he did to avoid giving rise to suspicion. Although he detested 'abroad', at the first suggestion of the trip, the possibility of arranging an accidental death at sea positively leapt to the forefront of his mind, where it remained until he turned possibility into fact. Torquay could wait.

They flew from London to Sri Lanka to join the cruise ship in Colombo. It was Polish owned, middle-sized and middle-aged. Its four week total itinerary took in ports around the Bay of Bengal, then Malaysia, Singapore, Borneo, and Java before it returned via the western coast of Sumatra. Passengers could engage for half the cruise, as Percy and Sybil were doing, joining or leaving the ship in Sri Lanka or Malaysia.

The two were given an outside cabin on the Second Deck near the centre, and close to the stairs to the Upper Deck where the restaurant and bar were located. Above the Upper Deck was the Boat Deck, for open-air promenading, with a swimming pool aft. Although their cabin had a porthole, Percy early determined with reluctance that it was too small to squeeze fat Sybil through, kicking or otherwise.

In the restaurant they were obliged permanently to share a table for four. The limited number of smaller tables was reserved for passengers taking the whole cruise. Their two female table companions were also the occupants of one of the cabins next door to their own: this was one of the earliest disclosures during the polite exchanges at the first meal.

The women, Kirsty Redley, a widow, and her unmarried younger sister, Rita Stork, were a vivacious pair of slim and attractive if somewhat brassy blondes. They both looked to be under thirty and were altogether a contrast to the other passengers who, in the main, were much older and decidedly staider. Indeed, people wondered what two such youthful, glamorous spirits were doing on such a predictably unexciting cruise. If they were here in hopes of making new men friends the girls must have been disappointed: the few disengaged males aboard were very old indeed. In consequence, the more perceptive wives kept watchful eyes on their husbands when Mrs Redley and Miss Stork were close. This applied especially in the case of Rita Stork, a competent and seemingly ever present amateur photographer, whose obsession with taking candid camera shots was not always appreciated by her subjects. She snapped the Crickles more often than others – perhaps because Sybil seemed to enjoy the experience.

Certainly tolerant Sybil did not regard the girls as predators. As for Percy, while accepting that his late mother would unquestionably have described Kirsty and Rita as common, he was delighted at being thrown with them so regularly, even if their frank conversation and sometimes their behaviour struck him as daring. If he had not had a more burning issue on his mind, he would certainly have responded to what he took to be Rita's occasional explorative advances under the table.

As it was, though, Percy was applying himself wholly to creating the perfect opportunity for pushing Sybil overboard – an exercise that was proving more difficult than he had expected. The deed could certainly not be done in daylight, nor from a place where her fall was likely to be seen or her cries heard. It also needed to be at a time when Sybil's absence would not cause immediate alarm. Above all, the circumstances had to be such that no blame or suspicion could be levelled at Percy.

Their time aboard was over half completed before Percy was satisfied that he had a usable plan. Even then he was to depend on the right weather conditions, and fearful that they might never occur.

Encouraged by her husband, every night after dinner Sybil took a turn around the Boat Deck in Percy's company. Since the nights were often quite cool, most of the few passengers who liked to walk at this time did so on the closed Main Deck, which also saved them from having to climb another flight of steps. After their exercise, Percy would escort Sybil to their cabin. Then he would ring for a pot of tea to be sent along to her before he returned to the Main Deck lounge to play bridge with a group of regulars. Sybil did not care for card games, and in any case she liked to go to bed early with a book.

The duty steward usually brought the tea promptly. If modest Sybil was still undressing when he knocked, she would call to him to leave the tray outside. Percy knew this because on one night it happened he was in the bathroom when she had done so – and on a subsequent night when he had purposely locked himself in there, at once to check that she would do so again, as well as to make an important preparation.

It was in the Adaman Sea that Percy pushed Sybil over. The ship was just out of Rangoon on the three day run to Port Kelang in Malaysia, where the Crickles were due to disembark. As they finished dinner a bout of heavy rain had just eased off. The night was uninviting – not cold, but dank and overcast. Altogether the conditions were perfect for Percy's plan. Sybil took some persuading to come to the open deck which was otherwise predictably empty, but she did so to please Percy, even though she had been feeling unwell. When Percy paused to look over the side, just behind the davit of the aftermost lifeboat, Sybil paused with him.

There was no one else in view. The lifeboat prevented the

couple from being seen by the look-out on the Bridge Deck, just as the same object shaded them somewhat from the general illumination. Percy had planned their position carefully.

'See the flying fish?' he questioned eagerly.

As Sybil leaned across the rail, squinting with enthusiasm, he stepped behind her, grasped both her ankles and heaved her into eternity.

The splash she made hardly registered in the rush of water along the ship's side. Her cry was lost in the churning made by the port screw close to where she went in. Any further sign of her was lost in the immediate tumult of the ship's wake, and then in the murk and darkness.

It is likely that Sybil died quickly – probably of shock rather than drowning. The metabolic imbalance that caused her obesity had long put her heart and life at risk. She had been taking treatment without telling Percy, while doing her best to teach him how to fend for himself without her.

After what had been at once the most frightening as well as the most despicable act of his whole worthless life, Percy finished his promenade alone. For the time being the balance of his mind was sustained by what he urged himself to regard as the justice of his cause. It happened he met no one as he went down to the cabin at around the usual time, but an encounter would still not have troubled him.

Sybil had complained of feeling off colour at lunch and dinner. She had mentioned it to several people. The cause was the cold cure capsule that Percy had surreptitiously dissolved in her early morning tea, after he heard the weather forecast: cold cures upset her. If anyone had asked, her indisposition would explain why she had returned to their cabin ahead of Percy. He had rung for her tea as usual.

When the steward knocked, Percy had played the tape he had made in the bathroom of Sybil's shrill: 'Oh, leave it outside please . . . Thank you . . . Good night.'

But before the man could do as instructed, Percy had opened the door. 'OK, I'll take it.' He had placed the tray just inside the cabin, as he called in the direction of the bathroom, 'Sleep well, darling. I won't be late.' Then he had stepped into the corridor and closed the cabin door. 'My wife isn't feeling well,' he had remarked to the steward as they moved together in the direction of the stairs. 'Needs sleep, that's all. Keep an ear open in case she phones though, would you? If she should need me I'll be in the main lounge playing bridge.'

'Very good, sir,' the Pole had replied, gratefully pocketing the over-large tip which had been intended to mark events clearly in his mind.

Two hours later Percy looked up from his cards to glance at the time. 'Oh lord, I promised to look in on my wife before now.'

'I'll go,' said his partner, the normally reticent Miss Mold, understood to be a retired nurse. She was dummy for the hand. 'I need to freshen up anyway. Give me your key.'

He had been relying on her to volunteer: her cabin was close to his. He had mentioned earlier that Sybil had not been feeling up to scratch.

Miss Mold returned shortly to report that Sybil was not in the cabin, that her bed had not been used, and that the contents of a sleeping pill bottle had been spilled on to the counterpane.

Percy affected puzzlement, not alarm. 'That's strange,' he said. 'Perhaps she found it too hot in the cabin. Or felt better, and went for a walk. D'you think I should go and look for her?'

'Who's lost? Not Sybil?' It was Rita Stork's voice. She had come up behind Miss Mold. 'I'm not sure, but I think I saw her going up to the Boat Deck. That was about an hour ago. She was ever so groggy at dinner.'

Percy found Rita's mistaken observation almost too good to be true. Now with a deeply concerned expression he asked to be excused from the game to look for his wife. Rita and Miss Mold went with him. After they had searched both promenade decks, the cinema and games rooms on the Third Deck, and checked the cabin frequently, it was Rita who suggested they should tell the Purser.

In another hour the Captain reluctantly decided to turn the ship about. By then the crew and most of the passengers had been engaged in a meticulous search for Sybil who had failed to respond to repeated summonses over the broadcasting system. A now distracted Percy was plied with the professional ministrations of Miss Mold and the warmly feminine ones of Rita Stork.

Sybil's body was never found, although the sea search went on well into the following afternoon with other ships in the vicinity assisting. Everyone agreed with the Captain's verdict – that sick Sybil had gone for a walk on the open deck and, fuddled by phenobarbitone, had fallen overboard. It seemed to be the only explanation.

People were deeply sympathetic to Percy, especially Rita, her sister Kirsty and quiet Miss Mold. He stayed in his cabin for almost the remainder of the voyage, appearing only once for a meal, and affecting then to be completely broken.

Late on their last night at sea, Rita came to see him from next door – to make sure that he was all right, she explained. It was nearly midnight, and after most people had retired. He was in bed already, reading a girlie magazine which he quickly hid at Rita's knock. He also adopted his bereft expression for her benefit, while not being able to resist stealing lascivious glances at her when he thought she wasn't looking. She was wearing a frilly negligée loosely fastened over a low-cut, diaphanous nightie.

After making a show of tidying the cabin, Rita poured a whisky and took it to Percy. 'Drink it. It'll do you good. Help you sleep,' she said. Her fingers stayed on his as he took the glass. 'Now is there anything else you need? Anything at all?' She sat on the bed and crossed her legs, allowing the negligee to fall open completely.

'You could . . . you could kiss me good-night,' he half stammered, hoping it sounded like an innocent request for further harmless consolation.

'Oh, you poor man. And I'd like that, Percy love,' she answered. 'I'd like that very much. So let's do it properly, shall we?' She stood up, letting the negligee fall from her. Then she opened the bedclothes and slipped in beside him.

The following day was to be an unnerving one for Percy.

Because of the delay in searching for Sybil, the ship arrived at Port Kelang well behind schedule and too late for departing passengers to reach Kuala Lumpur in time to catch their flight to London. Since the ship had to leave almost immediately, the passengers were sent by train to the Malaysian capital, to spend an extra night there, in an hotel, at the shipping company's expense.

There clearly being no purpose in Percy keeping Sybil's clothes, before leaving the ship he gave most of them to a stewardess who was more or less Sybil's size. As far as he remembered later, it was he who had suggested Rita and Kirsty should each choose a keepsake from Sybil's other things, in gratitude for the comfort they had given him – publicly and otherwise. Rita had chosen the bright red cashmere wrap Sybil had bought in Madras and had afterwards worn so frequently. Kirsty had selected a chunky and distinctive necklace.

After the short train journey, Percy had reported as instructed to the British High Commissioner's Office. He was there for some hours giving a detailed account of the tragedy. In addition he had to go over the Captain's and the Deck Officer's reports which arrived from the Polish Embassy after some delay, and then had to be translated, along with a deposition from the steward who was the last person Sybil was known to have spoken to before her death. In the English version, at least, the steward's statement implied that he had seen Sybil as well as heard her: Percy was glad to confirm that this had been the case, confident that the man was not likely to be available again to correct him.

The First Secretary who dealt with Percy was earnest, sympathetic, unconcerned with time, and quite unruffled that Sybil, a British citizen, had met her end while under Polish jurisdiction, in Burmese waters, with the case now to be cleared in conformity with Malaysian law. It seemed there were well-tried procedures to meet these complicated circumstances: only those procedures had to be observed exhaustively.

The matter seemed to be concluded at the point where Percy gravely signed a form stating that should Sybil's remains ever came to light he authorised that they should be reverently and promptly returned to Britain. His pen had hesitated over the choice of whether his wife's remains should in that event be despatched by air or by sea: in the end he opted for air as showing greater keenness on his part. He was thereafter free to go home next day. And free was the operative word.

'Would you like me to take you to the airport in the morning?' asked the First Secretary as they were about to part. 'I'll be glad to. Get you diplomatic cover through customs and so on. After what you've been through you deserve to be spared all that.'

'No thanks. I'll be fine on my own, really,' Percy answered, anxious above all to get beyond the reach of serious officialdom. Customs would be no problem.

'Very well. As part of a cruise group in transit you shouldn't really have any trouble,' were the diplomat's last words.

What had come after Sybil's murder had drained Percy much more than the act itself. Even the unexpected love-making with Rita had been the less enjoyed because of his deteriorating nervous condition. Now he just wanted to be left alone with nothing to worry about – and a fortune waiting for him to enjoy.

He was sorry not to see Rita again that night, but he understood why. The sisters had told him they would be out for the evening. It was after ten o'clock when he got to the hotel. Before going to bed he took coffee with the ever solicitous Miss Mold. This was hardly a substitute for Rita's amorous attentions, but it was good for appearances' sake. It still would not do for him to be seen too much in the company of nubile, younger females. Rita had seriously advised as much before she had left him the night before.

'Well you can't be in mourning for ever, can you, love? It's not natural. Wouldn't bring Sybil back either,' she had said while snuggling close to him. 'But you know how people are. You don't want this lot thinking you're cutting loose too early. Different when we get home,' she had ended, the words heavy with promise as she traced a finger over his lips.

It was why he had kept his distance from the sisters on the train, and would continue to do so for the rest of the journey home. Little did happy-go-lucky Rita know, he mused, that it was suspicion of murder he had to avoid, not just the idle gossip of the over conventional. But she had the right idea.

So Percy was surprised when Rita telephoned him early next morning pressing him to come to the room she was sharing with her sister. It was after breakfast, and nearly time for the bus that was taking their party to the airport.

'Sweetie, our bags are going to be overweight,' she complained when he joined her. 'It's Kirsty's fault. Always buying heavy presents.' There was no sign of Kirsty, only Rita, managing to looking pert, sexy and dependent, all at the same time. She wrapped her arms around Percy's neck and kissed him warmly. 'Will you be an angel and take some of our stuff?' she pleaded, in a little-girl-lost voice.

'Of course. Anything for you. Give me whatever you want to get rid of,' Percy answered expansively. He had remarked to her on the ship how little luggage he had, even allowing for what he had kept of Sybil's belongings.

'Just that bag. Then we shan't be over the top.' She pointed to a smallish but expensive looking canvas hold-all, then glanced at the time. 'Hey, we'd better get moving.'

'It's locked,' said Percy, surprised that the bag weighed quite as much as it did. 'Shouldn't I have the key in case. . . ?'

'Kirsty's got it. She's gone down already. She'll give it to you later. Don't worry, you won't need it. Oh, better put your name on the label.' She pushed a pen into his hand, and he scribbled on the shipping company's label she had tied to the bag handle. It was a similar label to the ones on his own bags. 'Now hurry, lover.' She kissed him again, but briefly this time, then pointed him toward the door.

He took the bag back to his room. Shortly afterwards the porter came and carried it down with the rest of Percy's things.

Since the girls were seated at the front of the bus, in keeping with his public appearance policy, Percy chose a place at the back, beside the safe Miss Mold. One of the elderly male passengers, across the aisle, leaned over to say: 'They're very hot on that here.'

146

'What?'

'Drug peddling.' The man pointed to the signs in several languages fixed at intervals along the luggage rack. In English the message read: 'WARNING. Drug trafficking punishable by death. Do not become involved – even innocently.'

'How could anyone be innocently involved in carrying drugs?' questioned Percy.

'Nephew of a friend of mine was. Right here at the airport.' The other nodded authoritatively. 'He was a student with very little luggage or experience. Only seventeen at the time. Someone claiming to be overweight asked him to take one of his bags. The customs people opened it. It was a spot check.'

Percy had suddenly gone cold. 'What . . . what happened?'

'He was in gaol for months. In the end they believed his story and let him go. It was a close thing though.'

'Such a very nice hotel, wasn't it?' Miss Mold put in from the other side.

Percy answered with a brief affirmative, then fell silent for the rest of the journey. Was he being duped in the same way as the student? It would explain why Rita had been so especially nice to him. Despite his natural conceit, he hadn't truly convinced himself it had been solely male magnetism that had compelled her into his bed. Now there was a sickly feeling in the pit of his stomach that she had simply been setting him up.

'We said we wouldn't let people know we were together,' said Rita later, without looking at him and pretending she wasn't speaking to him either. He had caught up with her in the airport's moving throng.

'What's in the bag. Is it drugs? Heroin?' he whispered back.

'Of course not. Now get lost, will you, darling?' She increased her pace.

'Open the bag then. When we get to the ticket desk.' Porters were bringing all the baggage on trucks from the bus. The passengers had been told to claim their own at the check-in. There were warnings all over the place about smuggling drugs even sterner ones than those on the bus.

'Look at the warnings,' Percy insisted. 'I'm not taking that bag through. Not without seeing what's in it. Where's Kirsty? She's got the key you said.'

Resigned to acknowledging his presence at last, Rita pulled him aside toward a magazine stand. Kirsty's busy, love. I'm sorry you're like this. It's only a little thing you're doing for me. Quite safe. I'd have thought it was the least you could manage after the other night. And the rest.' She eyed him accusingly. 'They won't be stopping you. Not after your bereavement. It's a natural. Don't you see?'

'It is heroin. Oh my God.' He looked about him as if for help. 'Well I'm not doing it.'

She had her handbag open now, resting on the stacked magazines. 'I'm afraid you are, love. Did I show you the snaps?' The tone was relaxed. 'This one's so good of you and Sybil.'

'I tell you . . .' The new protest somehow became strangled in his throat. The print she had slipped into his hand showed Sybil half way over the ship's rail with himself still holding her ankles. Both the faces were in full profile. He thrust the print into his pocket, while staring about wildly, terrified that someone else might have seen it.

'There's another one I took just before. Shows you bent down, catching hold of her legs,' Rita continued remorselessly. 'Don't worry, they weren't processed on the ship. I had them done overnight in Kuala Lumpur. The people who did them wouldn't have understood what was going on, even if they'd bothered to try. They're darkish exposures. I wasn't using flash. Just special film. The detail's all there though. The police wouldn't hesitate with these.'

'You're not going to. . . ?'

'I am. Right now as well, if you're backing out on the bag. Play ball though, and you can have the prints and the negs after wc're through customs in London. God's honour.'

'But they hang you here for smuggling drugs,' he hissed desperately.

'Very rarely, love. And only if they catch you, which they won't. On the other hand, they'd definitely hang you for murder.'

Percy drew in a sharp agonised breath, as though he had been lanced somewhere sensitive. 'But you only get prison in England for . . . for doing either.'

'But you're out here, darling, aren't you? So you don't really have a choice, do you?' She watched the look of mute acceptance growing. 'So off we go then. And keep away from me till we're through. Oh, and if they do ask questions, don't try involving me or Kirsty, will you? If you do, we'd tell on you over Sybil straight off. Understand?' She closed her bag and walked away firmly.

He stood there trying to collect his thoughts and dully watching Rita disappear in the crowd heading for the check-in area. When he moved in the same direction, he was trying to pull himself together, wishing Sybil was with him, needing to ask her what he should do.

'Your things are over there, Mr Crickle.' Miss Mold never used Christian names. 'All right are you?' she added with concern. She was in front of him at the check-in desk.

'All right, yes.' He must be looking as guilty as he felt. He wiped his forehead, feeling the sweat streaming all over his body.

They were his bags all right, lying on the floor with some others still waiting to be claimed. Now the airline girl was holding her hand out for his ticket. He was just about to lift the bags on to the scales when the armed, uniformed customs official came over and stood behind them.

'With the cruise group, are you?'

'Yes. We're in transit.'

'These three yours?' Now the dark-skinned officer was leaning down reading the labels.

Percy hesitated. He knew he shouldn't have, but he couldn't help himself. 'Er . . . yes . . . They're mine.'

'British?' Without waiting for an answer the man selected a large printed card from a pack of them under his arm. The big printed words were in English, constituting a list of dutiable or prohibited items. 'You know the regulations?'

The list appeared as a blur before Percy's eyes. He swallowed. 'Yes.'

'You have anything to declare?' The small Malaysian looked bored not suspicious.

'No, nothing.'

'Could you open this one please?' He was pointing to the hold-all.

Percy's knees nearly gave out under him. 'Actually that one's not mine.'

'You said it was yours.'

'I made a mistake. I'm . . . I'm mixed up at the moment. I lost my wife, you see. She fell overboard. From the ship. Just a few days ago.' He was blurting out words desperately, knowing he was entitled to sympathy: the First Secretary had said so.

The customs officer was totally unmoved by the news of the tragedy. 'This bag please. Open it.'

Percy shook his head. 'I don't have a key. I mean that proves it's not mine, doesn't it?'

His expression unchanged, the man produced a big bunch of keys from his pocket.

'Mr Crickle has just gone through a very terrible experience.' Miss Mold offered from behind in the imperious tone of a senior ward sister protecting a defenceless patient.

'That's right. Like I said . . .'

'You want to unzip your bag?' The official interrupted. He had already opened the lock.

'It's not mine.' Slowly Percy undid the zip, his hand brushing the label inscribed with his name in his own handwriting.

Inside the bag a transparent envelope containing a photographic enlargement lay on top of a bright red cashmere wrap. The print that showed through the envelope was a coloured close-up of Percy and Sybil, posed smiling in deck chairs. In the photograph she was wearing the wrap, also the long chunky necklace that was also half showing beside it in the bag.

The official looked at the print, then at Percy, then at the wrap and the necklace, and finally again at the label. Pushing aside the other items his hands burrowed deeper into the confines of the bag.

At that point it all became too much for Percy. He started sobbing uncontrollably.

*

'Fancy going all the way. Hanging him,' said Kirsty. It was six months since Percy's arrest at Kuala Lumpur Airport. She and the others were relaxing over drinks in a Los Angeles hotel room. They had reached California by different routes and already disposed of the drugs they had each been carrying. The evening paper had the report of Percy's execution following the failure of a last minute final appeal.

'He deserved it,' said Rita.

'Have a heart, it wasn't his own powder. It was ours.'

'I meant for doing in Sybil. And for stupidity. He's properly spoiled the cruise ship into Malaysia ploy. We can't do a pick-up again that way in KL for years.'

Kirsty sniffed. 'But it still wasn't Sybil he was done for. Anyway, she was different. I'd have shopped him straight off for that. On the boat. It was your idea to use him instead. To carry that extra load. I was never sure. Neither was Gertrude, were you Gert?'

'Not of him, no. Only that he should have been looked after at the airport. By someone from the High Commission. Anyone bereaved like that should have been given VIP treatment. Diplomatic immunity. Escorted through customs and immigration.'

'Anyway Gert, you did your best for him.'

'Trying to protect our interests, that's all. It was a shame we lost the package. But he did take the heat off the rest of us. Even so, it shouldn't have been that way. He should have been escorted. I don't know what the British foreign service is coming to, really I don't.' Pausing to sniff, Miss Gertrude Mold then went back to her knitting.

MR OLIVER

Claudia's flat was in Hampstead, not the posh side near the Heath, but nice enough. It was the converted upper floor of a small two storey house in an old terrace on a side street. She had her own private entrance at the stairs, beyond the front door. An old girl lived underneath. She was unsympathetic, I gathered, and allergic to noise, but you hardly ever saw her.

Of course, it was a lot different from the other place – when Claudia had been a call-girl.

There are worse and better names for what she was then, but call-girl about covers it. She wasn't at it full time, and she never had to solicit either. It was all done very discreetly through this so-called agency. That was how we met.

I was given the telephone number by my stockbroker. He'd never used it, or so he said. He'd got it from a high-up in the City. The system was all very reliable: very circumspect: very safe in every way – so my stockbroker advised me. There would be no need to give my name.

I was interviewed first, by appointment, in a service flat behind Park Lane. It had its comic side. There was this sixtyish lady of quality who sat beside me on the sofa of the chintzy drawing-room while I sipped sherry, answered and asked a few questions, and leafed through the photograph album of available talent. Nothing pornographic, either – and only the most tactful reference to 'preferences'. I was also told that if the first introduction wasn't a success I could come back and make a new choice.

The 'initiation fee' – payable there and then – allowed for

three introductions if required. Even so, I was assured archly, it was a facility seldom used.

To avoid misunderstanding, clients were asked to make appointments with their lady friends as far ahead as was convenient, and always to pay on arrival the agreed rate for the time and services required.

Every client was supplied with a pseudonym – mine was to be Mr Oliver. Total anonymity would be observed. I was given Claudia's address and telephone number, as well as a number to ring if not satisfied after our first encounter – the number was different from the one I had got from my stockbroker.

That was the last I ever saw of Lady Vi – as she was known to Claudia.

The arrangement worked perfectly from the beginning. Claudia was everything I'd been looking for, and even better than her photo promised – again in every way. She was tall, slim, wide-eyed and 29 – a dancer with too little work, a lot of wit, long black hair, athletic, and sexy as you liked when you liked. The deal was expensive but it came without commitment, risk, or obligation. I could afford it, it didn't bother my conscience – and it didn't hurt anyone.

I had retired early from the Ministry of Defence three years before. I still got a substantial pension and I wasn't senior enough to have rated a knighthood if I'd hung on. Anyway, I'm an engineer – no Eton and Oxford background: not knighthood material. The consultancy I started worked harder than any Honour's List award.

My job had been in purchasing, with good contacts abroad, especially in Africa and the Middle East. A whole string of British and American manufacturers were glad to hire me as a roving extra salesman – and my services don't come cheap either. For once we seemed to have more money than we needed. It made a change.

I should explain that my wife Maud has been in a wheel chair for ten years. I am devoted to her. I would never have let her guess even how much I yearned for the physical satisfaction she couldn't give me – or risk her finding out I was taking it from someone else.

I am not promiscuous by nature. It wasn't until Claudia that I discovered how possessive I'd become – or perhaps always had been. The fact is, after a year I still valued the lack of involvement, but I wanted exclusivity.

So when Claudia told me one afternoon that she'd been offered a permanent job running an aerobics class for pampered young housewives, that the pay, for two hours' work a day, would nearly cover her living costs, and that it almost meant she could give up her 'other work' – well, you can guess my reaction.

Of course, it meant she had to give up the tiny but very ritzy and rent free apartment in Chelsea provided by Lady Vi. I gave her half the cost of the thirty-year lease on the place in Hampstead, plus a quarterly allowance in advance – always in cash – for what we lightly agreed should give me reasonable access on an exclusive basis.

So, you see, the whole arrangement was made on trust. I didn't expect it would last for ever. I accepted her word that I was enough 'man in her life' for the foreseeable future. She accepted I would never leave my wife. Our time together we enjoyed to the full. Individual problems were not shared – not the kind that could have marred the relationship: her probable loneliness, my burden of a sick wife – these were things never discussed, only sensed: and there were some not even sensed, I realized that later – too late.

Perhaps the most singular aspect of the affair was that I remained Mr Oliver – that Claudia never addressed me in any other way, and never showed the least curiosity about my real identity. There were dozens of ways she could have found out. Simply she didn't trouble, and I suppose it suited me not to volunteer. 'Lady Vi promised you total anonymity. That's the way it should stay,' she said to me several times, even after the move to Hampstead.

Once I wondered if she was keeping her side of the bargain: only once, and she knew it. Before I asked she'd volunteered, 'The marks on my back. No one's been whipping me. My sun lamp's on the blink. It waffled me yesterday.'

I believed her. In the 'old days' she'd had an elderly client who'd enjoyed a mild bit of flagellation.

The black eye had been two or three weeks later. I don't even remember the details of the harmless explanation she gave for that – only that it had sounded like a genuine accident. And I didn't link those two things with the only hint of trouble Claudia ever confided to me – because although it came soon after the two accidents I suppose I was too tired to pay attention; too anxious to be pampered. That was the last time we met.

I'd done what I'd often arranged before – caught a night flight from New York to London. I told Maud I was taking a morning flight the next day. That way I wouldn't be expected home in High Wycombe till after midnight. I could spend a whole day with Claudia – with an easy conscience too.

I slept off my jet-lag for a couple of hours – while Claudia did her aerobics class, shopped, and made us some lunch. We spent the afternoon in bed, and walked on the Heath after tea. Then she gave me a massage – the world's best, I can tell you. We went out to dinner – a small, discreet place we like close-by, all candle-light and real French specialties. We made love again at the flat before I left.

We knew we couldn't be together again for two weeks – I had this African trip coming up. Claudia didn't want me to leave. It had been such a perfect day. In the end, I stayed too long, I'd drunk too much – and, to be frank, I was pretty bushed when we finally did part.

I knocked down the old woman in Willesden: at least it looked like an old woman. It was in one of a string of back streets I regularly use as a short-cut to my High Wycombe road. It was just habit, to go that way. There wasn't much traffic at midnight on a Tuesday. I could have made straight for the main road.

The figure stumbled out straight into me from between some parked cars. She hit my fender, then sort of bumped down the passenger side. It was ghastly. Of course I braked, but I was going quite fast. I don't know how fast. When I stopped I could see this bundle in the road through my rear-mirror – also another car that had just turned into the street.

The other car had stopped immediately. The driver was already out and running toward the figure on the road. He didn't seem to be looking in my direction. I had to make the decision there and then – go back and be involved, or drive on quickly and hope I'd never be identified.

It wasn't only that I'd drunk too much – except that was bad enough. It was also that I had no excuse for being in Willesden. It's the opposite direction to my home route from Heathrow: what would I tell Maud? Honestly I was more concerned about Maud than I was about the police: at that moment, anyway.

If the person I'd hit was dead, then that was terrible but there'd be no helping her – only the near impossibility of proving the accident was her fault, there being no witnesses, and my blood-alcohol level probably being over the legal limit. If she was alive then help was already at hand, with nothing more that I could do.

I switched off my lights and drove away fast. The other driver was still bending over the figure in the road.

Later I stopped at a call-box. It was ten minutes since I'd left Claudia. She'd just gone to bed. I told her what had happened. I said if the police questioned me later I'd say I'd been with her till 12.30 – it was then only 12.15. If I was questioned I promised to ring her again, except that might not be possible immediately because of Maud – nor prudent if there was any chance the police might be with her when I called.

I told Claudia that if the police did check with her she should ring me at home. I had to give her the number, and she had to write it down. She'd never had it before. That was the way it had always been. I said if Maud happened to answer she should say she was Mr Oliver's secretary phoning about an appointment.

There were other people I might have asked to give me an alibi, but not that many, taking all the circumstances into account. It would have been complicated too – especially explaining things at that time of night. I could hardly have left it till the morning. Claudia would be telling nearly the truth.

I wasn't worried about Maud. If in some way the authorities did get on to me, I'd fix it so I was interviewed alone in my study.

157

Afterwards I could tell Maud the police had made a mistake. With my watertight alibi that should be the last either of us heard about the matter.

They came next morning about 10.30: two of them – nice enough chaps. The senior one was a detective sergeant, quite young – late twenties – and very polite. They were both in plain clothes. I let them in – showed them straight to my study. Maud never even heard them arrive. She was in the kitchen.

It appeared there had been an accident. A woman had died the night before. The sergeant hoped I might be able to help his North London colleagues with their enquiries. I looked surprised, but said I'd help in any way possible. I invited them both to sit down.

'Could you tell us exactly where you were between midnight and 12.30, sir?' the sergeant asked.

'Certainly,' I answered. 'There's just one thing. I was with a friend. A lady friend. It would hurt my wife terribly to know that. She's an invalid you see . . .'

'We understand, sir,' my questioner interrupted tactfully, nodding to his companion: he was younger still – a detective constable. 'It's a question of elimination, at the moment, sir. Anything you say will be treated as confidential.'

So I gave him Claudia's name, address and telephone number. I remember adding, 'By the way, Sergeant, the lady knows me as Mr Oliver.'

'Indeed, sir.' He'd looked at the constable as he spoke. 'And you were with her till 12.30?'

'I was.'

'And you'll swear to that, sir?'

'Absolutely,' I said.

There was silence for a moment, then both policemen stood up. I thought they were preparing to leave.

No one ever traced Lady Vi. The flat behind Park Lane was one you could hire by the day in between longer lettings. According to the landlord's badly kept books it had been officially empty the day I went there. Neither of the telephone numbers I'd been given belonged to the flat. They were both answering services, and both discontinued some time before.

Claudia's old flat in Chelsea had been leased in her own name. Only I knew she'd never paid the rent herself.

She'd started to tell me Lady Vi's 'agency' people were angry with her – that morning when I got in. Something about her not agreeing to go on paying some kind of penalty charge when she left them. They'd guessed she was going it alone with a client she'd met through them.

As I said, I was too tired to pay attention at the time. Claudia hadn't made it sound that important. I suppose she didn't reintroduce the subject later because she'd figured it was something she ought to handle on her own. It was not so much that she was independent: we had this kind of tacit agreement we'd cope with our own troubles and problems.

The street accident never happened – not according to police or hospital records. Whoever I'd hit must have recovered. Whoever the other driver was, he hadn't reported to anyone. We even ran advertisements begging the victim or any witness to come forward. By this time I'd told Maud the truth: she was very understanding. I publicly pleaded to be accused of knocking someone over in that Willesden street at ten minutes after midnight: result – nothing.

Of course the marks on Claudia's back and the black-eye hadn't been accidents. She'd been beaten up – by the enforcement members of Lady Vi's mob. And whoever she had let in after I left had been intending to administer a progressively more hurtful lesson – that was before things had gone seriously wrong.

But why had she let anyone in at gone midnight?

The court took the view she hadn't had to let anyone in – that I'd been there already. The old girl on the ground floor had seen us come back after dinner. What's more, she'd seen me before often, and had no difficulty identifying me.

I'd guessed what really happened. Claudia had opened the door thinking I'd come back after I'd telephoned – that I was intending to make the alibi more convincing: nobody believed my theory. If I'd been coming back I'd have used my own key they said, the key I'd admitted owning – except a door key doesn't unfasten a safety chain which I'd pressed Claudia always to use.

She hadn't been beaten repeatedly: there hadn't been time. There were just the two marks of the rubber truncheon he'd used – one on her shoulder, the other lower down on her back. It was the fall against the bedroom mantlepiece that had knocked her unconscious, caused the commotion and made him run for it.

The old girl's pet Scottie must have been roused by the vibration of the fall. Anyway, it started barking. Its mistress got up and began shouting abuse in the hallway. She said later she'd heard screams – thought they were screams of delight because we'd always been noisy lovers, and sadistic: she'd noticed that black-eye. The villain must have panicked and crashed out down the stairs. The old girl didn't see him. She was just 'sure' it was me.

It was another seven hours before the stupid old bint realized Claudia's front door was still open. It was the dog that found the body.

The second truncheon blow had been much fiercer than the first. It had ruptured her spleen: chance in a thousand apparently, unless it had been deliberate, and if so, very accurate. I don't believe whoever it was had been sent to kill: it wouldn't have made sense. Probably he'd lashed out hard, fast and wild when she was falling, trying to get away from him. That's when she hit her head. Claudia had died from internal bleeding. She'd come to at one point, but they figured she'd been too weak to move, to shout for help – not loud enough to attract the old girl anyway. But they were convinced she'd managed to do one thing.

It was how they'd got on to me. There was nothing to connect me with Claudia otherwise. Despite our relationship, the 'total anonymity' had endured. Of course I'd have come forward after the murder, whatever the consequences – but as a volunteer, not as what looked like the self-confessed perpetrator.

If it hadn't been for the damned fool game of anonymity Claudia would have known the number, wouldn't have needed to write it down – not after two years, and not so that it looked like the victim's dying message.

Because that's exactly how they interpreted it. It was what had been on the message pad that had fallen with the bedside table. The pad and pencil had been under her hand when they found her – with what she'd written before she'd been attacked, not after.

The writing was awkward looking – obviously, as I explained, she'd been in bed, probably half asleep, the pad at an unnatural angle. They weren't interested – only in what she'd written. There was the High Wycombe number, then, in capital letters it went on: MR OLIVER – 12.30 – POLICE'.

The appeal court confirmed the verdict and the sentence.

THE GIFT OF THE GAB

Dona Isabela Mendez moved down the front steps of the hacienda on the arm of her husband. Any waning in her natural beauty was easily compensated by her increasing serenity in maturity. The couple were preparing to greet their important guest as the dusty limousine came to a halt. 'My God, he's aged,' she uttered quietly, as they first caught sight of the single passenger.

'Haven't we all, my dear. Except on you it doesn't show.' Don Carlos Romero Mendez was giving a somewhat stiff wave of welcome, and resisting the compunction to let the hand stay uplifted in a simulated salute. Old habits are easily revived.

The little chauffeur, grey-suited and wearing what appeared to be a parlously sat-upon peaked cap, was soon leaping from his seat to open the rear door of the vehicle. He did give a formal if hasty salute, before thrusting his head and shoulders inside, ready to assist the occupant.

But Federico Amanas rejected help. With only a little straining, he levered himself on to the smooth driveway into the waiting arms of his hostess. Sweeping off the Panama hat, to reveal a still abundant growth of steel grey hair, he embraced her warmly, before extending a hand to her husband. 'It's like coming home,' he said, straightening his body to its full height, his broad chest filling the well tailored jacket of the white suit. The slimness of his waist suggested to Mendez, uncharitably, that he might be wearing a corset.

'That's exactly how we want you to feel while you're here, Presidente. At home. With friends,' the host now insisted.

163

'Too kind, too kind,' repeated the man who hadn't been president of the country for more than one and a half decades, but who savoured the memory.

'Was the drive from the airport tiresome?' Dona Isabela asked.

'Yes, but it could have been a thousand times more so, and still been worth it to embrace the most enchanting woman in the world.' He turned to her again, and, smiling, took her hands in his and kissed them both.

'Thank you, Federico. Can I ever have been that?' she questioned lightly, but without hint of protestation. She glanced overtly at her husband who seemed as flattered by the compliment as she was. The Dona and the ex-president had been clandestine lovers years before, a fact known at the time, but studiously ignored, by their respective spouses. Amanas's feelings for her then would certainly have supported his present extravagant description. 'But your compliments are as beguiling as ever,' she went on, their hands still clasped. 'So, has the place changed, do you think?'

He looked about him. 'Not at all. Such tranquillity.'

The Andalusian style country house, with the matching white church and village below it, was at the head of a subtropical valley lush with vegetation. The sloping vineyards and the flatter farmland beyond had been hewn out of the forest, against the backcloth and shelter of the hill ranges on both sides. The hewing had been completed late in the eighteenth century. A previous Carlos Romero Mendez had built the property, which established the present occupant as very 'old money'. He had been born to inherit a title even grander than Don, but had abandoned it as a sop to democracy when the present government had been elected (after a fashion) sixteen years before this.

Even so, Carlos Mendez owed his way of life to the veneration with which he and his wife were held by the locals – people of mixed South American Indian and Spanish colonial descent. At the start of the bloody coup that had brought in the Amanas regime, Mendez, with other powerful landlords, had accepted high political office, as well as army colonelcies, to bolster the new government's standing. That was why Mendez had then been obliged to live most of the time in the Capital, eight hundred miles away over the mountains, deserting his country seat and agrarian life style. When a counter, but less sanguinary revolution had taken place, five years later, he had changed to the winning side at the critical moment. Indeed, his astute wife had several times proved singularly adept at choosing such moments for him. After that particular event, again on Dona Isabela's advice, he had abandoned all outward desire to continue in national office, returning to a life of comparative obscurity as a provincial administrator – a largely honorary appointment, except his standing in the community was to serve, once more, to bolster another fresh regime's credibility.

The last change of government had subsequently done little for the country in general, but it had certainly served to protect those who lived under Mendez's immediate protection. This happy issue had a good deal to do with Dona Isabela's conduct during the five years of the previous regime when, unlike her husband, she had been careful to divide her time between the metropolis and their country estate, with the balance favouring the latter. It was her continuing presence in the country that had sustained the old loyalties, whilst her closeness to the then President Amanas had ensured her husband's special place in the government – at least while that government had lasted.

The province in which the Mendez family had lived for centuries was, by general agreement, the most attractive in the land. For a local peasant, the alternative of life as a poor miner in the hills, or as a smallholder on the freezing high plains to the north, or, worst of all, as a small freeholder on the low lying, sweltering desert to the west, would have been purgatory in comparison. And Don Carlos was still powerful enough to protect the locality from bureaucratic encroachment by a far away central government, as well as from unwelcome infiltration by people from other parts of the country who could upset the balance of the local economy. Altogether, Carlos and Isabela Mendez had done as well for their dependants as they had for themselves.

'We only wish Consuela could be with us, Federico,' Dona

165

Isabela offered with a sigh as she linked her arm in her visitor's. And the sentiment she had expressed was quite genuine. The ex-president's wife had been a frail, retiring creature, in time past grateful for the sympathetic friendship of her husband's mistresses, of which there had been many more than one. She had been content to provide him with children, to support him loyally in his political career, and eventually to end her days in a Swiss convent hospital.

'Yes, I miss Consuela deeply.' This also was true, after the speaker's fashion, though his visits to his wife in hospital had been, to say the least, infrequent. 'It's been over a year now, of course. The children are a comfort, yet so scattered about the world. But I have no complaints.' He paused, pouting, after this lofty pronouncement, aware that his well informed companion would know he was living with a twenty year old Swedish waitress who had not been considered an appropriate companion for this trip. 'The boys have their own families and careers, of course,' he continued. 'They come to see me often enough. Switzerland suits me, especially for my health and . . . and creature comforts.'

'This country, your country, will soon be ready to welcome you back, Presidente,' Mendez interposed firmly. In a way, the comparative ease with which the present still very private visit had been arranged supported the statement. The government was in trouble, and the ex-president had a surviving and increasing following in the country. It had been Dona Isabela who, ahead of her husband, had concluded that the current president might soon be prompted to do something drastic – very possibly to resign before inviting Amanas to return as head of a coalition administration. Once again, the two people whose life style would be best protected by such a development would be the Mendez themselves. And, thanks to the present visit, they would certainly be credited with any initiatives that might stem from it.

For his part, Amanas had no expectation that the last scenario would become a reality – even supposing he would have co-operated in its making. He had ruefully accepted that his leadership capabilities had diminished, particularly his powers of persua-

166

sion. He shook his head. 'I may be allowed back for a private visit to good friends,' he countered philosophically. 'But for a longer time? I think not, Carlos. I made a promise, you remember?' He looked across at the other man for a moment with admonition in his expression. It had been his own exile that had enabled Mendez and others to remain. This was the first time that Amanas had revisited the country he had once ruled, and which he had left after agreeing never to return. If the administration had any new role in mind for him, it would need to show its hand fully, and he doubted that Carlos Mendez had a mandate to do that.

'Your promise was made a long time ago, Presidente.' Mendez had been embarrassed by the loaded question.

'But not long enough to permit me to return for good,' Amanas commented, then, without waiting for either of the others to respond, he tactfully dropped the subject. 'Well now, this is quite a reception I see you've arranged, my dear friends,' he offered with enthusiasm.

A group of servants, stable hands, and field workers was assembled at the top of the steps, around the door. The men were bareheaded and beaming, the women were in Sunday-best peasant dress – with their coquettish little black *chapaca* hats, and their colourful long *polleias* skirts. There were murmurs of 'Presidente, Presidente' as the three approached, to be greeted by curtsies and low bows.

Yet the little demonstration was somewhat lacking in spontaneity or convincing size. The veteran politician assumed, with grim amusement, that it was meant to offer a token show of how his hosts were defying the official conditions laid down for the visit, which banned his appearing at any indoor or outdoor assembly.

'Good day to you all,' he called, fulfilling the role allotted, and lifting his arms in his old style, with hands facing outwards, in a gesture of warm, enfolding appreciation. 'Thank you for your welcome. And I see many familiar faces here. Some very old friends.' He moved to shake hands with several of those in the group. 'Ah, and this is . . . Pedro, isn't it?' He questioned a grizzled, stocky but powerfully built individual whose skin was as pitted and parched as tree bark.

After some hesitation, and a furtive sideways glance at his employer, the man replied. 'No, Señor Presidente, it's . . . it's Luca.' The gravelled tone had been less apologetic than indifferent, as if he was still prepared to answer to Pedro if that's what the Señor Presidente wanted.

'Luca. Of course it's Luca. I'm sorry. I was thinking of San Pedro because he was a fisherman. You still fish, Luca?'

'Yes, Señor Presidente.' He looked again at Don Carlos for sanction. 'I think tomorrow, maybe, it's arranged . . .'

'Luca will take you fishing on the lake in the morning,' Mendez put in. 'That's if it pleases you as much as it used to, Presidente. Your favourite rods have been stored carefully against your expected return. Let's see how you feel in the morning.'

'I feel already I'll want to go fishing with Luca in his flat bottomed boat. It'll be like old times. You still have that boat, Luca?'

'He still has it, yes.' Mendez confirmed.

'And still with no motor, because motors frighten the fish?' Amanas joked.

This seemed to relax Luca a little, who stopped nervously moving his fingers along the curled brim of the sombrero he was holding in front of him. 'No motor, Señor Presidente. Only two strong oars, and hands and arms to match them.' His voice was firmer now, and prouder.

'Good for you, my friend. Till the morning, then.' Nodding and smiling, Amanas moved slowly into the house with his host and hostess.

The lake was small, and twisting. It was a little more than a mile long, and three hundred yards across at its the widest point. Thick pine forest sloped down to its edges. The boathouse and landing stage, both visible from the house, were at the bottom of the terraced garden, with a vista of the water beyond until it curved out of sight. For this last reason, a moving boat was soon lost from view from the shore, with the curtain of trees providing

168

a haven of silence as well as privacy. Amanas had always found the lake a blessed retreat.

At his own request, the old head of state had taken a light breakfast at six o'clock, alone in his room, then made his way to the landing stage. Luca, who had arrived there well ahead of him, removed his hat in respectful greeting.

'Good morning, my friend,' Amanas called as he came near. 'You think the fish will be biting this early, Luca?'

'For you, yes, Señor Presidente. Like always.'

The visitor chuckled. 'Well, let's hope they don't know I've come down in the world since I last tried to catch them. Thanks, I can manage.' He stepped into the solid wooden boat that was square ended as well as flat bottomed – a sturdy construction, longer and wider overall than a large skiff, with metal rowlocks and a seat for the oarsman set just forward of amidships. Across from this was a wide bench for a fly fishing passenger who could cast from there over the square stern. There was no tiller. It looked to be an unwieldy craft but, as the visitor remembered, it handled well if ponderously. 'You know, it's more than fifteen years since you and I last did this, Luca?'

The shorter, older man looked up slowly from what he was doing with the boat's painter. 'Fifteen years, eight months, and four days, Señor Presidente,' he answered stolidly, and with a surprising accuracy which the other took to be a compliment to himself.

'You remember that date as clearly as I do, Luca, I expect for the same bitter reason?' he questioned. 'Or was it your birthday, perhaps?' he added affably. After settling himself on the seat, he had opened the small box of coloured artificial flies he had brought with him, and was soon intently choosing a selection to interest the fish.

Luca pushed the boat away from the jetty and arranged his hands on the oars. 'I remember for the same reason as you, Señor Presidente. It wasn't my birthday.' He let out his breath with undue heaviness before pulling evenly on both oars. 'It was the day before the revolution. Before the bloody riots in the Capital,' he completed.

169

'It was indeed. I could hardly forget.' Amanas shook his head before looking up. 'I left here by helicopter next morning. Even earlier than we are setting off today.' He paused because he had returned to studying the contents of the box, not because his memory of events was vague. 'But the riots weren't so bloody, you know?' He was now eyeing the green feathered fly he was holding by the base of its slender hook. 'And they were over very quickly,' he continued. 'Once I'd sized up the situation, my aim was to stop unnecessary conflict. The civil unrest was finished that night. The occupation of the central barracks by my President's Guards was against my orders. The men meant well, of course, but their stand was impetuous, and, in the end, unfortunate.'

'People were killed, Señor Presidente?'

The words, offered quietly, were nearer a statement than a question, except that Amanas assumed them to be the latter. The conversation ceased for some moments, the only sound coming from the movement of the water and the rocking of the oar handles in the loosely fitted rowlocks. Eventually Amanas looked up from his fishing gear. 'People were killed that day, yes. Forty-seven died in the bombardment of the barracks. Some of my most dedicated soldiers, most of them very young. My order to surrender was transmitted too late. Before the shelling was over, I had already signed a settlement with the leaders of the . . . the new government.' He had long since ceased referring to them as revolutionaries. 'It would have been pointless to do anything else. You see, Luca, I'd always accepted that my regime was to be a transitory one. It was our mission to provide a strong military government for as long as it took to stabilise the country and the economy. Some said we were undemocratic because we weren't elected.' He shrugged. 'But the people we'd thrown out in the first place were a bunch of crooks. They'd come to power through rigged elections. If that was democracy, God help democracy.'

The speaker gave a tolerant smile at his companion who was pulling hard on the oars with a steady rhythm, and already moving the craft around the first bend in the lake. He sensed that Luca had been unimpressed with his last point, but he was equally sure that the earlier question about the killings all those years ago had been prompted by nothing more than curiosity.

'Except, why should you have known any of that, Luca?' he asked, following up his conjecture. 'The corrupt government I sent packing had kept the whole nation ignorant. Of course, we planned to have elections as soon as the country was ready for them.' Not that simple folk like Luca would have been interested to know then, and it did little good if they aspired to know now, Amanas mused to himself, wondering why he was troubling to give this unengaged peasant a history lesson.

'Would it have been another five years before you had the elections, Señor Presidente?' the other man questioned unexpectedly.

'No. Much sooner than that, Luca.'

'But they'd been promised in eighteen months from after you came to power.' Before he had spoken, Luca had stopped rowing. He had pulled the oars inboard, and was gently easing a canvas bag out from under his seat. The little vessel was now well beyond observation from the house, and with the oars still, even the lapping of water against the boat's sides had ceased.

'That was a stated intention, not a promise, Luca. As time went on we decided it would have been dangerous to hold elections too soon. It took longer to stabilize the country than we'd hoped.' The words had been delivered in a more brusque manner than before, showing that Amanas was tiring of this sterile exchange. 'And I doubt what happened during my presidency affected anyone in this oasis of calm and prosperity,' he completed, more amiably, while making ready to start the fishing.

'But some people here were affected, Señor Presidente,' Luca persisted.

Amanas looked up from fingering his fishing rod. 'A few people, yes, Luca. As you'll probably remember, Señor Mendez joined me in the government.' Though inwardly it wouldn't have surprised him to learn that Luca had been oblivious of even that fact.

'My only son was affected too,' Luca responded stonily.

171

'Indeed? You never told me you had a son, Luca. What's his name?' It was something that genuinely puzzled Amanas. In times past, the boatman had spoken to him often of daughters, but not of a son.

Luca was ponderously undoing the straps of the bag which was now resting on his lap. 'Most people here are too young to know I had a son, *señor*, and the older ones have forgotten, including Don Carlos.' He paused, frowning, before he added. 'And even, probably, Dona Isabela. We called our son José. His mother and I quarrelled with him twenty-five years ago. He was nineteen then.' The speaker ran a hand across his tanned jaw. 'He had taken up with a married woman in the town. Her husband had thrown her out for being unfaithful. She had been one of José's teachers at the school. He learnt literature from her. It was his best subject.' He shook his head in either disbelief or bitterness as he continued. 'He refused to stop seeing her. Their relationship was becoming common knowledge. He was bringing disgrace to our family. In the end, we disowned him. We never spoke to him again.'

'Or spoke of him to others, Luca.? To me for instance? That must have happened just ahead of the time when I started coming here. For those wonderful weekends, escaping from affairs of state.'

'I remember, *señor*. By then we were very ashamed of our son. But sending him away was something we regretted later. Much later.'

'I'm sorry, Luca. Have you made it up with him since?'

There was a breathy grunt. 'No, Señor Presidente.'

'Was that still because of the . . . this woman?' The whole community was strongly Catholic, and Amanas could understand that a parting in such circumstances could have endured.

'No, *señor*. One of his sisters found out the slut had left him for someone else. That was a few years later, after they'd gone to live together in the Capital. But by that time José had learnt to do without his family.'

'Have you ever done anything to heal the rift?'

'No, *señor*, that was for him to do. To make the first move. His mother and I were agreed on that. But José was stubborn.'

Except no more so than his father, perhaps, Amanas mused, wondering whether Luca's wife had been so adamant. This was before he asked: 'So what has become of José?'

There was a moment's hesitation before the reply. 'He joined the army, *señor.*'

'Was that under the old regime. Before I became president?'

'That's right, *señor.* He was a bright, intelligent boy. He wanted to be a writer. But he was a doer as well as a scribbler.'

'A soldier poet,' Amanas offered.

'Perhaps, *señor.* He did well in the army. Except he despised what you call the old regime.'

'I'm glad,' Amanas, still seated, was busy attaching the chosen fly to his fishing line.

'Oh yes. You would have been proud of him, *señor.* When you called for support from the army he was one of the first to lead his men over to your side. He was a sergeant then. Later he became an officer. In your . . . in your loyal President's Guards.'

Amanas looked up, his eyebrows raised. 'He was in the barracks during the bombardment?'

'Yes, Señor Presidente. He died next day of wounds.'

Hurt showed on Amanas's face. For the moment he ceased to be engrossed with the fishing rod. 'I'm sorry, Luca, there was . . .'

'We have José's diaries,' the old man interrupted boldly. 'He kept diaries for the whole time he was a soldier. He called you the country's saviour. He wrote that you'd become better than family for him. Better than father, mother, and sisters. Far better than an unfaithful wife. That's why he gave his life over to you, *señor.*'

'That makes me very proud, Luca.'

'Proud, *señor?*' There was something close to disdain in the tone, but this was too preposterous a possibility to register with Amanas, although he was aware that the speaker's eyes were resolutely – and irksomely – fixed on his own as the words continued. 'But my son died for nothing. The things he wrote about in his diaries, the things you promised the people, they never happened.'

'But I planted the seeds for their future achievement, Luca. It was for others to reap the harvest. As they should have done, of course. The next government . . .'

'The next government has been as bad as yours, and the one before yours. Things are no better now. Too many people have no work. There's still great poverty, except in a few places like this valley. Our schools and hospitals are falling down. There's only money for troops and armaments.'

'These things evolve slowly, Luca. And the country needs an army for protection.'

'That's what you told my son and his comrades twenty years ago, *señor*. José believed you spoke nothing but the truth.' Luca paused. 'But tell me, Señor Presidente, why do we need protection? The people would be better off if we'd been invaded, conquered. All our neighbours are more prosperous than we are. And, in any case, none of them wants to invade us. The protection our government pays for is from the fury of their own people.'

'That's an exaggeration, Luca. I'm ashamed to hear you say it, as I'm sure Señor Mendez would be too. Believe me . . .'

'José believed you, *señor*, and see what happened to him in the end.' This time the interruption had been savage. 'If you'd told him the truth he might have left the army and come home to us. His mother and I were sure of that, after we'd read the diaries. You took our son away from us, Señor Presidente. You killed him.'

As he had been speaking, Luca had withdrawn a revolver from the bag on his lap. It was a single action, 45 calibre, six cylinder Colt. Amanas recognized the model. It could be close to a century old, but there were no apparent signs of age or wear. 'I wish you'd put that thing away, old friend,' he offered coolly. 'I know you're not going to use it, but it could go off by accident and . . . and that's something we'd both regret.'

Luca shook his head slowly, and cocked the gun. Then, holding the weapon with both hands, his elbows tight to his sides, he levelled the long barrel so that it pointed toward his companion's heart. His movement of the mechanism had made a click that, in the stillness of the lake and the confines of the boat, was as intrusive as a thunder clap before lightning.

'I am going to kill you, Señor Presidente. On behalf of all the sons who died bringing you to power. Or the other sons who died trying to defend you at the end, like my José.'

'Don't be ridiculous, Luca. Shooting me would be like signing your own death warrant. You'd be executed, so what would be the point?' Except the speaker could see the point well enough. He'd already dismissed the first guilty conclusions that had assailed his mind. Mendez couldn't have sent him out alone with this motivated madman as revenge for his affair with Isabela. The cuckold had as good as condoned their relationship for his own benefit at the time. And surely Isabela hadn't knowingly put him in this peril because he had dropped her for another woman? She had never been that possessive. It had to be that those two really hadn't known, or had forgotten, the grounds for Luca's obsession – as Luca himself had said. Even so, Amanas was about to be assassinated through their joint stupidity. 'And what about your wife?' he uttered desperately. 'Think of the shame you'd be bringing on her?'

Luca shook his head. 'My wife died fourteen years ago, Señor Presidente. She died of a broken heart. And they won't execute me. After I've shot you, I'll kill myself. I'll have nothing else to live for.' His hold on the gun tightened. The weight of the weapon had begun to make it waver in front of him.

Amanas's hands moved slowly to grasp the edge of the seat. He was planning to hurl himself forward to the right of Luca, while knocking the gun away to the left. The distance between the two men was scarcely more than four feet – except age and arthritis made the leap seem at least three feet too far. Kicking the gun out of Luca's hands seemed a better proposition, only both Amanas's feet were lodged under the angled wooden stretcher which the rower's legs had been braced against. If the verbal exchange could be prolonged, it was possible Amanas would gradually be able to alter the position of his feet.

'You want to say your prayers, *señor*?'

The ex-president silently credited God for the intervention, and studied his adversary before he replied. It was in that moment that he hit upon his best strategy, and altered his expression to suggest both penitence and surrender to the inevitable.

'I want . . . I want to make my confession, Luca. You'll allow me that before you take my life?'

'I'm not a priest, *señor*.' The old man looked uncomfortable.

'But what I have to say is far better said to you, than to any priest, Luca.' The speaker's previously confident demeanour seemed completely to have evaporated. 'You deserve to be my executioner, just as I deserve what you are about to do to me.' The words came thoughtfully and slowly. 'As you say, I was responsible for the death of your son, and the sons of many others. You are right. I made promises, and offered rewards. But the promises were never kept, and the rewards were never enjoyed. Was that my fault? No, it wasn't, but I have always accepted the responsibility even so. People risked everything for me.'

'Why wasn't it your fault, *señor*?' The question had come after a silence of several seconds.

Amanas gave a deep sigh and clasped his hands under his chin prayerfully, eyes half closed. 'I never knowingly duped my faithful followers. As God is my witness, from my youth up I had pledged myself to lift the yoke from the shoulders of my oppressed countrymen. From those who, like me, had been born into penury and, yes, near slavery, but who, unlike me, had neither the drive nor the chance to create an opportunity to rise above their abominable lot. But I saw my ambition as something that created a chance, not for myself, but for the country. Not that there weren't times when it all seemed likely to fall apart.' The speaker hesitated, brow knitting as though he was having difficulty recalling events. 'My old father, a dirt farmer on the plain, he struggled all his life to earn enough from the unyielding soil to feed and clothe his family, and most of the time barely even that. He looked very like you, Luca. Very like you,' he repeated. 'Once, at the beginning, when I was near despair, he grasped me by the shoulders and said: "We only have one life Federico. I've wasted mine, lived it to no purpose except to father you. So don't give up now. If you die in the attempt to save our people from perdition, it will be a noble death. If you succeed, God and the nation will bless you." I remember that well.'

The ex-president looked up slowly, a convincing tear coursing down one cheek. 'From then onwards I had no fear of death, only a devout belief in my mission which my father had taught me was more important than any single life, my own included. And later, when it seemed I was going to succeed, I took it at face value that those who had been my enemies, the people's enemies, were ready to change sides, to promise me support because they had come to believe in the same values, of the need to make the same sacrifices. They were powerful men – the biggest landlords, and the owners of the mines and the factories. I believed I'd converted them, Luca, that they were with me. How wrong I was. Because, in the end, they deserted me, as well as your José, and an army of other good men, for their own selfish reasons. Oh, my aims were honest, but because of those greedy people, I failed. For that, for my sins of omission, I have never been punished. There have been times since when the weight of my guilt lay so heavily on me that I aimed to take my own life. Perhaps you find that hard to believe, but I give you my word it's true.'

'So what stopped you, *señor*?' There was no mockery in the voice, but little of conviction either.

'It was my dear wife. You know she was an invalid? Entirely dependent on me?'

'I didn't know, *señor*.'

There was a scarcely perceptive lift of the other's eyebrows before he responded. 'Yes. From soon after we left this country, she was confined to a wheelchair, and later, for a longer time, to her bed. That was until her death last year. We loved each other deeply. I was her devoted carer. That became my function. I never resented it, and I never avoided it.' He straightened defiantly. 'And I wouldn't want you to think I did it as a penance. It was my duty, and, much more than that, it was my selfish desire never to be parted from her. So I don't deserve sympathy from you on her account. It would have been much worse if, like you, I'd lost my wife earlier than I did.'

'You had children to mourn with you, *señor*?'

Amanas grunted bitterly. 'As you did, Luca. But did it help that much?' He waited for the other's reply, but, since there was none, he continued. 'I thought not. And my two sons made their lives in other countries. They were never interested in improving the lot of our fellow countrymen. Not like your José. I wish my death could bring him back to you. I'd give anything for that. In my fight for the presidency and afterwards, in my years of office, my sternest pledge was to make life more fulfilling for our young people. We so nearly achieved it too. You don't know how close we got. But circumstances were against us. I had hopes for the present government at the beginning. That's why I resigned so quickly, without a real fight. But their leaders soon became less dedicated. If I'd been more resolute, stayed on and opposed them—'

'There would have been more bloodshed, *señor*.'

Amanas nodded sagely. 'I believe that's true. But the weight of it all has been too heavy for me over this last lonely year. Again I contemplated suicide, but I was stopped by the church's teaching. Clearly you have made better arrangements with our all forgiving Lord, but that way was not for me, and not because of cowardice. But this I do know, I shall be more content in the next life than I am now, even if I have to pay a heavy price for sacrificing my life to help my fellow men, and failing in the task. So, you see, you are doing me a favour in ending my misery. It's curious that instead of fulfilling your intention, you'll be doing the opposite.' Moving aside the padded jacket he was wearing, he began to unbutton his shirt, baring his chest. 'Take good aim, my friend. And before God, I forgive you for what you are about to do.'

The shot had echoed around the lake, shattering the silence, and rousing birds to flight. The startled Carlos Mendez was breakfasting alone on the terrace. 'Who can be shooting on the lake?' he demanded of the maidservant, pushing back his chair. Not that he expected the girl to know or to answer. He was sure that the ex-president had not taken shotguns with him, and, in any

178

case, to Mendez's tutored ear, the explosion had come from a rifle or a handgun. 'Run to the kitchen and tell Stefan to meet me at the boathouse. Quickly girl.' Stefan was his valet.

Mendez reached the boathouse first. When Stefan arrived, his master was already in the launch wresting the cover off the outboard motor. In moments they were skimming across the lake surface, the noise of the engine loudly heralding their progress.

'There they are, Don Carlos,' the young servant pointed as they cleared the first bend.

The flat bottomed boat was a hundred yards ahead, moving back toward them slowly, almost reverently, the oars dipping gently in the water, while making little disturbance to its surface. The only figure visible was that of the oarsman – until the other boat drew alongside.

'Oh, my God,' uttered Mendez, horrified at the gruesome sight of the dead man lying in the forward well of the other craft. The head was shattered and bloody where a bullet had re-emerged after entering from the other side at close range.

Shipping the oars, their handler had already stepped over the body, and was holding out the painter. 'Tow it in with this,' he said, in a matter-of-fact tone, and very much in control of himself. He handed the rope to Stefan, who seemed more capable of action than his petrified master.

'Yes, Señor Presidente.' The man had moved to hold the boats steady while Amanas stepped over into the launch.

'The poor fellow was consumed with remorse at having disowned his dead son,' Amanas said to Mendez. 'He told me so in detail, then shot himself. I did my best to talk him out of it, but I fear my oratory is . . . is not as persuasive as it used to be.' He frowned, but silently consoled himself with the opposite view – while seriously reconsidering his future.

179

SECOND BEST MAN

I suppose I resented Harry Smith from the very start, deep down and without admitting it to myself. It's why I was ready to kill him in the end. Before that, there was always reason to keep the special friendship going – or what everyone saw as a special friendship, and that included me, best part of the time.

At school Harry was deeply unpopular. Short, fat and pale, he was supposed to be anaemic, wore thick glasses and was excused all games. None of that stopped him being bullied. Well it wouldn't, not in our part of South London – not in a run down comprehensive school where a bunch of dedicated yobos only stopped making life a misery for the weaker boys while they did even nastier things to the girls. Except I protected Harry. It was for a price, not money, but he always had more of that than I had, and it came in useful.

It was brains Harry had, brains and cunning – enough to get us both through the term tests, and the exams at the end. Harry turned exam cheating into an art, not that he needed to cheat on his own account. He just worked out all the answers fast, and found original ways of passing them to me. It was thanks to Harry I got five GCE passes, and thanks to me Harry never got his nose broken, or worse. It was a fair exchange.

I was always a well built lad, and handy with my fists. It made up for not being so brainy. My dad had been a professional boxer. He taught me the rudiments of the manly art early on – before he left my mum to join a circus act. That was the last we ever saw of my dad: I was twelve at the time.

When I got older, I developed what they call rugged good looks. It was Harry who said I ought to have been called Byron not Bryan, after Lord Byron the poet who'd had all the birds begging for it: we were doing Childe Harold and Don Juan for English class at the time. Harry started calling me Byron after that, and it stuck. Even my mum called me Byron. I didn't mind: I was quite pleased really. I was pulling more than a fair share of birds myself by then, young Debby Moxton for one.

I left school before Harry. He went on to London University too: well he would, of course. Me, I went from job to job. I tried to get into acting. My mum used to say I had everything it took for that, except there wasn't the money for drama school and you don't get far without. It was those GCE certificates that saved me from ended up in labouring, I suppose. They got me the interviews, and – no point being modest about it – my winning personality and looks got me the jobs. Only none of the jobs lasted: I don't know why really. Mostly I was in selling – a rep for dog food, lavatory cleaners, encyclopaedias, this and that. Of course, I deserved better, a lot better.

It was Harry Smith, the bountiful, who gave me my first good job.

Harry's old dad had always been in building supplies, in a small way. It surprised everybody when Harry joined him – took over the business really: that was after getting a degree in economics. Only there was method in Harry's madness. There was a big building boom on, with everyone short of materials. Harry specialized. He just bought and sold partitioning, all kinds of partitioning – wood, chipboard, hardboard, plastic, metal, you name it, for every kind of building – houses, offices, schools, factories. He bought big, too, going all over the world in the end to get what he wanted. At the start he cashed in on his dad's goodwill, and his credit rating – and his dedication. That was clever. People had always trusted his dad, and the old man worked for Harry like a stoat. After two or three years, Harry had all the banks queuing up to lend him money – first in thousands, then hundreds of thousands, then millions. Marvellous how that lot'll back you when you're successful: not a sodding one would lend me enough to see me through acting school.

I didn't know about Harry's success at the start: we'd lost touch for quite a while. That was partly because I'd given up living at home for a bit – until I found things too expensive and moved back. Harry and I met up again at a dance for old pupils in the school hall one Christmas. When I saw him, I wondered what the hell he was doing there: he'd hated the school and he didn't dance. Physically he hadn't altered that much, he was still small, fat and ugly, only the clothes he was wearing were smarter than anyone else's, and he seemed to breathe confidence. Debby Moxton was there too, with another girl we'd known called Beryl.

Debby had definitely been the best looker in the school in our day, and probably any other day, come to that. Three years younger than Harry and me, at twenty-two, which she was at this point, she was an absolute knock-out – a tall, natural blonde, with an English rose complexion and a smashing figure. I reckoned she'd still have been gone on me if I'd made anything of myself. We'd knocked around together for a while after I left school. Unlike the other girls though, she'd never given it away, if you see what I mean? Bit of petting and a kiss goodnight was all you ever got from Debby. She made it pretty plain she was saving the real favours for a husband, and whoever married her had better prove in advance he could keep her in the manner intended. Till then she was happy enough working as a director's secretary in some big Croydon company.

So the four of us ended up spending that evening together. It seemed almost that Harry had intended we'd do that from the start, though how he knew we were all going to be there I never found out.

It was while the girls were in the ladies' room that I told Harry about my career progress, or lack of it.

'You ought to come into my business, Byron, boy,' he said, straight off. 'Plenty of room. We're expanding all the time.'

'No, I couldn't do that. Couldn't take advantage,' I said, hoping he'd insist, and wishing I'd got on to him before this.

'Yes, you could,' he answered, on cue. 'Anyway, I owe you.'

In a way he was right. If I hadn't protected him at school he could easily have turned out an insecure adult with a persecution complex, prevented from reaching his true potential. I read somewhere about that happening to people who'd been bullied a lot.

'So what would I do?' I remember asking next, but in a positive way, not to encourage Harry to have second thoughts. 'I don't know too much about partitioning.' Except I knew even less about portable air conditioning units, which, as I'd told Harry, was what I was supposed to be flogging at the time.

'Anyone who can sell air conditioning can sell partitioning,' he said. 'It's all part of the building trade. And you've got the presence for selling, Byron. Always have had. And the looks.' He'd always envied my appearance.

I didn't bother admitting I hadn't actually sold any of the air conditioning units yet – and that I hadn't exactly reached star salesman status with the dog food, the lavatory cleaners, and the encyclopaedias either. Anyway, I think Harry had really guessed all that, and he wasn't asking for references in any case. So it was agreed I should start with Smith Partitions Limited two weeks from the following Monday. Harry told the girls when they came back from the ladies: it all happened as fast as that. The girls were impressed too. Well, with Harry they were – especially Debby.

At the end of the dance, Harry drove us all home in the new Jaguar he'd got parked outside in the school yard. Caused quite a sensation that car did, and it was meant to. This was Harry showing off in front of his old mates and enemies – mostly enemies – and you couldn't blame him either. He dropped Beryl and me at her place which was just round the corner from my mother's, then drove on with Debby who was looking gorgeous and regal with it in the front passenger seat.

Debby and Harry were married three months later. I was pretty sore about that. I didn't show it, of course. There was no point, especially since Harry had kind of asked for my approval in advance. He said he knew I'd have Debby's best interests at heart since he remembered we'd been close some years back, and did

I think she'd make a good wife for a rising industrialist who could afford to give her everything she'd want out of life? So what could I say, except wish him good luck? It happened to be the day after he'd promoted me by making me responsible for selling to the solid 'house accounts' – building firms who'd never have dreamed of buying partitioning from anyone else but Harry. All I had to do was make courtesy calls, buy the customers lunch sometimes, and collect the bloody orders. To have told him what I really felt about his marrying Debby would only have upset the apple cart, and risked my job probably with nothing achieved. I mean she wasn't going to marry me, was she?

So short arsed, four eyes, anaemic Harry Smith landed South London's most desirable dollybird – and he got a virgin into the bargain.

I was best man at the wedding. Beryl was chief bridesmaid. When it came to appearances, Beryl was never exactly a show stopper, not in the same class as Debby, not by a thousand miles. She looked pretty good that day though, which was when I took up with her seriously. We got hitched ourselves not long after. I figured she'd stay close to Debby, so it was a way for me to keep the business relations cemented, if you follow me? – not very high minded of me perhaps, but practical.

At first we saw a lot of Harry and Debby socially. When Harry moved the business out beyond Reading, in Berkshire, he bought a home there too, and we did the same – not on a golf course like his, and it wasn't a mansion like his either. Harry set up a factory as well as a warehouse in the new location because by then he was into more than just buying and selling partitions. He'd decided he was going to manufacture the stuff himself, and not just partitions either. In no time the company was making complete, integrated portable buildings for temporary and permanent use, and undercutting everybody else in sight. It was a gold mine.

All this moved Harry into the really big time. Of course, before long the people close to him had to be in the same league as he was, and for one reason and another that didn't include me. I'd already been shifted off 'house accounts' into office management. It seemed you had to be a qualified architect with an MBA to handle the big accounts at that stage, even the tame ones. I was paid a bit more, but it was a downward move since I had less real responsibility. If I saw Harry at all at work it was only in the corridor. I noticed he looked worn, and I swear sometimes he didn't seem to remember me: anyway, he was hardly ever in the office, or in the country for that matter, especially after we won a Duke of Edinburgh Award for Export. There was no holding him then. People said he had his sights on a knighthood, and every time a newspaper ran a list of the country's highest earners, Harry would be there in the top hundred.

I'd lost touch with Debby and Harry socially by that time too, though that was mostly because Beryl and I had got divorced. We hadn't been compatible from the start. I was only worried that if Debby sided with Beryl over our break up, it might lead to me losing my job, but it didn't. I came to the conclusion that Debby and Harry had probably moved so far above our level, neither of them knew about the divorce, or if they did, neither could have cared less. At least, that's what I thought until that Friday night in November four years ago when I had to take something from the factory to their house.

Don't misunderstand, I hadn't been reduced to delivering parcels for the company on a regular basis – not quite, anyway. A silver tea set, a wedding present Harry had ordered for someone, had been sent to the office by mistake. Harry had been abroad, and his chauffeur was already at Heathrow meeting him. His secretary was in a flap because the wedding was next day and the Smiths were supposed to be taking the present with them. It was already gone six and the secretary was late for a date with her boy friend. She knew my house wasn't far from Harry's, so she'd rushed into my office almost in tears to ask could I possibly?

Debby answered the door herself. I hadn't seen her for nearly three years, not to speak to anyway. At thirty-four she still looked smashing, figure a bit fuller which you'd expect after she'd had two kids, both boys incidentally, and both, I gathered later, already away at boarding school. Only I wondered why she was wearing the dark glasses.

She seemed glad to see me, kissed me warmly on the cheek, and invited me in. She wasn't much interested in the story of the silver tea set, and dropped the box it was in on one of the hall chairs.

I'd been to the house before, often, but not for a long time. They'd made some improvements. For a start there were a lot more expensive looking antiques and pictures about the place.

She linked her arm in mine. 'What'll you drink? Whisky still, is it? Water, but no ice?' she asked, steering me into their drawing-room.

I said, 'I don't think I'd better stay that long. Harry'll be home any minute won't he?'

'Harry won't be home till Monday, and only then if he remembers where he lives. I just got a fax from the Paris office. He has to stay over. Pressure of work, poor dear. Tough titty having to spend the week-end in Paris by yourself, I don't think,' she went on in a really acid tone as she poured my drink from a trolley across the room.

'What about the wedding tomorrow?'

'Screw the wedding. If he's not here to take me I'm not going. They're his friends, not mine. Business friends. We don't have any of the other sort, not any more.' She came over with my drink.

'Aren't you having one?' I asked.

'Of course I am. It's over here. I'm a . . . I'm slightly ahead of you. I'm sorry about your divorce.' So she did know about that. 'I meant to ring you. Haven't talked to Beryl either. She always had personality problems, of course. You two should never have got married in the first place. Applies to a lot of us. Let's sit here.' So I needn't have worried about the divorce costing me my job. She motioned me to the sofa in front of the blazing log fire in the huge open hearth. The fire was a gas jet and the logs were imitation, but it was all pretty cosy.

'Something wrong with your eyes, Debby?' I said when we were sitting quite close together.

'Yes. One of them got blacked by my adoring husband on Wednesday.' She took off the glasses. Her right eye was almost closed and the flesh around it puffed and bruised.

187

'Accident?'

'Yes. He was aiming for my ribs, but he was drunk, and missed. Made up for it though with the next punch. Want to see?' Without waiting for an answer, she put her glass down, sat up straight, and in one showy movement pulled off the cashmere sweater she was wearing over her head. 'How about that? I thought he'd broken a rib. Feel the lump.' She'd hollowed her back and leaned closer to me. Then she took my hand and ran it gently over the blue-black area above her midriff.

It was a massive bruise all right, but I was paying more attention to the the rest of what she'd exposed. All she'd been wearing under the sweater was one of those lacy, half bras. It was white, making a nice contrast against her smooth, tanned skin, and didn't leave much to the imagination. Her breasts looked as firm and perfect as they had when she was a girl, well, they did to me at least.

'Worn well otherwise, haven't I, Byron,' she said quietly, following my eyes as well as my thoughts. Then, without shifting her gaze from mine, she undid the bra and shook it off to prove the point further, and before putting her arms around my neck. 'Why don't you stay for dinner? It's all prepared. Pity to waste it. No hurry, of course, it'll keep.' Then she kissed me, on the lips this time, slowly and very sensuously while she began undoing the buttons on my shirt.

'Are you alone in the house?' I asked.

'No, silly, you're here. Handsome, adorable, sexy Byron,' she giggled, thrusting her arm down under my shirt, fingers exploring.

'I meant . . .'

'I know what you meant. But even the fabulous Smiths don't have living in servants. So you can stay the whole night if you want. But let's not wait till then,' she added.

And we didn't. After all, I'd been waiting over twenty years for Debby.

It was when we were upstairs in bed much later that she began pouring her heart out to me, lying close in my arms. By that time we'd eaten, and the stimulating effect of what she'd drunk had worn off – and I guessed she'd drunk quite a bit before I'd got to the house. Now she wasn't kittenish any more, a bit maudlin really, but very affectionate still.

She gave me more depressing details of her life with Harry, about the way he beat her up, his drinking, his frequent absences, his infidelities, his lack of interest in the children, and his always putting her down in public, something that hurt her as much as the physical cruelty, only in a different way.

'So why don't you leave him?' I asked.

'And leave all this too?'

She had a point there. She'd certainly come a long way from Mafeking Street, Lambeth. Even so, breaking with Harry didn't mean she had to go back to that kind of life style.

'In a divorce you'd get half his estate, probably,' I explained. 'He's stinking rich.'

'I wouldn't get half. Or anything like. You know what a clever sod he is. I'm scared he'd fix it so I'd hardly have enough to live on. And he'd get custody of the boys. I couldn't bear that.'

'But you're wrong there. The wife always . . .'

'Not this wife,' she interrupted. 'If we divorced, I'd be the guilty party. He's . . . he's got grounds. I know he's unfaithful to me, but, the difference is, I can't prove it.'

'So what sort of grounds does he have?' It was a funny question to be asking when we were lying beside each other in her matrimonial, king-sized bed.

She didn't say anything for a bit, just fingered the sheet, then she looked up and shrugged. 'What the hell, I can tell you. My darling, oldest friend.' She kissed me behind the ear before going on. 'Four years ago, I had a brief affair. Well, Harry was neglecting me. He'd insisted on both the boys going away to school. I felt unwanted, unnecessary, and so lonely. I . . . I needed someone.'

'I wish you'd needed me,' I said.

'You were still married,' she answered, with what I suppose was a good enough reason. Beryl had once been her best friend, after all. 'Anyway, the man I was involved with was a young assistant pro, here at the golf club. Harry got suspicious and had us both followed. That's how he got the evidence. Nothing's come out in public, but Harry made me sign a confession. And I had to promise never to see Rickie again. That was his name. Rickie. He was so beautiful,' she added dreamily, then completed quickly: 'Like you, Byron.' She squeezed my arm, but I remember thinking she'd been a bit late. 'Harry still arranged to have Rickie fired. And fixed it so he'd never get another job in golf. Not anywhere. God, he's a mean bastard.'

'I still don't think one affair should stop you getting a good divorce settlement, or custody of the boys,' I offered, although I wasn't exactly speaking from experience. Beryl and I never had any kids.

'Except there's something else. Something . . . something that turns off divorce judges more than casual affairs.' She sighed and clung closer to me, the fingers of one hand playing with the hairs on my chest. Her head was on my shoulder, but her eyes were now avoiding mine. 'You haven't seen me for so long, of course,' she went on. 'Three years ago I was a mess. After I'd had to break up with Rickie, I . . . I started taking drugs.'

'Hard drugs or soft drugs?'

'Both. Well, one sort led to the other. That usually happens, doesn't it?' I didn't answer. I've never been into drugs. 'I . . . I was a fool, I know,' she added, 'but what with the beatings and the loneliness . . .'

'You don't have to talk about it,' I said quietly.

'But I want to. To you. There's no one else I can unburden on. The drug bit's over now. I took the cure. In a clinic. In California. Harry told everyone I had a blood disease, but you can bet he's got the sodding details in writing somewhere. That's why I'm scared I wouldn't get custody.' She breathed out noisily. 'I hate Harry. And I hate my life. I often think of doing myself in. I'm so unhappy, and it's all so unfair.' She started to cry quietly.

It was my turn to sigh – because I was aggravated. 'But there's got to be some way out for you?'

She leaned right across me. I thought she was getting amorous again, until her hand reached out to unlock the drawer of the small table on my side of the bed. When she moved back she was

holding a hand gun. It was a smallish, heavy black revolver with
a short barrel.

'Suicide's not the way,' I said quickly, taking the gun from her
with care. 'You're still beautiful, with plenty to live for.' I meant
what I said, too, and was already vaguely trying to fit myself into
an on-going scenario.

'I've never thought of using the gun on myself' She paused.
'Sometimes I think of using it on Harry, though.'

That shook me, because I could tell from the tone she was
serious. 'Murder Harry?' I said. 'But that wouldn't solve your
problems for you.'

'It'd solve them if a burglar did it,' she answered coolly. 'Harry
had a pair of guns brought over from the States because we've
had three break-ins this year. He swears he'll shoot the next thief
if he gets the chance. The other gun's at the London flat. We've
been burgled there too.'

'Isn't there an alarm system here?'

'Yes, but the thieves always get round it. They're so sophisticated these days. If Harry went after the next one, if there was a
fight, and if it was Harry who got shot, I could be a witness to
what happened, that it was he who had the gun, not the burglar.
We could do it, Byron,' she whispered at the end, breathing the
words quickly close to my ear.

'It wouldn't be as simple as that,' I said.

'It would you know,' she answered. 'And then I'd be very rich,
and we could get married later, and live happily ever after. Isn't
that what you always wanted, darling Byron?'

There were any number of times later when I could have backed
down, but I didn't. Like she said, it really was very simple – and
the reward was so big.

It was one in the morning, on the Thursday, three weeks later,
when I left the car in a copse, close to the house. I remember
being glad it was cloudy and dark, with the ground bone dry.
Wearing gloves and a Balaclava, I went in through the unlocked
kitchen door. The gun was in one of the drawers where Debby
had put it that afternoon. I went softly up the stairs to their

bedroom. There was no alarm: she had switched it off earlier, after they had gone to bed, pretending she'd forgotten to do something downstairs.

When I got to the bedroom door I began taking long breaths to steady my nerves, going over the final part of the plan.

When I opened the door, Debby was to switch on the lights over the bed. I was to go straight to Harry and shoot him in the head while he was still searching for the gun in the drawer. Then I'd leave straight away, dropping the gun on the landing, and breaking the panel of glass next to the lock on the kitchen door as I left, but from the outside. Debby would wait fifteen minutes, the time it would take me to drive home on back roads. Then, feigning hysterics, she was to call the police. Meantime she'd have turned the alarm system on again, forced open the jewellery drawers of her dressing table, and arranged things to look as if there'd been a fight on the bed between Harry, who'd gone for his gun, and the burglar who'd woken him. There was less than no chance anyone would hear the shot and fix the time of it. The house was set in the centre of ten acres of garden and paddock. The bedroom windows would be shut; in any case they over-looked a golf fairway, and miles of common land beyond that.

That first comment of Debby's had been pretty accurate. There was really nothing to it if we kept our heads. And the more I thought of pulling the trigger on Harry, the more acceptable the idea had become.

Getting practical experience of the gun had helped a bit. Debby had brought it to the house one morning when he was away, and I'd taken it to practise with in the local wood where people were always shooting rabbits. I'd cleaned it afterwards, and refilled the chambers with the extra shells she'd brought. She'd collected it again later that day.

It was while I was firing the gun that I got to thinking Harry was right about what he used to say he'd owed me – except the menial job I'd had in his company over the last years didn't show lasting gratitude, or anything like it, not when you realized he'd become a multi-millionaire. As for what he'd done to Debby, well that put the lid on it. But I have to admit that what egged me on the most was I'd be ending up with Debby after all – and with Harry's fortune to go with her. There was sweet justice in that.

I was pretty calm when I finally opened the bedroom door. I wasn't three paces into the room before the lights went on as arranged. I kept going, the gun already held out in front of me in my right hand, left hand supporting the right wrist. My gaze was fixed on Harry, but in the corner of my eye I saw Debby slip out of the bed on to the floor out of the way: good girl.

By now a bleary Harry should have been fumbling with the drawer key – but he wasn't. He was sitting up in bed putting on his glasses and grinning. Grinning! He could see the gun. Did he have a death wish or something?

When I was two paces from Harry I stopped, straightened my arms, and levelled the barrel at his forehead. At that range I couldn't miss – but for a split second looking into his eyes made me hesitate. I might not have gone through with it, except Debby saw what was happening to me.

'Do it! Do it!' she screamed.

I pulled the trigger, my ears instinctively preparing for the explosion. There was a click but no bang.

I pulled the trigger again, and the same thing happened. I pulled the safety catch on, then off again, and pulled the trigger again, and again, and again – and all I could hear was the sound of Harry's mounting laughter. I was panicky and confused. I looked down at the gun. It had to be jammed.

It was then I decided to club Harry to death. I looked up and was about to spring at him when there was an explosion, and a flash. Harry was holding a smoking gun in his hand. He'd been holding it under the bedclothes. The shot he'd just fired could have killed me, no question.

'Keep still, Byron,' he said, eyeing me. 'And Debby, my love, come round and stand next to Byron where I can see you. And do it now or I'll shoot him in a tender place, and that'd be inconvenient for both of you.' He chuckled as she did as she was told.

'I'm afraid you've got the gun with no firing pin, Byron,' he went on. 'I use it just to frighten people. It doesn't frighten me, of course. I switched guns after Debby lent you the other one to practise with. Taking it to your house was a mistake, of course. Just made it easier for the people I had following her. You'd have been better meeting in a supermarket or on a park bench, even. Don't you watch crime movies? Oh, and Byron, please take that ridiculous sock off your head. Slowly though, no tricks.'

I took off the Balaclava.

'That's much better,' Harry said. 'Now we can see your famously handsome face again. I knew it was you, of course, Byron. I have a perfect recording of you both putting the plot together that night I was delayed in Paris. Only, as I remember, it was Debby who did all the plotting. Never really an original thinker were you, Byron? Not a thinker at all, come to that. You always relied on others for the brainwork, didn't you? Still do, of course.'

'How did you find out?' I asked.

'That you were planning to murder me? In cold blood?' Without taking his eyes off me, he tapped the bedside table drawer with his hand. 'Undoing this lock starts a miniature tape recorder at the back of the drawer. Simple but ingenious, don't you think? I never told Debby about it for . . . for various reasons. It's recording now, as a matter of fact. I like to have a complete record of things. By the way, the tape I referred to just now is lodged under seal with my solicitor – to be played in the event I should die in suspicious circumstances.'

That was enough for me. 'Harry,' I said, 'shoot me, or hand me over to the police. Either way, get on with it.'

Harry looked shocked. 'Shoot you? Shoot Byron, my old buddy? My childhood companion and protector? My best man? How could you think I'd do anything so barbarous? It'd be like beating up my wife. Giving her a black eye. Punching her in the ribs.' Suddenly his voice rose as his gaze turned on Debby. 'Tell him you lied about that, you little slut, you druggy, you bloody whore. Tell him how you got those injuries. Tell him now,' he shouted angrily.

Debby had been silent up to then. Then she sank on to the end of the bed and started weeping. 'I'm sorry, Harry, I didn't mean . . .'

'Tell him now,' he repeated with a roar.

She swallowed, wiping her eyes with her hand. 'It . . . it was an accident. I fell down the stairs.'

'You fell down the stairs when you were stoned out of your mind. One night when you had your teenage lovers here. Two of them. That's the truth isn't it?' he roared again.

'Yes, Harry,' she answered with a whimper.

Harry nodded and looked back at me. 'Curious that, after being a professional virgin up to our marriage, she's been making up for lost time ever since. Though not with me, I'm afraid.' He pulled a face. 'Now then, as for turning you over to the police, Byron, I don't think that'd do a lot of good, do you?' he asked, as if it was a perfectly normal question to which he needed an unbiased answer.

'What are you going to do then?' I asked.

'I'm going to let you go home now,' he answered, in the same serious tone as before. 'But you'll be taking my wife with you. She's leaving me, Byron. Leaving me for ever. Eloping with you, you might say. In fact, that's exactly what we will say. All of us. It's been bothering me for a long time how to get Debby out of my life. To turn her over to someone who'd care for her. Her and her problems, with drink and drugs and men. Big problems they are, too. Have been for me and my sons for a long time. We're all fed up with her, I'm afraid.'

'That's not true,'Debby screamed.

'Oh, but it is true, my love,' he answered quietly. 'You know, Byron, my sons begged me to send them away to school because they couldn't stand living with their mother any more, especially when I'm away. Did you ever hear of such a thing? I try to be here as much as possible, especially in the school holidays, as much as the business allows at least. That's often difficult but I'm making arrangements for it not to be in the future. And contrary to what you've been told, I don't have girl friends, oh, and I don't drink either. Well, you know I never did.' He waited for Debby to protest, but she didn't. 'No, it'll be much better if Debby goes with you. Then I can divorce her. I would have done it earlier, but the men she's been associating with wouldn't have stayed with her for ten minutes, not unless I'd paid them. And if she'd had money of her own, they'd have robbed her blind. And I care about her, and her future, you see? That's why I'm ready to trust her to you. Trust you to stay with her. To look after her. Especially since you have no alternative. Either of you. And I'll make it worth your while.'

'I wouldn't need paying to . . .' I began, rashly probably.

'No, but money will come in handy,' Harry interrupted. 'It's a big responsibility you're assuming, Byron. But in a sense you're right. This could be a case of true love where mine has failed. After all, you've been lovers since childhood.' He smiled gravely. 'I've often thought if Debby had ever really cared for me, and if I'd been able to spend more time with her, I might have been able to straighten her out. But she never did love me, you know? She was just after the good life. It's you she's always loved, Byron.'

'You can't do this to me, Harry,' Debby blurted out at last, and sounding desperate. 'I did love you. I love you still. I'm not going with him.'

'Oh, but you are, my sweet,' he replied. 'You've had your chances before, but they've all ended in broken promises to me, haven't they? If, as you said on the tape, if you were ready to marry Byron after he'd murdered me, surely you're ready to do it now? Surely you're relieved he hasn't had to shoot me after all? Don't all our years together mean you're glad my life's been spared at least?'

There was silence for a bit, except Debby started weeping again.

'If the two of you refuse to do as I say, then I'm afraid I'll have to turn the matter over to the police. Tapes and all,' said Harry solemnly. 'It'll mean a long prison term for both of you, of course. Some would say that's no more than you deserve. Anyway, it's up to you.' He was looking at me hard as he spoke.

'Assuming we leave tonight, what's the deal, Harry?' I asked. 'The whole deal?'

'That's more like it,' he said. He got out of bed, and pulled on a dressing gown. He still had the gun in his hand but we both knew he didn't need it any more, that he'd won: the tape at his lawyers saw to that, and he knew me well enough to accept I wouldn't make some dangerous and bloody pointless, heroic gesture. 'You always were a practical chap, Byron. Where your own best interests were involved,' he said, moving to the chair in front of Debby's dressing table, turning it round and sitting in it where he could contemplate us both, his chin buried in his neck like a Buddha. 'The deal is that you leave together now. Debby can pack a case for immediate needs, the rest of her stuff can be sent on. She'll leave me a note saying you've gone away together. That she never wants to see me or our children again. That'll be grounds enough for an uncontested divorce with no nonsense about huge compensation for an unfaithful, unworthy wife and mother.'

Debby drew in her breath sharply, but didn't utter otherwise.

'I shan't be able to go back to the company,' I said.

'I agree, that would be difficult for all concerned,' he answered with a half smile.

'So what are we going to live on. We'll starve,' cried Debby, and meaning it.

'You'll live well enough. In Perth.'

'Perth, Scotland?' I asked warily.

'Perth, Western Australia,' he answered, as I was afraid he was going to.

'There's been a vacancy on the general management staff of our distribution company there for some time. You're appointed, Byron, with a ten year contract. The salary's better than you're getting here. Great country, Australia. You'll leave before Christmas, all travelling expenses found. There'll be a generous annual bonus too, from me to you, Byron, so long as you two stay together. You can't do better than that now, can you? Not in the circumstances. So take it or leave it, both of you.'

He had to be right, of course. In the circumstances. Even Debby agreed in the end. She didn't relish the prospect of prison any more than I did.

Harry always was right, of course. Clever Harry. We've made a good life here, too. When we married, Harry sent us that silver tea set as a present.

THE EXTORTIONATELY
DEAR DEPARTED

'They are the perfect couple for your ... your very generous gift, Monsieur Talbot,' said Pierre Boulanger, a thin, gaunt, stooping figure, thin-lipped, hesitant, and unctuous in his choice of words. He wore small, steel-rimmed spectacles with round lenses, and walked always with straight arms held close to his sides. Never given to true familiarity with either of us, he was invariably deferential toward me, and somewhat nervous when my wife Helen was about. I kidded her that he probably lusted after her in spirit.

But, in the end, I was wrong, even about that.

To describe the scam we planned to pull as 'generous' was typical Boulanger euphemism. From the start, three months before this, he had chosen never to refer to the illegal side of it, nor even to admit that it owned one. True, we had encouraged him in this, but we had never expected to recruit a collaborator who would enter into the spirit of things with the righteous enthusiasm of a parish priest engaged in unimpeachable good works.

Aged forty-five – three years older than me – Boulanger was a minor official in the regional health office of the French Social Security Ministry, and lived with his widowed mother in a Bordeaux suburb. We had met him when Helen was reclaiming the cost of having had her appendix removed at the local hospital. Because we were both British citizens resident in France there had been extra formalities to go through.

Boulanger had volunteered to come to the chateau after Helen had explained on the telephone that since we were in the middle of the grape harvest, and she was still in a delicate state, it would be impossible for either of us to get into town easily for several weeks.

In fact, after speaking with him for a few minutes, my perceptive wife had concluded that he could be the helpmate we had been seeking unsuccessfully for months. His whole manner had exuded selfless, eager co-operation. In the matter of the payment for the appendicectomy, he had seemed to be almost ready to waive the formalities and approve it on the phone. But Helen, still following her hunch, had cunningly protested that we couldn't possibly allow him to do anything irregular or risky, and certainly not before he had even met us. He had replied that while the risk was immaterial, it would be a privilege to make our acquaintance.

He had arrived that first time in the most dilapidated little Citroën Dyane (the rattlebones model with the canvas roof) that I had ever encountered still capable of movement under its own power. The comedy was that he drove the machine as if he was competing in the Monaco Grande Prix – at all of thirty miles an hour maximum, and that only when he was travelling down hill with a following wind. It was droll to watch the car crawling up our curved drive, the driver's hands, arms and shoulders, usually so inert, wrestling as if he was desperately trying to control the wheel, before he brought the vehicle to a terminal sort of halt somewhat short of the front door. You felt the wheels might at least have thrown up a showering of loose gravel, but they didn't.

Boulanger had been dressed that day – as he was on most subsequent days – in a worn, fawn cotton jacket, equally shabby but well creased grey trousers, and a black beret. He had pulled off – the beret courteously but with great economy of movement head inclined to allow the minimum upward and downward action of his right hand and arm – the exercise exposing a glistening, prematurely balded head. To be honest, Boulanger's car just about compared with our chateau in the elegance stakes. The place was an unlovely, broken down farmhouse with three acres of not very fruitful vines, all on the wrong side of the hill in any case for the ripening of perfect grapes. We had bought it three years before in a moment of abandon because it was cheap, and seemed to us to be overflowing with romantic potential. We had tired of our humdrum London jobs – mine at a bank, Helen's at a bookstore – as well as our even more humdrum existence in commuter land. Confidently, we had opted to exchange all that for a healthy, French rural life, supported by the income our ownership of an honest brand of *paysant cru* wine would surely generate. The trouble was, it was only the peasants who benefited when we failed to sell the stuff to anyone in the higher echelons of society. Worse, selling the chateau itself was proving even more difficult than flogging the wine: we'd been trying since year two.

The only possible up-side to what had become our penurious state was one that offered financial succour for Helen alone. When we had sold our unpretentious London suburban house for a handsome profit (there had been an English property boom on at the time), Helen had insisted that we insure my life for two million pounds for five years – until we were well established in the new life. She didn't care for the prospect that if anything happened to me in the interim, she would be left with a wine-producing business to run single-handed, while, by then, possibly encumbered with young children, in a foreign clime. Her own father had been killed in an accident when she was fourteen, and her mother had struggled to keep his business and the family afloat before expiring a few years later herself – Helen believed from exhaustion.

We had paid the whole five-year life insurance premium in advance to qualify for a fabulously low rate. Even so, there was nothing fabulous in the fact that I had to expire before there could be any benefit.

'Have you ever thought that we could fake your death?' Helen had ruminated in bed one night. We were in the middle of our third abysmal grape picking season.

'You mean, have me fail to return from a sailing trip? Or have my clothes found abandoned on a lonely beach? They wouldn't pay out for years in case I turned up again. And if they figured it was suicide, they wouldn't pay at all,' I countered firmly. I'd checked the policy frequently with vaguely the same sort of idea in mind.

'No, I mean really die. Not you, of course, my sweet. Someone else who we'd pretend was you.'

'You're not suggesting murder?' My wife is a lovely, butter-wouldn't-melt in the mouth, English-rose innocent. Six years younger than me, she had been piously educated at an expensive Catholic school, at least until the family fortune gave out. The very notion of murderous . . .

'Of course not,' she responded primly. 'But there must be tragic cases of middle-aged Frenchmen dying of incurable conditions, with distraught wives worried like hell over what to live on when they're left alone. I know I would be.' She was good at entering into the spirit of her fantasies. 'Nobody gets much of a pension before they're past sixty, and the French state widow's pension is lousy anyway. We simply need to find an impoverished terminally ill patient who looks vaguely like you, so you can . . . can swop places,' she embellished, warming to the task.

'And swop wives too?' I questioned.

'Of course. But that bit's only pretend.' She frowned, as if I'd spoiled her train of thought with such a trivial point, then added. 'We promise the couple, say, ten per cent of what we'd get from the insurance company—'

'You mean, two hundred thousand pounds?' I interrupted.

'Yes. That's more than three hundred thousand US dollars, leaving us with . . . nearly three million dollars,' she calculated wistfully, as if we had the money already. She was thinking in dollars because we'd originally planned to emigrate to Oregon. That was before we'd both been seduced by the French château. 'The husband would have to come away with me somewhere, pretending to be you,' she continued, 'before he . . . he passes on. When he does, I identify the body as yours, and we quietly pay his share to his wife, or whatever.' She paused, then completed with a rare spurt of genuine commercial practicality.

'Perhaps it would need to be a down payment of a hundred thousand pounds, and the rest on death.'

'So how would we raise the first hundred thousand pounds, ahead of my untimely demise?' I questioned with feeling.

'We could sell the château for a really knock down price. We wouldn't need it any more.'

She was right there. The place would probably fetch more than that, even in a distress sale. 'And what about the "wife or whatever"?' I went on doubtfully. 'How does she explain what's happened to a previously ailing patient when what she ends up with is lusty me?'

'As I said, the couple would need to leave where they've been living, and come away to a place where none of us is known. The wife would want to be with her real husband in any case. To look after him till the end. And she wouldn't go back to wherever it was they lived before, that's until after his death, and after the divorce. Then it would be all right.'

'What divorce?'

'Well, she'd need to divorce you eventually, so you could marry me again. That's after you'd officially enjoyed a miraculous cure. She'd be left with all the money we'd given her. A middle-aged widow with capital shouldn't find it hard to attract a new man. I feel she'd want to marry again, too,' mused my romantic wife. 'The divorce would be uncomplicated. We'd get it some place where it's easy.'

'America,' I provided, just to add colour to the crazy scenario.

'Yes, perfect. I expect that's where we'll end up in any case.'

'You mean because I wouldn't always be running into old friends and colleagues there? People who'd read in the paper I was dead.'

'Mm, partly. But I think you'd probably have to grow a beard too.'

'Only if you will as well, darling, to complete our disguise.'

She giggled, then sighed. 'You know, the whole thing would be a true act of mercy. And we'd still be left with all that money, plus whatever remained of what we get for the château. We'd make a fresh start. Something in the country still. Not a vineyard, but with clean air for rearing the children.'

We'd put off having a family till things got better. 'What if the couple have kids?' I asked.

'If they do, we'll have to deal with that when the time comes. You're being negative, darling,' Helen remonstrated.

'Because the whole thing's pie in the sky,' I countered. 'We'll never find the luckless patient. And if we do, the idea's still too complicated.'

Except it was exactly three months later when Pierre Boulanger found what he had termed the 'perfect couple' for our generosity – and it was hardly complicated at all.

Boulanger spent most of his normal working day visiting hospitals, and the homes of invalids – which is what Helen had discovered during that first telephone conversation. When she was sure we knew him well enough to risk it, she outlined our plan, emphasising its deeply humanitarian aspect. She never mentioned the two million pounds, only the amount of the insurance money we were ready to give to some terminally ill patient and his wife if a swop could be engineered.

Our new acquaintance seemed so moved by our generosity that we seriously thought he would burst into tears. Later, he firmly rejected our offer of a finder's fee for himself. 'It's for the good of all,' he pronounced portentously. This had been during his third visit to the chateau in as many days. We had let him recruit himself as an honorary grape picker who stayed each evening to share our simple supper, and which led to his becoming our equally honorary scout for the patient we needed. And who better for the job, it quickly proved, than resourceful Pierre?

Henri and Michelle Rabut were a sad couple. She was forty-seven years old, still very comely, and working at the check-out in a supermarket in St-Jean, a small town close to Limoges. Or that was what she had been doing until her slightly older, farm labourer husband had been told by the doctors that he had a wasting blood condition for which there was no known cure. He had, at the most, six months to live. Boulanger first met them two months after this when they had applied for extra government assistance. St-Jean was a hundred and fifty miles north east of Bordeaux, well outside his normal territory, but he had been temporarily seconded there due to illness in the Limoges office. By this time Michelle Rabut had already quit her job to look after Henri at home – she wouldn't countenance his spending more time than necessary in a hospital.

Like his wife, Henri Rabut came of simple country stock, and was endowed with a heap of innate peasant common sense. He was fatalistic about his condition – a realist resigned to the inevitable, and concerned only to provide for his wife in her widowhood. The couple were childless like us, but, in their case, due to Henri's impotence. His blood condition had first been revealed during tests at a fertility clinic.

Miraculously, it was clear from our first meeting that Henri could be accepted as my slightly older brother. If it came to a border official's cursory glance at a passport photograph, we all believed there was no doubt he could be taken for me. The prospect of the two hundred thousand pound bounty (about two million French francs) had been explained to Henri by Boulanger, and it was a credit to our conscientious go-between that both Henri and his wife considered us heaven sent and inspired benefactors.

It had been my idea that Helen and the Rabuts should move to England for the remainder of Henri's life – with me nearby, but in the background. It was bound to be less complicated and quicker if the insurance claim on my life was made in my native country. It would also be wiser, I thought, if no one in the community where the threesome settled had sight of me. In public, Michelle and I would have looked a touch less convincing as a couple than Helen and Henri, a point that might have prompted suspicion or at least nosy enquiry if the four of us had been living together. Better, I thought, to keep things simple, with Michelle posing as the friend and helper to Helen and her sick 'husband' Henri.

Henri, although by now seriously debilitated, could still cope with the journey across the Channel with the help of a wheel-chair. He didn't own a passport so the plan made a useful opportunity for him to acquire one. The photograph used in it was of me, with my eyelids drooped a little, my hair cut short like Henri's, and my cheeks sucked in to emulate his. We took it as a good omen that the photo fooled the local priest in St-Jean, who signed it on the back, as a true likeness of Henri, before it went to the passport office. This encouraged us to have Henri travel as me on my passport, and for me to travel by separate route as Henri: that worked too.

As predicted, we had disposed of the chateau within a week of it being put up for sale, and the money came through much more quickly than expected. This was because the asking price had been so low that the buyer was scared we might change our minds. In fact, we got far less than we had paid originally for the place, but it was sufficient to provide the Rabuts with their down payment, with enough left over to cover our expenses before poor Henri passed on.

Since it was now midwinter, it was easy for Helen to rent a seaside cottage at short notice in a thinly populated part of Devonshire, within reasonable reach of a doctor, and a town with a hospital, in case such a facility proved necessary. Once the three of them had settled in, she put it out at the village post-office-cum-store that she, her gravely sick husband Edward, and their indispensable friend and housekeeper Michelle, were there because, despite having lived in France for several years, Edward wanted to see out his last days in the area where he had spent a good deal of his childhood. In fact the true Edward Talbot had never been to Devon in his life, so that the possibility of anyone local recognising my name but not Henri's face and build as quite matching it was remote. Helen also told the chatty post-mistress that Michelle's husband was not with them because it would have meant giving up his job in France – an unnecessary sacrifice when it was known that Edward had so little time to live.

We had a stroke of luck in the village doctor. His name was Jacques Egbert, and he was a Frenchman who had settled in Devon after marrying a local girl in the mid-1980s. What brief conversations he had with Henri (whom he knew as Edward Talbot) he was delighted to conduct in French, to the great relief

206

of his patient. My surname happens to be as common in France as it is in England, and Helen had explained to the doctor that her husband had been brought up to speak the other language fluently by French grandparents – which, in my case, was not far from the truth.

Jacques Egbert was a competent doctor, who kept his searching enquiries at the medical not the social level. Helen insisted on retaining him privately and not as a National Health Service physician. She explained that she and Michelle were determined to nurse Edward at home for as long as it was possible, which could involve an excessive number of house calls. The house calls didn't bother Egbert at all, while the private arrangement pleased him a great deal: he had very few fee paying patients.

On his first visit to the cottage, Egbert took blood samples from Henri for analysis. These confirmed the patient's condition, also the advanced stage it had reached. The doctor was relieved that the two women were well aware that there was no cure for what ailed Henri, only pills and injections to make his life more bearable. Helen played the part of the shortly to be widowed spouse with great conviction, something made easier by the fact that, in the circumstances, Michelle herself showed almost superhuman stoicism.

The burden of frequent house visits did not, after all, come to test the doctor. Henri died of heart failure one night in his sleep, five weeks after he had arrived in England. This poignant event, predicted but deeply sorrowful, in the end came as a relief for Henri as well as for the rest of us. Helen, in particular, had grown immensely fond of him, and the feeling had been mutual. The funeral was a quiet one, attended only by Helen, Michelle, the doctor and his wife. The body was cremated. Helen kept me informed by telephone at the small Ashley Hotel where I was currently staying, in the inland town of Boddlestone. As a general precaution, I had been changing locations and hotels a good deal since our arrival. I had moved to this one just before the cremation. I missed the service. Apart from the reason that had kept me away to date, I had persuaded myself it wouldn't have been fitting for me to be present since I was shortly to make off with the deceased's wife. Also, to be honest, I didn't fancy attending my own funeral.

After a copy of the registered death certificate had been received by the insurance company, they sent a representative named Plumridge to call on Helen by appointment. She described him as a quiet person with the demeanour of a senior clergyman. He also called on Dr Egbert, but this, he explained, with a touch of embarrassment, was normal practice, the sum insured being relatively large. Indeed, he went out of his way to assure Helen that his company had no reservations about the nature of her husband's sad and untimely demise. It had certainly been untimely for the company.

Before the policy had been issued, nearly four years before, I had been subjected to an extensive medical examination. There had been no suspicion of a rare and terminal blood condition then. Plumridge had earnestly observed as much to Helen, something he combined with his renewed condolences, and the information that the two million pounds would be paid in seven days – which it was.

Shortly after this, Helen had arranged for the second hundred thousand pounds to be transferred electronically to Michelle's new bank account in Lyons, which Henri's true widow had set up under Boulanger's instructions. He had stressed that it would be less noticeable for her to be with a branch of a large bank in a regional French capital.

It was the day before the money was due to be transferred that Pierre Boulanger turned up at Boddlestone. I had discreetly kept in touch with him during our time in England, so he knew where I was staying, as well as about the progress on the insurance pay-out. We were relying on him to guide Michelle on how to look after her money, as he had done with the first instalment when her husband had been alive – and very competently, according to both of them, particularly Michelle. He was hardly a professional 'money man', but was proving a prudent, honest, down to earth adviser, which is what Michelle testified he had been to them from the start. He had told us, in his modest way, that he handled his mother's financial affairs in the same practical fashion.

It was good to know that Boulanger stood so high in Michelle's esteem, particularly as she had no near relation or friend in business to turn to otherwise. I certainly didn't wish to become too closely involved in her affairs since she would shortly be divorcing me.

I hadn't expected Boulanger to come over from France unannounced. Unfortunately, I had been out when he had telephoned from Dover at nine o'clock in the morning, and left a message with Shirley, the Ashley Hotel's not very bright, but curvaceous and leggy receptionist. He had come by car, a new one he had said, and he estimated he'd be in Boddlestone by one o'clock for lunch.

'Must be a really fast car,' Shirley offered in an awe-struck way – fast cars probably equating with rich and equally fast owners in her estimation.

'It won't be,' I answered, unconvinced that the thrifty, minor civil servant had treated himself to something capable of covering the distance in the time.

In fact, Boulanger arrived at twelve-thirty in a new beret and a not quite so new, but dashing, open, white Porsche, looking flushed and shyly pleased with himself. It went through my mind that the car, though two or three years old, must have cost him a lot more than I would have expected him to spend on a replacement for the Citroën. But then, to my knowledge, he had never over-indulged himself before. It occurred to me, also, that I might offer to pay for the car as a present, in lieu of the finder's fee he had rejected. Indeed, it seemed possible that he now regretted this piece of self denial, was too meek to say so, but had come in the new car naïvely hoping I'd take the hint and offer to defray the cost.

By keeping watch for my visitor, through the lounge window, I had managed to stop him as he'd been about to climb the hotel steps. It was the kind of establishment where conversations were easily overheard. 'Let's have a late lunch along the coast. It'll give me a chance to ride in your splendid new motor,' I suggested firmly and loudly after we'd shaken hands. 'There was really no need for you to come over, you know?' I added, once we were out of earshot of the building. 'And it would have been wiser if we hadn't been seen together in public.' I had sandwiches and some beer in a bag under my arm for our lunch. 'Terrific car,' I added, as we got into the Porsche, and to soften the affect of my admonition. 'How much did it cost you, Pierre?' I watched to see if the enquiry would please him as much as I'd surmised it would. But he completely ignored it.

'We have important matters to discuss,' he responded solemnly. 'Am I right in believing you originally proposed paying Michelle and her husband five per cent of the insurance money, monsieur?' He was still addressing me in his formal way, despite the number of times I had pressed him to call me Edward.

Helen and I had never divulged to Boulanger what the total insurance pay-out would be. 'No, we'd always committed a much larger percentage than that,' I answered, as it happened, quite accurately. Nor did his reference to what had been 'originally proposed' register with me when he said it: we had only ever put up one proposal to him. 'But, with great respect, Pierre, I don't think the actual percentage is any of your business,' I ended.

At this point I was directing Boulanger to head the car out of town on to the coast road. He was driving with the ferocity that was so wildly out of keeping with the rest of his persona – and which made him a good deal more menacing to other road users than when he had been at the wheel of a clapped out jalopy. I had already needed to remind him several times that in Britain we drive on the left-hand side of the road, not the right. It surprised me that he had reached Boddlestone unscathed.

'Ah, but in the matter of the percentage you are mistaken, monsieur. It is very much my business. Mine and Michelle's. I am here to tell you we now require the whole of the insurance payment you have received, less two hundred thousand pounds,' he completed.

As if to underline this aggressive and preposterous demand with a matching bellicose action, he gunned the accelerator, forcing the Porsche around an electric milk float whose astonished driver had been easing it out to the centre of the road prior to making a turn. We were still in a built-up area. After completing the foolhardy manoeuvre, my companion frowned intensely, but not at the milkman whose arm-waving protest he had totally ignored.

'What do you mean? It's Michelle who gets the two hundred thousand,' I expostulated. 'And she's had half of it already, as you well know.' I was now very uneasy – and with good reason.

'But that was only the ... the provisional arrangement, monsieur.' We had left the town now, and he had begun racing along at over eighty until I shouted at him that we'd have the police on our tail if he didn't observe the speed limit. 'Michelle has run the greatest risk in all this,' he went on, easing back a little on the pedal. 'She deserves the, how do you say, the lion's share. I believe you and madame have received four million pounds.'

Nonsense, it was only half that,' I exclaimed without thinking, consumed by a mixture of anger and outrage, but then immediately regretting the disclosure.

'So it was two million, monsieur.' He seemed to have accepted this as fact. 'It wasn't very generous of you to offer Michelle only ten per cent. So it's justice that we match you. You must pay Michelle one million, seven hundred thousand. That's the total, minus ten per cent and the hundred thousand you have already advanced to Michelle. We shall be scrupulously fair in keeping to the revised agreement. Only we need Madame Talbot to transfer what we are owed to Michelle's bank in Lyons by this time tomorrow.'

'Drop dead, Pierre,' I answered, nearly speechless with fury.

'It would not be in your interests if I dropped dead, monsieur ...' he began, as I thought, arrogantly to imply that we were still dependent on his involvement for the pittance being offered.

'And what's all this "we" business when you speak about you and Michelle?' I broke in before he had finished his sentence. 'I don't believe she's ready to renege on our original deal.'

Boulanger laughed aloud at this, well not all that loudly, but he seldom made any noise at all when he showed amusement. 'Michelle and I had been in love with each other for several months before I met you and your wife, monsieur.'

'You mean she was unfaithful to Henri? I don't believe it.'

'I never said she was unfaithful to him. Only that we were in love. We planned to marry after his death. But then, with my sick mother still alive, and needing to go into a private nursing home soon, it was a question of finding enough money for everything. Your . . . your gift was providential.'

'And generous enough as first agreed. So why are you now being so damned greedy? It won't work, you know?' I pressed, but aware already that we were his hostages.

It was clear now that we had played into Boulanger's hands by exposing our scam to him in the first place. It must have offered the perfect fulfilment to his wildest dream. And if he shopped us to the insurance company, it was Helen and I who'd go to goal, not him. He was clean, and we'd never be able to prove differently.

'We are all greedy, monsieur,' he replied in the tone of a sage philosopher.

'But Michelle . . .' He seemed to have forgotten her – and her complicity.

'Is greedier than anyone,' he broke in primly, as if he regretted her weakness.

'But she's involved in the insurance fraud too.'

He outwardly winced at the word fraud, the hypocrite, before he responded. 'Only because you took advantage of her simplicity, monsieur, and the plight of her poor sick husband, now dead. Any court, in England or France, would sympathize with her position. Especially if she confessed to everything and appeared as a witness for the prosecution.'

So he had it all figured. 'Except, if you shop me and my wife, you'll lose the money. All of it. The lot,' I said, increasingly convinced that he wasn't really expecting to get ninety per cent of it, that his demand was just an opening gambit. He had to be ready to negotiate. The question was, should I play ball with him, or simply call his bluff?

'If I shop you, monsieur, you'll go to prison,' he uttered flatly, but, as I knew, accurately.

'Nonsense. We'd just be fined and made to give the money back.' Only I wished I could believe my own words. 'Tell you what, Pierre,' I continued, 'disappointed as I am in you, and my wife will be more so, I'm ready to offer you another . . . hundred thousand pounds. But that's absolutely as far as I'll go. So you can take it or leave it. It's that or nothing. And remember, if you report us to the authorities, and even if Michelle does testify against us, she'll even have to give back the money she's already got from us.' I was not absolutely sure of my ground on that either. Since the first hundred thousand had been paid before we had the insurance pay-out, it was technically nothing to do with the scam. Even so, it seemed a telling threat.

Boulanger shrugged his shoulders prior, possibly, to challenging the supposition. Except that was the very moment when he'd suddenly had to brake the car hard. He had been travelling too fast again on the approach to a traffic roundabout, and the braking counted for nothing in view of what he did next. Briefly disorientated, he'd followed habit and swung the car right, instead of left. The road had seemed empty, but not once we were driving on it in the wrong direction.

The driver of the articulated truck did his best, but he still hit us broadside. Boulanger was killed outright.

I was still in hospital at the end of two weeks, but mending fast by then. My injuries had been multiple, but not permanent or disabling. I had also been fully conscious when they pulled me from the wreckage, and capable soon afterwards of concocting a story explaining who I was, and why I was in England. I identified myself as Henri Rabut, and explained that I had come over from France to collect my wife, Michelle, who was staying in a rented cottage close to Boddlestone with her friend, Mrs Helen Talbot whose husband they had both been nursing up to the time of his recent death. Since Mrs Talbot had not been in any state to be left alone so soon after her bereavement, and since the cottage was small, and I hadn't wished to intrude on a widow's grief, I had been staying at a local hotel. About my presence in Boulanger's car, I said he was an old friend on holiday in England, and that we had arranged to lunch together.

Of course, it had been urgently necessary to deal with Michelle. In the new circumstances, I didn't believe she would have the nerve to persist with Boulanger's blackmail plan on her own, but I had to be sure. Happily, I was right. I confronted her with his admitted perfidy as soon as she and Helen came to the hospital. Helen was profoundly shocked, and Michelle broke down in tears of shame and embarrassment – which to outside observers passed for tears of joy at her 'husband's' survival. Even so it was as well for our general credibility that this scene took place in a small four-bedded hospital ward, in which I was the only patient that day.

Michelle showed surprisingly little grief over Boulanger's death. It seemed that there had not been much true affection between them – he had simply been using her as he had used us. She more or less threw herself on our mercy, saying that he'd forced her to go along with his disloyal plan against her will. Then she begged us still to give her the second hundred thousand, and to let her go back to her birthplace near Lyons. It was significant that, according to her, Boulanger had only declared his love for her, and proposed marriage, the week *after* he had engineered the Rabut's involvement in the insurance scam.

The unhappy woman now planned to buy a farm to work with her brother and his family. She volunteered that she would still co-operate willingly over the divorce, putting proceedings in hand in France immediately. We had already discovered that a 'quickee' divorce was as simple there as it was in England or America. Since, by this time, the money we had agreed to pay Michelle would be in her bank account next day, the simplest and smartest thing to do was to pack her off to France straight away. Indeed, for her to go back by herself, leaving her putative husband to be cared for by another woman, would provide useful grounds for the divorce.

So poor misguided Boulanger got his deserts, and a happy ending seemed to be in store for the rest of us.

*

It was at the end of my third week in hospital that the police came to see me again. At first I assumed the visit was to clarify points in my first statement about the accident, until I realized that these were a different type of police – plain clothes officers, not uniformed, three of them in all, and one of them French. Helen was with them, looking miserable.

My mistake had been in interrupting Boulanger in the car when he was saying it would not be in my interests if he dropped dead – which, of course, is exactly what the wretched man did a split second later. He had pretty certainly been about to inform me that he'd left a letter with a Bordeaux lawyer to be handed to the police if he died suddenly in suspicious circumstances – showing that he trusted me a good deal less than I had always trusted him.

It had been ten days before the lawyer, hearing of Boulanger's demise, and the manner of it, had decided to take what, on lawyerly consideration, seemed to him the proper action. After that things had moved fast, with the French and British police and the insurance company working in friendly co-operation.

I was right about one thing. After getting all their money back, the British insurance company decided not to press charges. They didn't want the case advertised because it would have made them look stupid or careless, or both.

After investigation, the police also dropped the idea that I could somehow have been responsible for taking Boulanger's life – which I clearly couldn't have been, not without putting my own life in equal danger. Even so, the Crown Prosecutor still put me on trial for impersonating a dead person, with criminal intent. Helen and Michelle were charged with complicity.

The hearing took place in England. Michelle was acquitted because her lawyer claimed she had been a grieving widow callously led astray. She'd had to return the second hundred thousand pounds to the insurance company, of course, but she had kept the first one, and there was no legal way of making her give that back to us. We'd hoped she might have shared it with us at least, but it had already been invested in that family farm, or her brother swore it had been, and he was a hard and unsympathetic man who overruled her as easily as Boulanger had done.

Helen was convicted and fined £20,000 – which cleared us out. She has returned to her old bookshop job in London, and glad of the chance. The judge gave me eighteen months. Thanks to good behaviour, I shall be released next week after serving only half the term.

Except for what Helen brings in, we're penniless. This is why we are delighted to know that your production company is ready to consider making a film of our true story which has yet to be told publicly in the detail I have set down in this account.

I anxiously look forward to hearing from you.

THE FINAL CHANCE

James Ratkin-Finch was my last resort, my very last resort. I
hadn't intended to kill him either, well, not when I got there.
It was because of the way he treated me – something that hadn't
altered one bit since my schooldays.

Ratfink, which is what the boys, and a good many staff
members called him, had been my housemaster at Gorelake, a
boarding school in Surrey. It wasn't one of the posher English
private schools – or 'public' schools as they're misnamed to the
confusion of most foreigners. And, again, unlike Eton,
Winchester, and the others, Gorelake didn't date back to the
dark ages either. It was founded, in the 1880s, intentionally to
educate the male offsprings of not overly well-off parents posted
overseas in the then far flung British Empire. So far as Gorelake
was concerned, it seems that the female offspring of the same
families were to be left to fend for themselves: but then, that was
in the nineteenth century.

The original investors in Gorelake must have calculated that
most of the school fees would be paid as 'extra staff benefits' by
Queen Victoria's armed services – the country's largest overseas
employer. My father, for instance, was a regular soldier in the
Royal Engineers, where he eventually rose to the rank of staff
sergeant. He was never made an officer, but was a sought after
specialist all the same – in the practical aspects of bridge
building. My mother had died having me, their only child, in an
up country Malaysian hospital where officially she shouldn't have
been at the time in any case. My birth was something for which

217

my father would never forgive me: I learned that much at a very tender age. He never remarried either. Instead, he immersed himself in his work. He applied for one overseas posting after another – some of them official secondments to friendly foreign governments, to territories where frequent wars – mostly civil ones – made bridge building, or re-building, a major strategic preoccupation for the most recently victorious faction.

Up to my reaching boarding school age, I was passed from one grandmother, aunt or older cousin to another, with increasing ill grace on all sides. I was a difficult child from the start, and didn't become any less so as the result of being farmed out to a series of reluctant relatives.

So everyone was relieved when, at six years and eight months, I was packed off to Gorelake whose junior school accepted boys at that age. For an extra fee, the establishment also housed and fed its pupils through the Christmas and Easter holidays, and even made arrangements for them to be looked after in the long summer vacation too. While this was a facility the school had been providing from the beginning, it had continued with it after the Second World War for reasons mostly to do with its own economic survival. In short, Gorelake found it profitable to go on offering holiday accommodation after other schools dropped it – when air travel was enabling loved ones to be brought together quickly. Needless to say, this last and desirable piece of social evolution had been studiously ignored by my father, though it was steadfastly quoted by my other relatives as the reason why he should be responsible for me during vacations – an idea he flatly never accepted.

It was Gorelake that continued to get my father off the hook, on a long term basis, with the British army footing most of the bill. It was also why Ratkin-Finch first came into my life.

At Christmas and Easter the junior school's earnest head-master and his scrawny wife cared for the pathetic handful of pupils of all ages who had nowhere else to go. The couple shouldered the chore, I suspect, only for the extra income it earned them personally. The atmosphere during the holidays was more like that of an orphanage than that of a private school – though

218

the difference would not have been all that marked at any time.

So, at first blush, Ratkin-Finch came as a blessed relief to me when, after my first year at Gorelake, I was turned over, with eight others, to his especial care for the summer hols. In a sense it was a sort of promotion for me. After all, I was in the Junior School while he taught geography in the Big School, and was a house-master there. Where the Junior School headmaster was weedy and studious, the inappropriately named Ratfink was a huge, burly blond bachelor, who, despite middle age, was a pillar of strength, energy, and spiritual zeal. He ran the Gorelake summer holiday camp for us otherwise abandoned pupils as though there was nothing else in the world he would rather be doing through half of July and all of August every year.

That first time we travelled by train, bus, and, for the last mile and a half, on foot, to the banks of a remote Scottish loch. It was a pattern I was to get used to over the coming years, along with transporting tents, sleeping bags, quite sophisticated cooking utensils, including a portable stove (Ratfink was keen on his food), prayer books (he conducted a daily chapel), and clothing suitable for all seasons. This last was because while the camp sites changed each summer, they had it in common that they seemed to be even more subject to the vagaries of the British weather than most other places. Which is how I contracted viral pneu-monia.

Ratfink was a 'strength through misery' fanatic when it came to facing up to the elements – meaning thunder, lightning, gale force winds, and torrential rain for days on end. 'Making men of you all' was his often stated objective. For my part, being not yet eight years of age, I was far from contemplating imminent manhood, and was much more concerned with my, for me, shameful, enduring bouts of infantile bed-wetting.

My inclination to hero worship our leader evaporated on the second night when all the tents blew down, and he had us huddled together in our sleeping bags in the lee of an inade-quate boulder, instead of finding the means to transport us back to civilisation and hot baths. Next day we fed off soggy bread and cold baked beans, while toughing it out till the wind and rain abated, playing boisterous games, climbing hills, and even swimming in the freezing loch. Later, while there was still no sun, there was an improvement in the weather, so that we got the tents up again and the stove functioning.

I was physically a tall, willowy weakling, naturally pale, underweight, subject to coughing bouts and lacking in energy – nothing there, according to Ratfink, that couldn't be cured by exposure to fresh air and healthy living. I wasn't a whiner, though, not at that point – which is why my illness wasn't noticed until I collapsed halfway up a hill on day five and was hurried off to hospital in an ambulance, 'just to be on the safe side' Ratfink explained defensively at the time. He was far from sure that there was anything really wrong with me, even after pneumonia was firmly diagnosed. I'd had flu in the previous spring and had never got rid of the bronchitic aftermath, bronchitis being something that hadn't responded to syrup of figs, the Junior School remedy for all ills.

The following year, far from being turned down by Ratfink as a candidate for his summer camp, he couldn't have been keener to have me along, I suspect because he was convinced I'd been shamming illness before, and needed to be taught a lesson in manliness. You'd have thought that my collapse when previously in his charge might have prompted some responsible relative to demand that I shouldn't have to run a similar risk again: but not a bit of it.

My middle-aged, spinster Aunt Deirdre, who lived in Surrey, and managed a small sweet shop, wasn't a particularly responsible relative. She was just the closest geographically to Gorelake. She took me in for a few days at the end of term, but was soon seeing me off – this time to mountainous North Wales – from London's Euston Station, under the Ratfink wing. She remarked to him, when they met on the platform, how well I'd recovered from the pneumonia. He gave a guarded grunt to that. Anything more would have meant acknowledging that I'd really been ill. 'Pity about the bed-wetting still,' Aunt Deirdre had added, in the full hearing of three other older boys.

'Bed-wetting, you say? There are ways of curing that, of

course,' Ratfink had replied confidently, the now broadcasted news of my demeaning weakness being fresh to him because I had been careful to cover up evidence of it in the previous year: we campers looked after our own bedding, whereas at school there were housemaids for such potentially revealing chores.

'I know there must be ways of curing it,' my aunt had responded, without, I'm sure, accepting that love, affection and a regular home life figured prominently amongst them. Ratfink's remedy consisted of my taking a foul tasting homeopathic relaxing tablet each night, going to the camp latrine before *and* after I undressed, repeating to myself 'I will not wet my bed tonight' ten times before going to sleep, then saying a prayer about it. Finally, I had to keep a battery operated alarm, that Ratfink had posted to him at the camp, under my legs in my sleeping bag. The alarm went off when it got wet – and, often, as I discovered, when it didn't get wet. None of this did anything to alleviate my occasional affliction, while the unreliable alarm would have ensured that I didn't get a proper night's sleep for the whole holiday – except that, after three nights I kept it switched off. I told Ratfink that I was completely cured. It was the first lie I ever told him, and because it reflected well on him, he swallowed it whole.

'There you are, young Chivers,' he boomed in response, 'only took a bit of effort on your part, didn't it?'

'Yes, sir.'

'Right. Next thing is to teach you to hold a cricket bat straight? Make a man of you yet, won't we?'

'Yes, sir.'

I hated cricket. I was once hit hard on the nose by a cricket ball, and in any case I was no good at games.

I didn't move up to the Big School until I was nearly fourteen – more than a year after my contemporaries. This was because I had lagged behind them all in reading, and thus in every other subject except woodwork. Nor had there been family cries of protest that the school had failed to *teach* me to read, or questions about whether I might be dyslectic – I wasn't, but it might have been worth proving the point. So far as I know, my

221

father, who'd been on secondment in Pakistan around that time, might have been planning on my becoming a carpenter: it's possible.

By this time, I had come to live in fear and trembling of Ratfink who, for five successive summers, had been attempting to overcome my weaknesses in body, mind and spirit with his purported morally and physically uplifting regimens. It was as though he had dedicated himself to turning me into a joint candidate for the Olympics and holy orders – an ambition, he divined, which could be better realized if I was under his direction all through the year. This is why I was put into his house.

The more evidently I failed to match up to Ratfink's ambitions for me, the more zealous he became in their cause. This brought out a kind of defensive streak in me, which eventually I honed into a talent for cunning and deceit – the basis, probably, of my subsequent criminal career. I make no bones about this.

I was effectively an orphan forced to fend for himself from a very early age. Although this had prompted me to develop native guile, I had limited academic ability, remained physically weak, and had no financial means. Although my school fees were paid for, I was allowed very little pocket money. This was why I began thieving.

I nicked small amounts of money, and insignificant but saleable things, from other boys, but mostly from Ratfink's study and his bedroom. I had been doing this for over a year before he or his housekeeper realized that there was a thief about the place. To counter Ratfink's aim to turn me into a pious cherub, I had got my agnostic father to write to the headmaster that I was to be excused morning chapel on religious grounds – because my mother had been Jewish. It was one of the few useful things father ever did for me. The development was a shock for Ratfink, but one he could do little about.

As the only pupil allegedly of the Jewish faith in the whole school, I was set to read from the scriptures by myself in the house common room while chapel was on, an arrangement that gave me the run of the building for twenty minutes every weekday morning, and for over an hour on Sundays.

It was on a Sunday that Ratfink caught me in his bathroom. I was lifting a pack of razor cartridges from the store cupboard, in which he kept about a year's supply of everything, when he walked in on me.

'Excused myself from chapel too, this morning, Chivers,' he said, standing four square in the doorway. 'In a worthy cause, it seems. So it's you who's been robbing us. Shame on you.'

I either had to suffer a beating from him then and there, or be taken before the headmaster. There was really no option. I was pretty sure the headmaster would have chucked me out of the school. Although I hated the place, it was the devil I knew. A fresh school could have been worse.

In fact, I was surprised that Ratfink took such lenient action, although he did seem to get his pound of flesh out of it. The corporal punishment was preceded by a five minute lecture intended to have me shedding tears of shame and contrition – so I let it, as I thought, to give Ratfink some self-satisfaction, and maybe reduce the severity of what was coming next. The beating was administered with a birch cane. He gave me five hard swipes on my bare bottom: allowing for the calculated mitigation, I had still expected six. I'm pretty sure that was what Ratfink had intended as well, except, after the fifth stroke, he dropped the cane, turned away, and told me to pull up my trousers. Then he had us both on our knees reciting, in unison, the general confession from the prayer book. He seemed to have forgotten I had changed my religion, and I didn't remind him. He was so fervent with his praying, it sounded as though he felt more in need of forgiveness than I was.

But it was after that day that Ratfink turned against me – disowned me, if you like. He'd pick on me, make me look stupid, show me up in front of others, in class, at games, in the house, really needling me whenever he got the chance, in the main for being a moral, academic and physical failure. With my background, his new attitude didn't hurt me that much, it just surprised me. It was as if he regretted having let me off lightly with a beating when he could have had me expelled from the school – and out of his life.

I never stole again, though. But it wasn't because of the beating. I'd hit on a bigger and better source of income.

Around the same time that I was caught by Ratfink, two slightly older boys really were expelled for smoking pot. The headmaster solemnly addressed the whole school to say he was satisfied his prompt action in getting rid of the boys had eliminated a source of great evil in our midst before it had taken root. I figured his action hadn't done anything of the sort, because I happened to know the two had not just been smoking the stuff, they'd been trading in it, satisfying a need which would now require filling by someone else. I struck while the iron was hot, contacted one of the boys at his home, and, for a consideration, got the name of their supplier in the local town. I was in business the following weekend.

At the time, I didn't think there was much harm in cannabis. That was before I let one thing lead to another. It was through that first contact that I moved on to dealing in more expensive stuff. Nobody in authority at Gorelake found out that I was into drug pushing till my last term, and even then nothing was proved. It was Ratfink again who nearly caught me – did catch me, really, selling ecstasy tablets to another boy in the changing-room of the school gym, except I was too quick for him. I saw him bearing down on us with the glint of victory in his beady eye.

'Stay where you are, Chivers,' he bawled, 'I want you.'

I grabbed the tablets back from the boy, raced into the loos at the back of the building, locked myself in a cubicle, and flushed the stuff away. Ratfink even climbed over the partition with the intention of stopping me, but only after he'd wasted precious time trying to force the doorlock.

I took the initiative then, came the high horse, and said I'd tell the headmaster that Ratfink had chased me into the loo in a frenzy, but for no reason I could fathom, making me run for dear life after screaming 'I want you, I want you,' at the top of his voice – and in front of a witness for whom I'd only been changing a five pound note. That would have left it to the headmaster to draw whatever nasty conclusions he chose. The ploy worked.

From then on, of course, Ratfink redoubled his efforts to get me. He failed, mostly because there was so little time left, and I was extra careful. Three weeks later, on my last day at the school, he called me into his study.

'Chivers,' he said, 'I've dealt with a lot of ungrateful, dishonest and stupid boys in my time. Nearly all of them had some redeeming features, but you have none. And no scholastic qualifications either.'

'I may get some A Levels, sir,' I put in. National exam results were never announced till the following month.

'I doubt it, Chivers. I seriously doubt it,' he replied. 'You've let me down. When you came to the school, and then into my house, I was ready to befriend you, knowing your background, and so on.' He looked out of the window, as though the view there was more comforting than the sight of me. 'But you spurned my friendship,' he went on. 'And worse than that, you've been involved in criminal activities. We both know what I mean.'

'Not really, sir,' I answered, all innocence.

'Nonsense. You know well enough and that makes you a liar into the bargain.' He shook his head. 'I don't know what you'll do for a career, and despite your attitude, that worries me. Perhaps I can help—'

'I'm going into the entertainment business, sir,' I interrupted quickly, before he could start arranging a place for me as a gardener's apprentice in some municipal park – it was the kind of thing he'd offered to other, what he called, misfits.

He turned back to me with a glower. The entertainment business could have meant a lot of things – and the ones he was thinking of were all obviously unsavoury. His face remained clouded until he made up his mind not to enquire any further about my career plans. 'Crime doesn't pay, Chivers. Not in the end. Try to lead an honest life from now on. Don't bring shame on yourself, your family, and your school, which is what'll happen if you don't go straight. Apart from anything else, you'd be bound to get found out. Remember I told you as much. That's all. Goodbye.'

He didn't shake hands with me, and the look in his eye

seemed to indicate he never wanted see to me again. He was right about the A Levels. I didn't get any. Not one. It didn't stop me telling future employers I'd got four, at high grades. Nobody ever asks to see the certificates. In any case, my first job was lined up – as a trainee manager in a disco company where Bert Pinker, a cousin of my father's, was in charge of accounting and recruitment. He'd never helped me in any other way, and, like a lot of my relatives, I think that made him feel guilty.

The company had six disco halls, all in London. Straight off, I had to get to know them so that I could step in as management support during illness or holidays. Wearing a second-hand dinner jacket, I had to answer customers' questions in what Bert had stressed to the owner was my authoritative private school accent, make sure people were decently dressed, spot the drunks, see there was no drug taking or pushing (ho! ho!), relieve the disc jockeys for spells during the evening, and check the box office and bar tills with the managers at closing time.

The pay was lousy, and the job didn't exactly offer glittering prospects, but, as you may have deduced, in one brilliant move I'd got the exclusive drug selling rights to a few thousand young punters – a task for which I was already well qualified. What's more, I exercised my instructions to keep all drug pushers away from my discos with a positive and often commended dedication. Altogether, I couldn't have asked for a better deal. Within twelve months I'd made a hundred times my official salary out of my side line.

The pity of it was, I got careless. Half way into my second year, I sold some heroin to a plain clothes police woman. Pretty thing, she was, and flirty with it, until she slapped the handcuffs on me.

Because it was a first offence, although I had to pay a hefty fine, I was only sent to jail for six months, and excused two of them for good behaviour. Naturally, second cousin Bert disowned me after that, so, when I was freed, there were no more jobs from that quarter. I forged a reference from him all the same, and on the strength of that, the dinner jacket, my posh voice, and my fictitious A Levels, got a place as an assistant manager with a cinema and pizza chain in the north of England. Of course, I should have seen the light then, and gone straight. Despite the fine, I'd managed to stash away a bit of a nest egg. But soon after starting in the new job I came to realize that it was almost as good as discos for carrying on the business I really preferred.

The judge was harder on me the second time.

Yes, I'm afraid there was a second time – and a third, and a fourth, as a matter of fact. No matter how careful I was, I seemed always to get caught. By the time I was thirty-five, I'd already done five years behind bars. My marriage had foundered by that time as well.

But it was then that I got the break. My father was killed when a bridge he was supposed to be mending fell into the river somewhere in Somalia. He hadn't made a will, so, after a lot of legalities, his whole estate, including some insurance money, came to me, because, even though he'd effectively abandoned me too, I was still his nearest if not exactly his dearest relative. My total inheritance came to just over £80,000, which, after some persuasion, I invested in a half share of a run down, back street pub in Earls Court, a part of west London that was being rejuvenated. The pub was screaming to be modernized and turned into the kind of spot where well-heeled young executives could get a drink, a meal, live music, and dancing at weekends, at reasonable prices. I recognized the potential in the place the moment I was taken to see it. And it was the sort of legitimate business I'd come to understand – as well as the sort I should have switched to seriously long before this. The idea was that I should manage the enterprise when we reopened it.

My partner in all this was Gregory Elliott-Smythe, a highly qualified accountant, very conservative sort of chap, a bit older than me, who looked a professional right down to his fingertips. He'd given up his accounting practice to devote himself to property and business development, working with different investment partners, like me, who had expertise in different fields. Fiona told me all this. It was she who introduced me to Gregory. She was a temporary secretary with the law firm who handled the legalities on my father's estate. That's how I'd met her. She was quite a looker, and she was also crazy about me.

It was Fiona who'd advised me to take Gregory's advice on how to use my new found wealth. She knew the law firm had processed a lot of successful business for him over many years, and she'd heard the senior partner say that Elliott-Smythe was the shrewdest money man he'd met in his whole life, and that he'd go far.

Gregory went far, all right, probably to somewhere like Hawaii, a few days after getting his hands on my money – and Fiona went with him. They were a couple of con artists. Later I discovered that the law firm had never even heard of him. He'd used a different outfit to legalize our partnership.

If there was any time in my life when I was entitled to feel hard done by, this was it. The idea of going straight had turned into a sour dream for me. I was dead broke. What money I'd had, apart from the 'invested' inheritance, I'd blown on giving Fiona a good time. There was no relative I could turn to, and, all of a sudden, I didn't seem to have any friends. As I said at the start, that was why I went to see Ratfink.

I rang the school, but the headmaster's secretary explained that Mr Ratkin-Finch had retired two years before this. After I told her my name was Henry Roberts, an old boy of the school, she gave me Ratfink's address. Something told me not to use my own name. Henry Roberts was a real person: he'd been at school with me, and had gone on to be a clergyman. The address was in Brighton, on the south coast. I had to hitch-hike there: I was that hard up. It was mid-January, and raining.

Ratfink lived alone in a terrace of small, recently gentrified, two-storey houses with no front gardens, but each rendered in contrasting pastel shades of biscuit, pink or cream. The street was at the back of the town, though with a view of the sea if you stretched your neck.

'Come in, Chivers,' he said, immediately on opening the door. It was as if he'd been expecting me. There was no other greeting, no smile, or – more predictably – frown of recognition. Yet he hadn't set eyes on me for over eighteen years. 'Leave that wet

coat there,' he ordered, indicating a mahogany hall stand, as he
led the way down the narrow, carpeted passage.

The room I followed him into was more or less a replica of his
study at school, but on a smaller scale. I recognized the pictures,
and the pieces of silver and bric-à-brac – in particular, four
matching George II candlesticks, two Russian icons, a gold
handled Indian dagger encrusted with rubies, and his collection
of carved ivories. There was also a small, valuable Victorian
painting: an Edwin Landseer. This showed a stag and some
hounds by a bubbling brook, on a hillside covered with heather.
The hounds were having a ball, while the stag was bleeding to
death: not exactly my style of wall decoration, but we'd always
been told it was worth a mint. Ratfink's father had been a
diplomat and had collected most of the stuff on his travels except
for the Landseer which had belonged to his mother.

'You've been . . . at liberty again, for a while,' he said. 'Four to
five months, is it?' It was only half a question, as if he knew the
answer close enough already. As it happened he'd been dead
right. He'd sat himself behind his desk. I took the seat on the
other side without being asked. I was damned if I was going to go
on standing like a naughty schoolboy.

Ratfink had hardly changed. His hair was still blond, with very
few fresh lines on his face and neck. He was wearing a Viyella
check shirt, his Oxford college tie, and what looked like a cashmere sweater over well cut tweed trousers and brogues. He
carried himself well, and the voice was as confident as ever.

'So you've kept up with my . . .' I began.

'Your regress,' he put in sharply, at my brief hesitation. 'Yes.
There's a Gorelake boy in a senior position at Scotland Yard. He
keeps an eye on your . . . your comings and goings for me on
their computer. In case you do something unspeakably foul
which would get the school into the national media. So far your
miserable criminal career hasn't promoted you out of the local
papers. Can't think why not. You've been a total blackguard and
a failure, of course.' He cleared his throat and leaned forward
suddenly as if he was going to spit at me.

I jerked back involuntarily, which seemed to amuse him. 'I'd decided to go straight, since serving my last sentence,' I insisted. 'Except I've been done out of a substantial inheritance by a swindler.'

He nodded. 'The money from your father's estate?'

'Yes. You knew about that too?' I was frankly taken aback at how much intelligence he'd gathered on me.

'Not about the swindle. The ... alleged swindle.' He was staring me straight in the eyes as he continued. 'There was something in the paper about your father's death. As I recall, you were his only child.'

'I wasn't lying about what's happened to the money,' I went on, then gave him the story in detail.

'A fool is still a fool whether it's with money he's come upon honestly or otherwise,' he responded loftily. 'I told you years ago you didn't have the brain power even to be a passably efficient crook. Clearly your dimness was apparent to Mr Elliott-Smythe.'

'That wasn't his real name,' I put in hastily, before regretting it.

His eyebrows lifted. 'Well, I never. So you twigged that, did you? How brilliant, but too late, of course. And now you've come to me for help, because you've exhausted every other avenue. Not that there could have been many other avenues on offer.'

'I want your advice,' I answered, and pretty tight lipped about it.

He gazed at me with feigned astonishment. 'But I gave you that nearly twenty years ago. Go straight, I said. Go straight in your own interests, because you're not bright enough to go crooked. Well, all you're likely to get from me is a cup of tea and a digestive biscuit, and that's only because it's still raining outside. Come into the kitchen.'

He got up, and moved off through the door, obviously revelling in my plight. I followed, getting angrier by the second. What right had the self-satisfied swine to treat me this way? To make me feel like dirt? It wasn't Christian of him for a start, but I'd always reckoned he was a hypocrite. I thought I knew him well enough to realize he truly wasn't going to help me either. The tea was just to string out the mental torture a bit longer.

It was as he was filling the kettle that I decided what to do. I'd never attempted anything violent before, but I was bound to get away with it, and it would solve my problems.

No one knew I was there. If I killed him, I'd have plenty of time to sift through the contents of the house, and fill one of his suitcases with whatever was valuable and small enough to shift. There'd be money as well. I even knew where he'd always kept it, from the last time I'd rifled his desk. I could be in France, with the loot sold, before the body was even found. The candlesticks alone would make up for the money I'd lost. And I knew someone who'd fence the Landseer for me, though that would take longer.

There was a big old-fashioned, cast iron frying pan hanging on the wall with other utensils. He had his back to me when he moved to the gas cooker with the kettle. That's when I grabbed the pan, raised it above my head and brought it down with all the force and hate I had in me.

'Glad you're conscious again, Chivers,' said Ratfink in that smug tone of his. 'Try to stay that way this time, will you?'

I could just make him out, sitting a few feet away from me, but my vision was very blurred. I was lying nearly flat on my back. There were wires and tubes sprouting from me. My left arm was in a plaster caste which was supported in some way. My head was bandaged too. As my free hand went to touch my brow, the pain was excruciating. 'Where . . . where am I?' I asked.

'In hospital. Not in a prison cell where you deserve to be, you stupid idiot,' he answered, quite amiably for him, but quietly. Every painful blink was getting him more in focus. He leaned closer to me, as though he didn't want us to be overheard, although there was no chance of that. I was in the only occupied bed in a small observation ward where patients were put after being moved out of intensive care. 'What happ . . .' I began.

'What happened was, you tried to do me in,' he answered contemptuously. 'Only you bungled it. I saw you coming. You were reflected in the glass panel on the cooker, bringing a pan down on me with a sledgehammer blow. I moved out of the way smartly, so

231

you missed me, broke your arm on the cooker, then slipped on some grease attached to your shoe, and which, I may tell you, wasn't picked up from my immaculately clean floor. You fractured your thin skull, again on the cooker. You've been in a coma for three days. Came out of it this morning. That's why they sent for me.'

'You've told the police?'

He gave a long sniff. 'No. Decided against that.'

'For the sake of the school?'

'Only partly.' He paused. 'Been expecting you for some time. When you concluded you weren't up to standard for a life of crime. I was testing the depth of your resolve when I insulted you with tea, biscuits, and no sympathy. I needed you as a supplicant before you'd avail yourself of your . . . your last opportunity.'

'Which . . . which was you?' I offered.

'Yes. Sensible thinking on your part at last.' He nodded. 'Logically, you'd have to end up with me. And that's a less immodest statement than . . . than a selfish one on my part. You see, retirement's not been fulfilling enough. I've been looking for something extra. Something challenging.'

'Like reforming a lost soul?' I couldn't decide whether to be glad or terrified.

He cleared his throat. 'There was once latent good in you, Chivers. With effort, we may be able to revive it.'

'What if I try to murder you again?' I asked weakly.

'You won't. Even the first time was entirely out of character. In an educated person, murder needs guts of a specially undesirable kind. You don't have it. I could take the precaution of making you sign a statement, confessing to what you . . . you tried to do to me, then lodging it with my bank in case, as you say, you should be prompted to try again. Instead of that, I'm going to trust you.' He paused. 'Just as you are going to trust me. Years ago, I got it wrong over that pneumonia of yours which you'd been bearing like a man. I never wanted to admit as much, and I did offer you atonement later, not least by taking you into my house. But you spurned that by stealing from me. I should have put your lapses down to feeble immaturity. I didn't, and more's the pity.' He frowned.

There was silence for a bit. 'So what happens next?' I asked.

'I propose you come to live at my place for a bit. There's a spare bedroom. After you've recuperated, there's a priest friend of mine in the town, Father Gerard. He specialises in placing chaps of your sort. He'll find useful employment for you.'

Working for the Brighton Parks Department was more interesting than I expected. Then, after two years, Ratfink and Father Gerard found me a job helping to run a small garden centre just outside the town. That was shortly after I'd married a local girl. Ratfink died a year later. He left me enough money in his will to buy a controlling interest in the business. It's a good healthy, outdoors life I lead. From time to time, I take on youngsters Father Gerard sends me – offenders on probation. I teach them the trade, and point them toward an honest life. I've just straightened one of them out. He was growing a narrow patch of cannabis in one of our heated greenhouses. It was at the back, under a long seedling table where nobody would have noticed except me, because I'm regularly on the look out for such things. There was enough pot there to quadruple his week's wages if he sold it.

'Give us a break, guv?' he begged me, after I'd read him the riot act. 'It's my first lapse.'

'So long as you'll accept you've no future as a crook,' I advised bluntly.

Then I told him my life story. It usually works.

THE OTHER WOMAN

'Thanks Gary. You can kiss me if you want,' she said.
And all I had to do was step closer. She did the rest: the first time, at least.

Well, she took me a bit by surprise: even me.

It was only my second day in the job.

We were in the master bedroom. I'd just driven her back from Guildford. She'd sat with me in the front of the Jag.

On the inward journey, her husband had been with us and they'd both been in the back. We'd dropped him at the station, then she'd gone shopping.

She hadn't said much in the car; just watched me a lot, especially my hands. I'd taken the dress-shop bag upstairs as she'd ordered. It wasn't a heavy bag. I mean she could have managed it herself: no strain. I'd wondered if she had anything else in mind. Then I'd thought, no such luck: I was wrong about that – if you'd call everything else that happened lucky.

'Not bad at all,' she said, taking her mouth off mine, as if I was something she'd just eaten. Except the words had sounded more like a challenge than a compliment; that she'd expect me to do better next time. She hadn't let go of me either. 'So when are you picking up Rick?'

'At five.' Up to then, I'd called her madam: now it didn't seem right, not with the way she was groping me.

'Five? So what you waiting for?' She swivelled in my arms. 'Undo my zip. Silly boy.'

She was a fantastic lover.

'You really a public school drop out?' she asked later, when we were just lying on the open bed: it was mid-June, and very hot. She was smoking a cigarette.

'I dropped out after school,' I told her. The public school bit always created interest – because I was a chauffeur. Not that I'd ever been near a public school, but the idea went with the posh accent. I'd worked a lot on the accent since leaving my Comprehensive in Manchester.

'My husband was impressed with your army service,' she said.

I'd guessed that much. And my service record was pretty accurate: it needed to be, because it was easy to check – not like the other stuff. Like a few of the references for instance. People never check on references. If they checked mine they'd find most of the writers had gone abroad or died.

But the story of my five years in the REME was kosher. The army taught me everything I'd ever need to know about car engines – enough to be an over-worked fitter in a garage if I'd wanted. Only the part about refusing to go forward for a commission was invented.

'Why didn't you want to be an officer?'

I knew she'd be asking that. It works every time, especially with the birds. 'Didn't want the responsibility,' I said. 'I like my freedom. It's why I stopped soldiering in the end, too.'

The last part was mostly true. Fact is, I've never really been a drop-out. I'm just someone who uses his skills to work for the biggest return over the shortest period, and always with an eye to the main chance. But that's not the kind of thing you mention at a job interview.

Her husband was Colonel Rick Brota, mercenary extraordinary. He was retired, or else the call for hired assassins had dried up. That was what some locals in the village pub had said to me the night before. They didn't seem to like him.

I'd known already that Brota's speciality was masterminding military coups on islands where the government troops were under-equipped or potentially disloyal, or both. He'd done a bit of the same in submergent Central Africa too. He hadn't always been successful. Except the word was, win or lose, he got paid in advance. The 'freedom fighters' he'd worked for were always well bank-rolled.

You could tell Brota had done well from the shapes of his house and his wife. Mark you, he was getting on – over sixty I reckoned, and writing his memoirs. With one eye and one arm lost along the way, (he wore a black eye-patch but no artificial substitute for his right arm,) he looked a bit of a crock, and he couldn't have been exactly a dashing military figure to begin with. He wasn't British for a start: Spanish or Portuguese, I'd guessed, up to then. He was small, gaunt, wizened, and asthmatic. He hardly ever spoke.

Of course, if he'd been in better nick I wouldn't have risked taking instant liberties with his wife.

The house was stockbroker Tudor, air-conditioned throughout, with five acres of grounds, and a chauffeur's flat over the garage. It stood by itself, backing on to woods, on the outskirts of a village south-east of Guildford, about thirty miles from London. I was engaged for chauffeuring and general maintenance. There was a lot of plant and machinery. Beryl, a middle-aged biddy from the village, came in early every day to clean the place and prepare the food. She left at noon and came back at six to cook and serve the dinner. There was a regular gardener on Mondays, Wednesdays and Fridays.

It was now one p.m. on a Tuesday.

'You've got a very sexy body,' she said, fingering bits of it.

'Not as sexy as yours.' I was reciprocating in all senses.

I'd figured she was around thirty-five, three or four years older than me. Her first name was Connie and she was an old fashioned blonde bombshell. By which I mean she wasn't one of your flat-chested, underfed dollies, held together with eye shadow. She was more the Marilyn Monroe type, if you remember her in her prime or maybe just a bit past it.

Connie was tallish and well-built all over, not fat, but plenty for a man to get hold of. She had big brown eyes, pouty lips, and tousled gold hair that she probably paid a lot to keep looking untamed. You wouldn't call her a raving beauty – her nose was a bit large – but she had real magnetism. She carried herself like an athlete, or a dancer maybe – plenty of energy, with an urgent thrust in the upper leg movements. And she had a grip like steel.

Socially Connie wasn't top drawer. The heavy Mayfair accent had touches of Bermondsey that the charm school, or whatever, hadn't been able to iron out. It takes one to spot one.

'I've waited a long time for you to come along,' she said later. We'd just finished another little orgy. She was sitting astride me at the time, massaging my chest. She seemed to like doing that.

'You mean you don't screw with all the new chauffeurs?'

Without any warning she slapped me hard across the face. Well I suppose I'd asked for that. Then she slid off me and started weeping, her back towards me.

'I'm sorry,' I said. 'I didn't mean that. I was only joking.'

She didn't answer for a bit, just went on sobbing, fit to burst. Then she said: 'You wouldn't joke if you'd been stuck here for five years with a has-been. It's no life for me. We've no friends. He never takes me anywhere. All he wants every night is to listen to Wagner recordings. And that's really all.' She turned to look at me. 'And I thought you were different. I could see you were interested. When we were in the car.' She dabbed at those lovely eyes. 'I'm not promiscuous, just desperate for affection. I have so much to give to anyone who'll really care for me.' She'd ended sounding bitter.

'I've said I'm sorry.' I was too, for nearly blowing everything. 'So why do you stick it? A gorgeous woman like you?' I kissed her on the forehead.

'Because I used to think the swine couldn't last for ever. There was never any love between us. It was a marriage of convenience. We met through an up-market dating bureau. My previous husband ran out on me. Left me with a load of debt. Rick needed British nationality. He got that through the marriage.'

By now she was recovering pretty fast.

'Why did he need the nationality?' I asked.

'In case they ever try to extradite him.'

'Who?'

'Take your pick. There are half a dozen governments in exile who hate his guts. The ones he got deposed. If any of them ever got back in power, they'd want him strung up. After a show trial. It's an obsession with him. But he's sure the British would protect him.'

'So what nationality was he?'

'Argentinian. Only they don't like him either. They'd have shopped him any time. To the first bidder. His first wife died years ago in Buenos Aires when he was away. The death certificate said heart attack. I've seen it. He thinks she was murdered.'

'And he married you to get a British passport? So what did you get out of it?' I knew the answer, but it was polite to ask.

'His money. He's very rich.' Well she was honest, at least. 'As his wife, I get everything. That was the deal. Except he can go back on it. I can't.'

'How can he go back on it?'

'By leaving me. Divorcing me. He's got what he wanted after all. They wouldn't cancel the nationality.'

'But why should he divorce you?'

'Because he's found another woman.'

'You're kidding?' He looked to me hardly capable of a good cough let alone . . .

'I wish I was kidding. I had him followed once. To where she lives in London. Afterwards I followed him myself. Twice last month. It's a block of service flats in Victoria. That's where he'll be today. Why he took the train. Otherwise you'd have been driving him. He's deadly secretive about her. Anyway, I've seen her. She's . . . she's older than me.'

That last bit seemed to hurt the most.

'Why not tell him you know?'

'I wouldn't dare. In case he walks out on me.'

'But if he did that, it's you who'd have the grounds for divorce.'

She shook her head. At first I thought she wasn't going to explain, then she said: 'He caught me with a man. It was two years ago. His name was Paul. He's an actor I'd known before. When I was on the stage. We ran into each other again when he came to Guildford. To the theatre there. It wasn't an affair, just a . . . a . . .'

'Renewing of an old acquaintance?' I helped her over the awkward bit.

'That's right. Rick didn't see it that way. He's insanely jealous. Possessive, even though he hardly ever wants me himself. I swore there was nothing lasting with Paul. But Rick made me promise in writing I'd never see him again. And I had to put that Paul and I'd been – been to bed together.'

'Pity you did that.'

'I'd no alternative. And now he's got that to hold over me.'

She'd forgiven or forgotten my mistake by this time, and was snuggling in my arms again.

'So what are you going to do?'

'Sometimes I think I'll kill myself. I would too. Or else kill Rick.'

I didn't take the suicide bit seriously. It sounded too much as if she was playing for sympathy. And the idea of killing her husband was even less believable, at the time. It seemed to me she was a highly sexed, unsatisfied wife urgently in need of regular relief. So who better than Gary Powell to provide the necessary? And there were long term possibilities on the cards as well.

The job was going to be even more perfect than I'd hoped. The wages were well over the odds, with short basic hours, and paid overtime to include all weekend work. Brota wasn't mean in that department. I had my own furnished flat, and the off duty use of a four-year old Honda 450cc motorbike.

It was the sort of billet I'd been after for years. And while keeping madam happy would be no effort, I'd make sure I wasn't caught at it like Paul, her actor friend. Meeting discreetly was easy – even on the days the gardener was around. There was no joy in the mornings because of the daily woman, but the afternoons were a cinch. Brota always slept a while then, if he was home. Later he'd go to his study and work on his memoirs. Connie would slip up to the flat, usually while he was sleeping. There was a door into the garage off the kitchen, and an inside stairs from the garage up to the flat, so no one ever saw her.

She still kept on about how miserable and trapped she was –

and worried about Brota leaving her for this older bird. It was because I couldn't credit the other woman really existed that Connie finally got me to follow Brota and see for myself.

On the days I drove him to London – once or twice a week – I knew there was no chance he was seeing a woman. The routine was dead regular. In the morning I'd drop him at the British Library in Bloomsbury, pick him up and take him to his club in Pall Mall for lunch, then back to the library, and home from there at five. Sometimes it was other libraries or museums he worked in, but the routine was the same. I mean this life story he was doing was serious work. Connie said he needed the book to throw a whitewash over his nasty past: she kept saying it.

Anyway, she was right about what he did in London when he went by train. On the day I mentioned, Connie drove him to Guildford station in her own car. She made the excuse that she'd sent me off early for an important errand on the Honda. That was nearly right, too. I was parked opposite the house in Victoria when Brota arrived there in a taxi.

He didn't stay long; about half an hour. But when he left, the woman was with him.

Connie was right. Her rival might have been a bit older, but that was the only minus. She was quite a looker – very dark, good figure, and the face of a Madonna. They got into a taxi. I followed closely on the Honda. With the crash helmet on, my own mother wouldn't have spotted me. We finished up in Bedford Row. They went into a lawyer's office there and stayed two hours.

That convinced me.

Meantime my affair with Connie was getting pretty torrid. I was crazy about her. She behaved in bed like no-one else I'd ever known; don't get me wrong, but she had a real professional touch. The idea of losing her for any reason got to be unthinkable. Maybe you know how that can happen to a man with a very special woman?

'There's a way we could be together for always,' she said to me one afternoon, as if she was reading my thoughts.

'How, lover?'

We were in my bed in the flat: it wasn't as big as hers in the house, but it was cosier.

'You know what he did for a living?' Connie asked, instead of answering my question.

'He was a mercenary.'

'He murdered without cause or justification. For money.'

'Other soldiers.'

'Soldiers, civilians, women, and children.' She shuddered. 'He didn't discriminate. It's all in the filthy record. The one he's trying to cover up with this obscene biography. How can such a man live with himself?'

'I wonder that as well.'

I remember her pulling her naked body closer to mine as she said. 'If he committed suicide, no coroner would be surprised. With all that guilt weighing on him. I could say I'd seen it coming for years.'

'He'd never do himself in?'

'But we could make it look as if he had. It'd be easy. And think of what we could do after? All that money? He's got millions. Just for the two of us?' She thrust her open mouth over mine before I could answer.

In the next ten minutes Connie gave me a fantastic, unforgettable demonstration of what daily life could include, alone with her. It made all our other times together seem tame and lack lustre. It even made the money look simply like the icing on the cake.

It was then I agreed to murder Colonel Brota.

Connie had the whole thing worked out.

She had a dental appointment in London on the following Thursday afternoon. She would arrange with her husband that I should drive her there and back in the Jaguar, in case the treatment was painful. She knew he wouldn't want to go to town as well on Thursday because he had fixed to go up the day before.

On the day, Connie and I would set off at one fifteen. Close to London, I'd leave the car and switch to the Honda where I'd left it the night before. She would drive on, while I doubled back, stopping in the wood behind the house. I'd hide the bike there, and at two thirty – the time Brota took his nap – slip up to my flat, using the garden gate to the wood. I'd change out of the clothes I was wearing, then go through the kitchen and hide in the hallway until Brota went to his study. He worked at a desk facing the window with his back to the door. He always left the door wide open.

Once he was busy, I'd creep up on him, and shoot him with one of his own revolvers through the left side of his head. After I'd made it look like suicide, I'd change clothes again, pick up the Honda, and meet Connie at six o'clock where I'd left her. Later, we'd both swear we'd been together off and on all afternoon; that I'd waited outside in Sloane Street while she was at the dentist, then behind Harrods where she'd have done some shopping.

We'd stop at the service station on the A3 near Esher. Connie would call the house from there. She'd speak to Beryl, the help, who'd be in the kitchen by then. Connie would explain we'd been held up by traffic, and tell Beryl to warn Brota in case he got worried.

It was tough on Beryl, but she was a solid citizen, well able to stand shocks. We both agreed it was definitely better that we didn't find the body ourselves.

Connie had thought of everything. She even had a ready made suicide note. It was a card written in Brota's own hand that said: 'Forgive me. Rick.' It wasn't perfect, and it wasn't new, but it looked convincing enough. It was a note he'd done to go with some flowers he'd bought her after a quarrel three years before. She'd saved it: afterwards I wondered if she'd been planning her husband's 'suicide' all that time ago. I was to plant the note after I'd done the shooting.

The gun was no problem. There were four hand guns in the house – two service revolvers, and two small automatics. One of the automatics was in the bedroom, but the others were kept in a locked drawer in the study: Connie had a duplicate key. It was she who decided I should use one of the revolvers, a single action Webley 45. If Brota really had shot himself, she said, he'd have used a heavy gun: he thought of automatics as weapons for women. This was all right with me: I knew how to handle an army revolver; except I'd never shot anyone before.

Somehow Connie had me feeling that in wasting Brota I was doing a public service. I suppose it was easier thinking I was avenging all those women and children he'd liquidated.

When it came to it, the first part of the plan went like clockwork.

At three I was standing in the hall closet, watching Brota go into his study for what was to be the last time. Five minutes later I crept in behind him.

He was bent over his work. There were open books all over the desk. He wrote everything in pencil, with his head close to the paper. He didn't wear glasses for his working left eye.

The carpet was thick. I had on rubber sneakers. I know I made no sound getting up behind him. I moved slightly to his left as I started to raise the gun. I was holding it with both gloved hands: it was already cocked.

It was then that he sensed I was there. I'm certain it was nothing he heard: it was his training or something – uncanny. With no warning, without looking round, he rammed his chair backwards into me, throwing his body forwards and downwards, twisting around clockwise, to the right, scattering books and papers like confetti.

The next moment he was crouched in the knee-hole of the desk, then he was starting at me like a spring uncoiling and there was a bloody great flick knife gleaming in his only hand.

The chair had caught me in the groin, off balance, and off guard. I'd fallen back, nearly fallen over, but I didn't panic. It stayed in my mind that I had the best weapon, that I had to shoot him, that I had to shoot him close-to, and that nothing else would fit for a self-inflicted wound.

Although I was scared, I let him come at me. He'd used the chair again, jumping on to it, levering off the seat like a cat, so he ended aiming himself downwards at me, like he was flying. He didn't shout or speak: just made sharp groaning breaths that I'll never forget.

For a split second I didn't move, then I ducked and feinted to the left. As he passed me, I brought up the revolver again, double handed, and squeezed the trigger. The gun went off with a roar. I thought the muzzle was pretty close to his head.

Brota hit the floor with the far side of his skull exploded by the exit wound. There was blood splattered all over him – none of it mine though. It had been a good try for an older guy, but he hadn't touched me. I'd managed to stay out of knife range. He'd been leading with his left, it was all he had to lead with, poor sod. I'd dodged the other way.

I'd dodged to my left.

It only came home to me the second time.

Even then I had to look again before it sunk in.

His skull was a mess all right, because of the heavy calibre of the weapon – except the clean bullet entry hole was on the right side of the head. I'd missed out on one thing when he'd turned on me.

I suppose I'd been so obsessed about getting the gun close, and so thrown at his resisting at all, I'd forgotten I had to shoot him on the left side. Not that I could have done much else anyway. If I'd feinted the other way, he'd probably have got me with his knife.

As I moved the chair behind the body, I was telling myself that a man with only a left arm just might decide to shoot himself through the right temple.

I kept telling myself that.

Otherwise things weren't a lot different from the way we'd planned.

I didn't try putting him into the chair. It would have to look as if he pushed it back, stood up and turned around before he'd shot himself. I left him exactly where he'd fallen, being careful not to step where there was any sign of blood. There was some blood on the sleeves of my shirt, but I'd allowed for that.

I took the flick knife from Brota's hand, and put the gun in its place. I wiped the knife, closed it, and put it on the desk, then buried it under books I picked up off the floor. It was where it must have been at the start.

I left the suicide note on the desk blotter – lying on the centre of a clean sheet of paper.

Going back to the flat, I took off the shirt and jeans, and made a bundle of them. I put on my chauffeuring clothes again, under my bike gear, all except my suit jacket which was in the car.

I left the property the same way I'd come, without being seen by anyone: I was sure of it. Once on the road, I was just another motorcyclist buried under tin-lid and ton-up gear. I stuffed the clothes bundle into a half-full builder's skip outside a clearance job.

I was back at the meeting place ahead of Connie. We'd fixed it that way so she wouldn't be seen sitting in a big parked car, looking conspicuous on the edge of Merton. It was safe enough to leave the bike there.

She was over the moon that I'd done the job. She wasn't so pleased when I told her exactly where I'd shot him, not any more than I was. We'd both known the importance. After a bit, she agreed the police would accept that Brota had chosen to shoot himself in a cack-handed way – because what other explanation was there?

Connie made the phone call at the service station.

'OK?' I asked, when she got back in the car.

'It should be, in a minute,' she said. 'When Beryl gets to the study.'

'If she rings the police straight away, they ought to be there in ten minutes.' I was timing it so we'd be home in half an hour.

Connie didn't say anything for a bit.

'You all right?' I asked later. She was frowning.

'Look, in case anything goes wrong, that's for both of us, or just one of us, let's make a pact.'

'About what?'

'The money. Rick's money.' She paused. 'Half each.'

'But we'll be spending it together.' I was trying to be cheerful, but I knew what was in her mind, and why. It was I who'd cocked things up.

'I mean if things go wrong, if one of us has to skip, or anything. We should be prepared.'

246

'And by anything, you mean me ending up in the nick?' I said, and I wasn't joking.

'That could happen to both of us. But if it does, or just to one of us, when it's over, still half each?'

'That's fair.' What she meant was if I got rumbled, and she didn't, my half would be waiting for me when I'd done time. 'But I still don't see—'

'And neither of us admits anything,' I remember her interrupting, her voice very firm. 'Whatever happens, we agree to stick to the story?'

'Sure.'

I think my optimism started draining from then.

When we got to the house there were two police cars, two ordinary cars, and an ambulance in the drive. Beryl had done her bit.

Connie acted like she'd been born to the part. Surprise, shock, horror, hysterics, all came in the right order. In no time she was being helped to her bedroom, weighed down with inconsolable grief.

It was left to me to explain where we'd been, except Beryl had done a good advance job over that too.

I was just as bowled over as the loving wife, but in a manly, loyal way.

'Yes, the colonel had been depressed. For the last three days,' I answered the direct question. It seemed to satisfy them at the time. 'I couldn't say whether he had frequent fits of depression. I've only been employed here five weeks.' Then they wanted to know how I'd got the job, where I'd worked before, and before that. They seemed almost as impressed with the army bit as Brota had been. I didn't bother with the up-market trimmings though.

The questions seemed pretty routine, but they went on a bit: 'Yes, I knew the colonel had been a mercenary,' and, 'No, there hadn't been any visitors expected that afternoon,' and again, 'No, I hadn't seen any strangers hanging about the place.'

There were two of them doing the asking, both CID – a Detective Inspector Stewart and a Detective Sergeant Montgomery.

'It's pretty certainly suicide, Mr Powell,' the inspector said, like he was taking me into his confidence. 'But we have to check all possibilities, you understand?'

'Of course,' I said, relaxing a bit.

'Where's the motorbike, Mr Powell?' Montgomery asked suddenly.

I'd been ready for that one. I said I'd taken it to Merton the night before, to a special dealer, because of a dodgy clutch I couldn't fix myself. But the dealer had been closed. So I'd left the bike and thumbed a lift back, not wanting to risk any more damage to the gearbox.

'You didn't use it this afternoon?' That was the sergeant again.

'No. How could I? I was driving Mrs Brota.'

'Of course,' Stewart chipped in. He nodded, and smiled before he changed the subject. 'The colonel and his wife, what sort of terms were they on?' he asked. 'Good terms, would you say?'

'Very good terms. Very loving. So far as I could see. But like I said, I haven't been here that long.' I didn't want to overdo it.

And that was nearly it. I had to give them a timetable of where we'd been in the afternoon, and they wanted to know exactly where the Honda was, as well as its licence number. More routine, the inspector said. They didn't mention exactly how Brota had shot himself. There was nothing said either about how the shot was fired, or about his only having one arm – the wrong one for aiming a gun at the right temple.

There were police about the place till nearly midnight. They left then. The body had been taken away earlier. It looked like it was all over, except they locked and sealed the study – door and windows. Said it would have to stay that way till after the inquest: it was understandable, I thought.

Connie was left to herself, but not totally alone. The local doctor came, and gave her a sedative. He said she should have someone sleeping in the house for the night. Beryl volunteered, so we had no celebration that night – not that we'd have risked it in any case.

Stewart and Montgomery came back next morning at 8.30. I was hosing the Jag when they arrived. They waved to me but didn't speak.

It was a detective constable who came later who asked to see my crash helmet, and the rest of my bike gear. His car was pulling a trailer. The Honda was on it.

The two senior coppers were in the house for over two hours. When Beryl brought me a cup of coffee at 10.30, she always did that, she said they'd been alone with Connie since before nine.

When they came round to the garage I was doing a job on the work-bench. They asked to talk to me in the flat upstairs.

They wanted to know again if I'd used the bike the previous afternoon. I answered the same as before. Then they said someone had been seen getting out of a blue Jaguar in Wimbledon, dressed in identical bike-gear to mine, at 1.58, and then ridden off on a bike like mine. I said it couldn't have been me. Montgomery said Mrs Brota had just had to admit it was me. That I'd left her around two, and met her again later.

Apart from sweating all over, wanting to be sick, and wishing the world would stop, I had to think like lightning.

If Connie had said that much, she'd have to have been desperate.

I made the decision: 'OK. It's a fair cop,' I said, looking a bit ashamed. 'The colonel never gave me time off in the day. Mrs Brota's more understanding. When I drive her to London, she sometimes drops me off for the afternoon. There's a girl in Croydon I've been seeing if I've got the bike handy. She works nights. It's what happened yesterday. Except the girl's gone away.'

'Why didn't you tell us this before, Mr Powell?' Stewart asked.

'Because when we got back, with the suicide and everything, I thought I'd best stick to what we'd have told the colonel. That's if he'd asked.'

' "We" being you and Mrs Brota?'

'I didn't want to let her down, like.'

Montgomery stood up after his boss gave him the nod. 'Mr Powell, ' he said, 'I have to tell you we have reason to believe that after you left Mrs Brota, you came back here, concealed the motorbike in the wood, shot Colonel Brota dead, and later rode back to Merton.'

'That's a lie,' I said. 'A diabolical lie.'

But I was convicted of murder three months later.

I never talked to Connie again, but I stuck to our agreement. I never admitted anything: still haven't. I always reckoned it was police harassment that got her saying I'd left the car.

The rest of the evidence was all circumstantial. The shot had been made too far from the right temple for Brota to have fired it himself with his left hand. There were fine traces of his blood on the knife, even though it had been wiped, closed and hidden under papers on the desk. The house had been locked tight, as always because of the cooling system, with no signs of a break-in. I was the only one with a key besides Beryl who'd been at a Mother's Union meeting all afternoon. Two local women had seen a motorbike in the wood when they'd walked a dog there at three. They'd thought it was my bike, and it was gone when they came back later. The ink on the 'suicide note' showed it was more than two years old.

None of these things amounted to that much on its own. But when you put them all together they were enough for a jury - and an appeal court later.

My story is still that I'm the victim of a miscarriage of justice. That way there's always hope that if you keep on, some do-gooder will take up the case, shake somebody's testimony, and get you pardoned: it happens all the time, if you wait for the dust to settle and memories to dim. You have to stick to your testimony though.

Connie never got implicated. There was a time at the start when I thought she would be for sure. That was when they tried to get me to involve her, saying that if I admitted she put me up to the murder, I'd get a lighter sentence. They said the same to my lawyer. But I couldn't see any real benefit in it, even if I'd been ready to shop her, which I wasn't. Whichever way you looked at it, I'd have had to admit I'd committed a crime in the first place. There was no point in both of us serving time if one could stay in the clear, looking after the money.

They suspected her all right, but no jury would have convicted Connie in her widowhood. The Director of Public Prosecutions must have seen that even if the police didn't. In the end it was his decision not to charge her, or so my lawyer said. They figured a jury would say I hadn't been around long enough to have had anything going with the colonel's wife, on top of which her grief had everyone convinced. In court it bloody near convinced me. She came there as a prosecution witness against me: that must have been part of the deal with the DPP. Of course, she didn't shop me altogether – only said I'd been off alone for the afternoon. Well, she'd been made to admit that already. I've never found out how. Anyway, I didn't blame her. The foul-up was still down to me.

I think they lost interest in Connie when something, or someone, put them on to a motive for the murder that didn't involve her, and made it seem I'd used her without her knowing.

At the end they'd definitely persuaded themselves I'd been put up to the job, as a contract killing, by one of Brota's old enemies, and everyone knew there were plenty of those to choose from. It was why they didn't expect me to grass. My being an ex-soldier fitted too.

I thought even if I had to do eight years of the life sentence before parole, I still had something to look forward to. I didn't include Connie as part of the something: that was being realistic, especially after her actor friend Paul got permission to see me following the appeal hearing. He was a good-looking bloke, officer class from birth: I could see that. Connie had sent him to tip me the wink that my share would be waiting as promised. At the same time he made it pretty clear I wasn't to expect a share of Connie as well.

So imagine the shock when I saw this court report in the paper. It said Mrs Eva Brota, second wife of Colonel Rick Brota, had been awarded the whole of her husband's estate. Fair enough, I thought at first, wondering why she'd had to go to court, and why they'd got her first name wrong. But it went on to say it was Connie who'd lost the case. It was then I noticed there were pictures of two women. I recognized the dark one as well, from the time I followed her and Brota from Victoria to the lawyers.

This Eva had been his second wife all right, with an Argentine wedding licence to prove it. He'd married her, then later deserted her and two children, years ago. That was in some South American outback village, where he'd been hiding while the heat was on. She'd been no more than a peasant then – so she'd improved herself since. But she'd still thought he was dead until a few months before, the same as he must have hoped she was: to my certain knowledge he'd never mentioned her to Connie.

When Eva found out her husband was alive, and loaded and living in England, she'd come over demanding maintenance. The report said they'd had several meetings alone and with their lawyers to work out a secret settlement. The circumstances for Brota, it said, had been 'very delicate'.

Well dying had settled every kind of delicate circumstance for him, but not for her: it also produced an outsize delicate circumstance for Connie.

Brota had been trying to keep Eva's existence quiet to protect his British nationality – because he'd known she was putting that on the line. Eva could prove his marriage to Connie was bigamous, and like all bigamous marriages, the paper said, this one was null and void, 'along with all benefits stemming to either party.'

But even though one of those null and void benefits was Brota's new nationality, you wouldn't have guessed that could hurt anyone now. It did though. A bigamous wife has no rights.

The report said the judge expressed his sympathy to Connie.

But Eva got all the money.

THE RUDE AWAKENING
OF SYBIL FLITCH

'*Mademoiselle*, I think you have dropped your sunglasses.'
The voice came from behind Sybil Flitch as she was mounting the solid flight of concrete steps that led from the beach to the Promenade des Anglais. The accent had been French, the tone cheerful but concerned. When she turned, the speaker was revealed as a man of around forty – which was her own age. Wearing a white T-shirt, blue shorts and sandals, her benefactor was a fraction shorter than she was, lithe and bronzed, with neat black hair, active blue eyes, and a firm, good-humoured mouth. In Sybil's own immediate, self-belittling opinion, he was a lot more confident than she was, but then, most people were. Nor was she surprised that the man had assumed she was English, because most of the other people in Nice assumed that too, despite the copy of *Paris Match* pointedly left protruding from her canvas shoulder bag.

'Oh . . . *merci, Monsieur, merci beaucoup . . . Je suis très, très . . .* grateful.' She took a loud breath, 'I mean . . . *reconnaissante*'.

'They're prescription lenses, perhaps?' He smiled approvingly at the timid woman, and the earnestness of her halting expressions as he handed her the glasses.

'Yes, they are. It was . . . it was careless of me to drop them.' She put the glasses on so that she could stop squinting at him against the sun.

'It's easily done. But you are English, yes, *Mademoiselle*? With an excellent French accent and vocabulary.'

'I'm studying French. In my spare time. A correspondence course.' Sybil felt herself blushing after blurting out the unnecessary details. She moved involuntarily from one foot to the other, then back again – a maladroit, nervous habit that had beset her since childhood, and which inevitably manifested itself when anyone paid her a compliment. The shy girl had long since developed into a gauche and overly inhibited woman.

'Then, *bonne chance avec vos études, Mademoiselle.*' With that, the handsome Frenchman quickly mounted the remaining steps, and made off along the wide sidewalk.

Sybil sighed to herself as she checked the bag to be sure it wasn't in danger of shedding any more of her precious belongings. All the same, it seemed odd that the glasses had fallen out. She was quite sure they had been firmly stuffed into the open side pocket. As she looked up again, she caught sight of her reflection in one of the sheltering glass panels of the Neptune private beach she had been using every morning, and for lunch. It was no wonder the man hadn't wasted any time getting to know her better. Her mousy hair appeared to be less 'tousled cut' than downright unkempt. Her face was blotchy because she hadn't rubbed in the après sun cream properly. And the barely thigh length, rust-coloured linen shift she had on made her look like an undernourished Roman slave, a maturing waif, not a carefree, rich, twenty-first century unattached Parisienne – which was the way Dilys Morgan had described what the garment did for her when it arrived from the mail order company.

Of course, it was unfair to blame Dilys for anything except for not being here – and that hadn't been her fault, Sybil remonstrated with herself as she waited for the pedestrian crossing light to change. She regularly crossed the wide thoroughfare at this point, opposite the Négresco, one of the most prestigious hotels on the French Riviera, in the hope people would assume she was staying in it. Sybil was prone to harmless if also pointless fantasizing. She gave a surreptitious pull at the right side hem of the shift where it seemed shorter than it did on the left. Altogether it felt too short all round, especially now she had left the beach. At home, in Wimbledon, she wouldn't have been seen dead on the street in a skirt that finished so far above her knees. Walking in a very short skirt made her want to crouch like Groucho Marx. How different it would have been if Dilys had been here as planned, building up her courage.

When the traffic halted, Sybil made the crossing, while trying to ignore the very old man who was moving half a pace behind her, keeping up with difficulty, and with the help of a stick. She imagined his disgusting, lascivious gaze was boring into the back of her naked knees, or worse. In truth, the fellow was half blind, and was stalking her only for protection from the traffic.

The unattached, morally rigorous Sybil worked in the production department of a small, specialist South West London publishing company. She had been a late, only child. Her parents were now both dead. Her father, after surviving his wife by eight years, had eventually departed this life three years ago. Sybil's inheritance had included a substantial house, and an equally substantial holding in Government bonds. She had decided to stay in the house, having no desire to leave Wimbledon where she had grown up. She still attended the Anglican church there, except this currently had less to do with her enduring faith than with her regard for the new curate. It also involved a degree of optimism in view of the rumour that the forty-four year old curate was celibate, a possibility that provided material for one of Sybil's wilder fantasies – until she had absently implied as much to Dilys. Her friend had immediately insisted that a bachelor clergyman wasn't the stuff for fantasy but rather a lively challenge, and that Sybil should 'go for it'. Altogether, Dilys had been good for Sybil's morale, though Sybil rarely acted on her more audacious promptings. She had yet to 'go for' the curate, at least by any route that might seriously have alerted him to the fact.

Sybil enjoyed her job, and had risen to be the firm's Deputy Production Manager – though, since there were only three people in the department, that wasn't saying a great deal. She was careful to live within her modest salary, using the income from her inheritance to pay only for treats, such as visits to the theatre or the ballet. Increasingly she had come to think of those funds as the sacrosanct nest egg that would see her through a comfortable, if still single, old age. For Sybil had abandoned serious ambitions involving romance and marriage. The older she became, the more such hopes were replaced by fantasies often more deliciously wanton than any she would knowingly confide in anyone, including Dilys.

She was now striding inland toward the Hotel Pleasance. It was early afternoon still, but unusually dry and hot for April. At least she had been lucky with the weather, and although this was the last full day of her holiday, she was still being careful not to expose herself to too much sun.

The hotel, on a quiet street off the rue de la Buffa, was a small and older establishment, its 1890's exterior now shrouded in purple bougainvillea. It had no restaurant, nor any true view of the sea, but the interior had recently been refurbished, and there was a tiny garden with cushioned chairs, and a stone fountain that played gently in the background. The place had been especially commended in the holiday brochure as a comfortable and modestly priced base, convenient for the beach, as well as for the many cultural attractions that Nice offered. Early season single guests, like Sybil, were given the use of 'doubles' at no extra charge. She preferred a double bed for the admitted reason that she found it more comfortable, and the unacknowledged one that it fitted the scenario of several of her holiday fantasies.

Sybil had made few really close friends in her life, partly because of shyness, but as much because she was naturally wary of such relationships. This was why her burgeoning friendship with Dilys Morgan had latterly become so important to her. She found Dilys uniquely sympathetic from the start. The two had met more than a year ago, over coffee and sandwiches before a symphony concert at London's Festival Hall. Dilys also lived alone, in a flat not far from Sybil. A legal secretary in the City, she was two years younger than Sybil, and divorced. The two women had similar cultural tastes and lifestyles, though Dilys's bachelor existence was of her own making. She was an exuberant personality, outgoing, gregarious, and pretty with it. Although attractive to men, a bad marriage had soured future relationships in that context, at least for the time being, but she took a vicarious interest in helping to improve what she called Sybil's 'prospects' which, she insisted, didn't necessarily need to involve specifically marriage prospects. Sybil had found that insistence not only challenging, but also releasing – and definitely not off-putting, at least not in the way Dilys put it.

The holiday the two women had planned together had been something that Sybil had looked forward to with immense enthusiasm – until the sudden serious illness of Dilys's widowed mother in West Wales had made it incumbent on Dilys, also an only child, to go to her side and to stay there. This had happened only a few days before the two friends had been due to leave. In the circumstances, travel insurance had covered the cost of Dilys's cancellation, but not Sybil's. It had been Dilys who had persuaded her friend that it would be profligate to waste the cost of the trip. But now, nearly two weeks later, the holiday without Dilys had proved deeply disappointing.

Sybil and her father had regularly taken their annual vacation together in the English Lake District – always at the same hotel, and always during the first two weeks in July. In the year following her father's death, Sybil, more obliged than actually anxious to strike out on her own, had joined a conducted art tour of Rome. All the other participants had proved to be either elderly married couples, or even more elderly widows whose conversation had centred around bodily ailments or on new ways of enquiring why Sybil hadn't married yet. There had been no widowers in the party, eligible or otherwise.

In the second year Sybil had returned to the Lake District.

The idea of joining a singles or under forties holiday club at some exotic location had been anathema to Sybil – and not only because she imagined she would be older than everyone else. One of the early bonding ties with Dilys had been that the other woman also abhorred such arrangements, though not for the same reasons as Sybil. As Dilys had put it bluntly, she objected to parading herself as an unwanted female who was 'bursting for it'. There were much more subtle and civilized ways of enjoying yourself in company of your own choosing, she had insisted. The holiday in Nice had been intended to prove the point.

'Good afternoon, Mees Fleech,' beamed Maurice from behind the hall desk. 'You 'ave a good morning, yes? And nice lunch on the beach again? So, this afternoon you visit another museum?' He reached behind him for Sybil's room key. Maurice was a fay, engaging, even ethereal looking youth, slim, with close cropped hair, gold earrings, and delicate hands. Officially he was the live-in hotel concierge, but on most days, from dawn to seven in the morning, and nine in the evening until midnight (when the front door was locked), he was also receptionist, telephonist, barman, and room service waiter. Until Easter, which was much later in the month, the hotel was understaffed to balance with its being under patronized.

Maurice had been taking a caring interest in Sybil. 'You go to the Chagall Museum again, perhaps? Or the Matisse? You enjoyed the Chagall very much, yes?' he questioned again, while still holding on to the key.

'I'd like to go back there, but my museum pass expired yesterday. How much is a day ticket at the Chagall?'

'*Voila!* Mees Fleech. I 'ave this for you.' With a graceful, balletic movement of one arm, Maurice handed her a card, along with her key. 'Some guests who left this morning gave it to me. It's a weekly museum pass for two, expiring tomorrow. They got it from their travel agents. You're welcome to it. No charge.' He beamed.

It was two hours later when Sybil moved through the entrance of the Chagall Museum on Nice's Hill of Cimiez. She had washed her hair and spent a little time reading in the hotel garden, before walking most of the way to her destination on the shady side of the streets. She was now wearing a cotton and polyester dress which she considered a lot more decorous than the shift, and which was actually more flattering to her figure, as well as less of a strain on her nervous system.

'So, we meet again, *Mademoiselle*, do you think it can be fate?'

It was the Frenchman from the beach. Sybil's knees weakened

under her – but the feeling was intensely agreeable.

'You're a Chagall addict too?' she uttered, trying to behave with the nonchalance of a Dilys Morgan. He was such a beautiful man, with a quite radiant smile, and a voice even deeper and more captivating than she remembered.

'I've no idea if I'm that, but I'm here to find out,' he answered her question, then posed one of his own. 'Perhaps you can teach me about him, *Mademoiselle . . . Mademoiselle . . .* er?'

'Flitch. My name's Sybil Flitch. And I'd be glad to go round the galleries with you.' Although she had already twice rocked from one foot to the other, she was suddenly full of courage, doing what Dilys would have done – steeling herself to capture just one sweet human experience from this miserable, totally unremarkable holiday. And she did know a lot about the artist. She had borrowed several books on him from the Wimbledon Public Library before she came, and this was her third visit to the museum.

'And I am Anton Remand. You must call me Anton.' They shook hands, and she was conscious that he had held hers a touch longer than was necessary. 'You must let me buy the tickets,' he insisted as they approached the counter.

'Please, no. I've got them. Well, a double ticket, for the week.' Why did she feel as though she were inviting him to share her double bed?

'Oh, but you have someone else coming? I'm intruding.' He stopped, and drew back a little.

'No, no.' She took a breath. 'He . . . he had to leave Nice this morning.' Now she was telling lies, and was not in the least ashamed of it.

And so began the most exciting, romantic experience in Sybil's life. They toured the museum, with Anton as a willing, intelligent pupil, something that increased Sybil's confidence by the moment. Afterwards they took a bus down to the Old Town, had several drinks at a café in the Place Rosetti before dining – slowly, and with increasing intimacy – at L'Escalinada, a pretty restaurant perched up two steps in the narrow rue Pairoliere. The food and wine, both chosen by Sybil's gourmet French escort, were superb, particularly the wine, which Sybil consumed in uncustomarily large quantities. At the end, she had insisted on paying her share of the bill, which her companion had at first refused to let her do. Finally, though, he capitulated only, he said with a tolerant smile, to make her happy. Certainly, by this time, she was very happy indeed.

Anton had gathered a good deal of information about the increasingly loquacious Sybil, though, fortunately for her, he had asked nothing about her companion whom she said had left that day. She had learnt, in turn, that Anton lived in Lyons, was a long distance truck driver (and a commendably cultured one), who owned his own rig, and operated on routes all over Europe, including Britain. On medical advice, he was taking a few days off from work after treatment to dispel a stomach ulcer. He was staying with married friends in Nice. When he casually let slip that he was a widower with no children, Sybil had been ready to burst into a spirited rendition of the Hallelujah Chorus. Instead she drained her glass again, and didn't demur when her escort refilled it – nor when his leg engaged hers even more closely beneath the table.

Later, delicious tremors had run through Sybil's body when the two had strolled, hand in hand, along the moonlit and almost deserted promenade. When Anton stopped, and took her in his arms and kissed her, first gently then ravenously, she matched his ardour with an alcoholically strengthened passion that she hoped was promising nothing less than headlong, amorous surrender.

It was nearly a quarter to midnight when they finally reached her hotel. 'You'll come in for a drink, won't you?' she pleaded rather than asked, and with high hopes and no concerns about the possible, delicious consequences of the suggestion.

Anton gave her a conspiratorial smile. 'I'd like that very much, my darling.'

The normally ubiquitous Maurice was not behind the hall desk, nor could he be seen at the little bar in the lounge. The ground floor of the hotel appeared to be empty.

'The bard ... the barden ... the garden is beautiful,' Sybil offered solemnly, but without attempting to move her guest in the garden's direction, and before adding. 'One can almost see the ocean from the balcony of my room.' She ran both hands through her hair, vaguely simulating what the almost sea breeze on the balcony might do to it. 'I've got a small bottle of Scotch there, too. For emergencies.'

'Then I'd definitely like to sample the view and the bottle,' Anton responded.

'Right,' said Sybil rather loudly, then put an upright, silencing finger to her lips before confiding: 'It's a double room.'

'Indeed?' His eyebrows lifted a fraction.

After the defining statement about the nature of her accommodations, Sybil, somewhat unsteadily, went behind the desk, and helped herself to her room key. 'Now, where's the lift gone? she asked, stooping a little, and turning in a half circle, then back again. 'Ah, there it is,' she giggled, pointing. 'Come on then.' She attempted to move boldly across the hall, tripped, and was caught by her attentive escort. She then straightened her dress – before managing to repeat the performance.

Sybil was never able to recall in absolute detail what happened during the ensuing quarter of an hour. Sufficient that, no matter how rapturous the experience, at a moment when, as she'd often been led to expect, that rapture should have ratcheted up a notch (ahead of it racheting up several more), she had been unceremoniously jerked out of paradise and into a sobering, devastatingly earthy reality.

Without warning, as they lay hotly entwined on the bed, Anton had been consumed by a fit of violent and agonising, physical distress. Moaning and gasping for breath, he separated from her, clutching at his chest, his expression transfigured by the pain he was enduring. Then his back arched and twisted in a hideous way before his whole body froze, and with an awful, sepulchral groan, he totally collapsed, limp and inert, face buried downwards on the bed sheets.

At the exact moment of Anton's final prostration, the petrified and nearly naked Sybil was conscious of a church clock starting to toll the hour, and then of an incongruous, urgent knocking at her door. Grateful for the promise of some other human involvement in her plight, and oblivious of what impression an outsider would make of her appearance and, more, of her compromising situation, she scrambled to open the door, grabbing her nightdress as she went.

'Mees Fleech, I saw your key was gone. You're OK, eh? I 'ope...'

She pulled Maurice inside, closed the door and propelled him toward the lifeless figure on the bed. 'My ... my friend, he's ill. It's some kind of seizure. Please fetch a doctor.'

'Oh, *Mon Dieu.*' Maurice quickly felt for a pulse at Anton's wrist, then at his neck. Next, in an unexpectedly professional manner, he raised the still face-down body slightly, thrusting his ear against the chest. A moment later he shook his head. 'I regret, Mees Fleech, your friend is dead.' He caught her as she appeared to be about to collapse, and helped her into a chair.

'He can't be dead,' she murmured insistently. 'A minute ago we were ...'

'Mees Fleech, until last summer I was a medical student, failed, I regret, but I know 'ow to take a pulse. Also I know when a man is dead. This one is. He 'ad been ill?'

Sybil nodded, and began to weep. 'He was recovering from something. I think he said a stomach ulcer.'

Maurice pouted incredulously. 'More likely, I think, a 'eart attack, like now, only this one was massive.'

'But shouldn't we still get a doctor in case ...?'

'It would be no 'elp for your friend who is very dead,' the young man interrupted. 'Only very dangerous for you, Mees Fleech.' He paused. 'These are 'is clothes?' He picked up the shirt, then the blue slacks Anton had been wearing, and searched the pockets. From the trousers he withdrew a small, hinged, plastic pill case. Inside were four small tablets. He put one of the tablets to his tongue. 'So, it's as I thought. These are for angina attacks. Your friend should not have been exerting 'imself too 'ard.' The look he gave Sybil was not admonishing; only sympathetic.

Sybil gave an agonised gasp. 'So what should I do?'

'You should do nothing, except go to the bathroom, and close the door. Better leave everything to me than to . . . to make your agony greater.'

'But he's my responsibility. Oh God.' She covered her face with her hands while her shoulders began to heave in concert with her sobbing.

Maurice knelt beside her chair. 'Listen, Mees Fleech. If a dead man is found in your bed there will be a big enquiry. You will be interviewed by the police, er . . . detained in France, while the authorities discover exactly 'ow he died. Also what he was doing in your room. If you invited 'im in.' The speaker clenched his teeth as part of a painful grimace. 'The newspapers will report all this. It will be embarrassing for you, or worse. You could be arrested, who knows what will be decided in such a matter?'

She uncovered her tearstained face. 'Oh no. I can't bear it. It was all so . . . so innocent.' Except, even in her still half bemused, intoxicated condition, Sybil realized that, by her standards at least, the last description was hardly apposite.

'Of course it was innocent, Mees Fleech. But better you don't 'ave to explain that to anyone except me. One other thing, do you know, did he live in Nice?'

'No, in Lyons. He was staying with friends in Nice, near the airport. He wasn't married,' she added in an expiating tone.

'That's good. So please, into the bathroom.'

Her expression was now half enquiring, half supplicating. 'But what are you going to do?'

'I dress 'im, then move 'im to an empty room down the corridor. Later tonight, I arrange for my cousin to come with 'is car. He'll drive your friend to a quiet place on the beach, near the airport. He will be found there in the morning. A poor fellow who 'ad a 'eart attack when walking 'ome.' Maurice shrugged, before his face clouded a little. 'The two of you were alone this evening?'

'Yes. We met for the first time at the museum this afternoon.'

'Good. So no one else was with you, to remember you were together?'

'No one. Oh, except the waiter in the restaurant where we ate?'

Maurice thought for a moment, then shook his head. 'OK, that's a small risk.' He helped her out of the chair, then to the bathroom door. 'Stay there for five minutes. Then come out, and go to bed. You 'ave sleeping tablets with you?'

'Yes. They're very mild.'

'Take one.'

She nodded, and for the first time there was a ray of hope in her eyes. 'I don't know how to thank you enough. If there are expenses . . .'

'I regret, such 'appenings cost a little, of course,' he interrupted awkwardly. 'For myself, you are welcome to my 'elp. For my cousin, who takes a great risk . . . yes, we'll 'ave to pay 'im, but I think it's better than spoiling your reputation, no? Your life?' he completed dramatically.

'Oh yes, Maurice, and of course I'll pay.'

It was six-thirty when Maurice knocked gently on the door with Sybil's breakfast tray. She felt she hadn't slept at all, before she remembered waking twice in the night hoping the whole Anton episode had been a bad dream – and grimly realising that it wasn't. She had certainly lain awake contemplating the awful things that could happen to her in a foreign country where she'd been caught in bed with a dead man she hardly knew, and then had someone else dispose of the body. Apart from the possibility of being arrested, even imprisoned, she would never have been able to face Wimbledon again, or the firm. The last two consequences were immediately more dreadful even than the prospect of incarceration: she was so dreadfully ashamed.

Maurice opened the balcony window wider, and put the tray on the table outside in the sunlight. It was a ravishing day. He turned to face Sybil. 'So everything is fixed, Mees Fleech. There is nothing to worry about. Nobody will ever know your friend was 'ere. It's all over.' He gave her a confident grin.

'You mean your cousin did . . . did everything?' She half whispered, pulling the collar of her negligée tighter around her neck, and leaving a good deal less of her bare flesh exposed than on the last occasion Maurice had been present.

He nodded with great assurance. 'And no need to whisper, Mees Fleech, the rooms on both sides are empty.'

'I see, yes.' She wondered if one of those rooms had been used as a temporary resting place for Anton Remand during the night, but didn't propose to ask. Instead she said: 'And how much do I pay your cousin?'

'Ah, I regret, more than I expected.' He brushed a hand over his stubbly-haired head, something she had noticed he did whenever he was embarrassed. 'It was all more complicated, you see? My cousin had to er, how you say, involve someone else. Someone he 'as to pay more than 'imself. The speaker hesitated. 'But it's better you don't know the details, Mees. And I will pay some of the cost for you.'

'Certainly not, Maurice. I owe you everything. Just tell me how much your cousin needs.'

Maurice swallowed. 'I regret it's . . . it's twenty-five thousand francs. Most of it he will need today . . . to pay 'is collaborator.'

Sybil had hoped it might be less, but had been prepared for it to be even more – possibly a great deal more. It had been something else she had worried about during the night. She told herself now that two and half thousand pounds, the equivalent of the sum Maurice had named in British currency, was nothing compared to the value of the freedom it had bought her. Her nest egg could and would have to stand it. 'Your cousin shall have it, Maurice. Only I don't know if I can get that much transferred to Nice today. And you know I'm leaving this afternoon. Could I send part of it to you at . . .'

Maurice was looking relieved. 'I know 'ow, Mees Fleech,' he broke in. 'Last month another guest arranged to 'ave a bigger sum sent 'ere from England quickly. To buy a painting. It took an hour only to arrange. I can show you the bank he used.'

Maurice was right. For a hefty management charge, and after several telephone calls from the Nice branch of an American bank to the manager of Sybil's bank in Wimbledon, 30,000 francs were placed at her immediate disposal. She had increased the sum because she wanted to reward Maurice himself. She had explained to her own, sensibly cautious bank manager on the telephone that she was using the money to buy an oil painting offered to her at a knockdown price, and that she would be selling bonds to cover the temporary overdraft at the bank immediately on her return.

Sybil gave Maurice the money over coffee at a rear table in an otherwise deserted café near the bank. He was even more reluctant to accept the extra 5,000 francs than the late Anton Remand had been about allowing her to pay half the bill for dinner – but, like Anton, he had eventually given in, with profuse thanks.

Maurice had the rest of the day off. He said he would like to have been with Sybil until she left, to keep her spirits up, but that it would be unwise for them to be seen together. Thus, they had said their farewells at the café, when he had suddenly taken her hand and kissed it profusely, while repeating his thanks for the money. She had found his action quite touching, and, in a way, curious in view of the risk and effort he'd taken for such a relatively small and unasked for personal reward.

At Maurice's earnest request, Sybil agreed to go to the beach in the usual way, and to have lunch there, except, on the way back to the hotel from the bank she felt impelled to enter a church, the one whose clock had chimed the fatal hour the night before. The interior smelled of incense, a familiar enough scent to her since the Wimbledon church was 'high', though less gilded than this one. She knelt at the back and silently confessed her shame and penitence for what had happened From now on she promised to cleave to her normal moral standards, and to avoid heavy drinking. She thanked God for sending Maurice to help her. Then she thanked God again for sending Anton whom, she believed (this after some intricate mental gymnastics) a caring divinity had intended should be the love of her life, her future husband, and the father of her children. While Anton had been denied fulfilling this destiny, through untimely illness, and with their love unconsummated (just), his memory would remain in the forefront of her being, a real and enduring presence that would (very possibly) transcend any future need for other men in her life.

After all that, Sybil felt a good deal better – especially about Anton's role. Her well-being improved even more after she happened to see the local news on television in her room. There had been no mention of Anton. Maurice had already told her that the death was unlikely to warrant more than cursory investigation by the authorities, fatal heart attacks being common in holiday resorts where many people came to recuperate. In any case, he insisted, there was nothing now that could possibly involve Sybil with the tragedy.

With everything packed except the shift she was wearing and her travelling clothes, Sybil had walked to the beach, returning to the hotel again after lunch. The tour company's airport coach was due to pick her up there at two-fifteen. It happened, though, that she had left herself too little time to shower and change, and because the coach had arrived early she had ended up boarding it in some haste and confusion. It wasn't until they had been moving for more than a minute that she missed her wrist watch, and figured she must have left it in the bathroom. It had been her mother's watch, quite valuable, and sentimentally irreplaceable.

'Stop the bus! Stop the bus! *Arrêtez, s'il vous plait, monsieur!*' she cried, rising from her seat, grasping her case from the rack, and struggling forward along the aisle. '*J'ai laissé ma montre dans l'hôtel.*'

The driver, a reasonable man, stopped the vehicle quickly enough. Even so, he explained to the mademoiselle that he had other pick-up points to reach. His schedule didn't allow for passengers to return to hotels to retrieve abandoned watches. If she got off now, she would have to hire a taxi if she still wanted to catch her plane. Sybil said she understood, left the coach, and hurried back to the Pleasance.

Again the reception desk at the hotel was deserted. Instead of waiting for the lift, she dropped her case in the hall, and ran up the stairs. The door to her room was open. The regular maid was changing the bed linen. Sybil explained about the watch, but

267

failed to find it in the bathroom. The girl hadn't seen it either. She suggested that Maurice at the desk might have it. Sybil, her frenzy mounting, explained that Maurice wasn't at the desk, and that it was his afternoon off. The maid countered that he was probably in his room in the basement, the third on the left from the bottom of the stairs. Although it was wildly improbable that Maurice would have the watch, Sybil reasoned that at least he could be relied on to look for it, and post it to her if it was found. She raced back down the stairs to the basement.

Frantic with haste, concerned about the chances of finding a taxi, and in any case doubting that Maurice would be spending his time off in a basement room, instead of knocking politely on his door, Sybil called 'Maurice are you there? and turned the knob. The door opened wide to her touch.

It was a small whitewashed room with a single high window letting on to an area wall. There was a bed, a dilapidated wardrobe, and a chest of drawers with a small television set on it. The walls were decorated with magazine posters chiefly of bronzed male couples, clad mostly in bikini briefs, and photographed in affectionate poses. But it wasn't the couples in the posters that were riveting Sybil's horrified gaze, it was the couple on the narrow bed. They too had been engaged in an affectionate pose when she appeared, but were now grabbing at the sheet to cover their understandable embarrassment.

Nor was it what the two were doing that had shocked the prudish Sybil, it was who they were – Maurice whom she had expected to see, and Anton Remand whom she never expected anyone would see alive again.

'Mees Fleech, I can explain,' Maurice began, distractedly pulling on some shorts under the sheet, before sliding off the bed.

'No he can't, Sybil,' Anton offered woodenly, sitting up and steadily fixing his eyes on hers. 'I'm sorry. Only, you see, we watched you leave some time ago.' He shrugged his bare shoulders before adding. 'I'm afraid it's what you call in England "a fair cop". We are both underpaid minions in the hotel trade forced to take advantage of unsuspecting guests.'

Fighting back tears at first of humiliation, then of rage, Sybil Flitch kicked the door shut behind her. The whole confidence trick was suddenly exposed to her, like its two perpetrators, right down to the fake seduction, aborted, she realized, through the cueing of Maurice in the corridor by the tolling of the church clock – and, no doubt, to the relief of her gay seducer. The last conclusion hurt her a lot.

She breathed in deeply and slowly. 'I want my money back now. All of it,' she said in a cool, commanding voice, both feet surprisingly well anchored to the threadbare carpet. 'Otherwise I call the hotel owner and the police. I'll tell them everything.'

'Everything, Sybil?' Anton questioned quietly. 'But there's no proof of anything. Not even that we were together.'

'There was the waiter at the restaurant . . . and the one at the café. I'll tell everyone why I needed the money from England. The police will believe me.'

Anton hesitated, his gaze still locked on hers, then he gave a slow nod to Maurice who hurried to open the wardrobe and to pull an envelope from it. 'It's all here, Mees Fleech,' he offered plaintively.

The other man chuckled. 'You see, there's been no time yet to share it out.' He levered himself from the bed, stepped boldly to the chair where his clothes were lying, and pulled on a pair of briefs – all with an insouciance calculated to make Sybil cringe. Except the histrionics failed to affect or to impress her.

Sybil took the envelope from Maurice, and checked the contents – three still tightly banded packets of 1,000 franc notes. When she opened her handbag to put the money away, her mother's wrist watch detached itself from a side fold of the lining. She gave a little sigh of pleasure, then stepped across to Anton with a disarming smile. 'Anton, or whatever your name is, there was no chance before to say goodbye, was there?' she remarked lightly. Then, without warning, she slapped him so hard across the face that, taking him off balance, it spun him back to the bed. Her powerful, lightning backhand had always been her tennis strong point, as befitted a daughter of Wimbledon.

With that, Sybil left, confident of herself, of finding a taxi, of catching her plane, and, she realized with mounting satisfaction, of having a tale to tell Dilys Morgan that would rock her sideways.